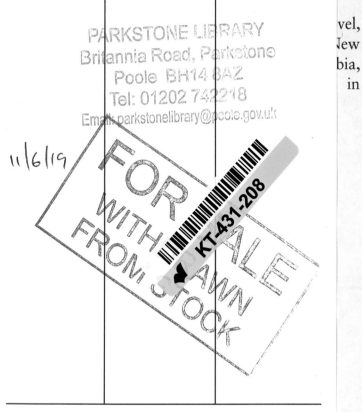

Also by Irene Sabatini

The Boy Next Door

IRENE SABATINI

corsair

CORSAIR

First published in Great Britain in 2014 by Corsair

Copyright © Irene Sabatini, 2014

The moral right of the author has been asserted.

A CIP catalogue record for this book
is available from the British Library.

ISBN: 978-1-47211-416-7 (paperback)
ISBN: 978-1-47211-417-4 (ebook)

Typeset in Sabon by SX Composing DTP, Rayleigh, Essex
Printed and bound in Great Britain by CPI Group (UK) Ltd, Croydon, CR0 4YY

Corsair
is an imprint of
Constable & Robinson Ltd
100 Victoria Embankment
London EC4Y 0DY

An Hachette UK Company
www.hachette.co.uk
www.constablerobinson.com

To R and G

This is a story of a hero, but it took me a long time to figure out who the hero was and how to fix things. I went on an adventure. There were raging forests in Kenya, muddy battlefields in France, and Bob the Butternut in Zimbabwe.

My brother showed me this YouTube video with this random butternut called Bob dancing the Macarena (53,000 views; it was wearing a pink tutu), but then we made it be about the president of Zimbabwe because he's called Robert, like me. I don't know why Robert becomes Bob and not Rob (not all the time) or Bert, it just does.

But most of the action happened here, the best place in the world, so it's also the story of my family. It all began with Monsieur Renoir, and I guess it ended with him too.

Chapter One

Monsieur Renoir

School finished early for the half-term break, and George was actually playing tag with me, in the foyer.

Usually when we came home from school together he acted like I didn't exist; he was always way out in front, headphones clamped on. It was the only time he ever walked like a normal person, because he had to get home, have his high-protein snack, just like the pros, pack his football bag and make sure he didn't miss the tram to go to training. I ended up walking and talking and singing to myself and finding distractions like sticks to wave around, or reading the referendum posters on the walls and trying to decide how I would vote if I was a grown-up, even though Mum wasn't around to discuss it with me. The good thing was that they put new ones up every month, about other stuff. And I wasn't talking to imaginary creatures or friends either; I was saying out loud anything that came into my head, maybe bits from a book I was reading, or I was busy trying to invent something. Every now and then I guess

George remembered that he was actually supposed to be looking out for me; he would turn round, see whatever I was doing, shake his head and just carry on walking. He thought I had problems.

George: Fourteen years old.

Me: Ten.

I was running around the lift, screaming whenever he came close and then dashing for the stairs, shrieking and yelping, no, no . . .

George acted like he was tired; he stretched and yawned.

'That's your problem,' he said. He picked up his backpack. 'You get way too hyper, calm down.'

I think he was just mad he couldn't catch me. He kept tripping because of his jeans. They were halfway down his butt.

I ran up the stairs, base. He made one last grab for me and then he roared. I screamed and scrambled up two more steps.

I was panting on the stairs, safe. No way was he going to follow me; we weren't allowed to use the lift without an adult, but he said stairs were for babies and he was a man, supposedly. There was also that funny smell that was always around. It came down from Monsieur Renoir's landing, which was between the ground floor and the first floor, technically, floor half. It was called *entresol*. Between floors. That sounded really spooky.

George flung out his arm, which meant whatever, and turned his back.

I wanted the game to go on.

'Coming!' I shouted. And I was about to leap down again when it happened.

'Taisez-vous! Ce n'est pas la rue!'

The words jumped and snapped after each other.

Shut up! This is not the street!

And then . . . the 'm' word, which is the 's' word in English, or the 'c' word.

I don't know why, but I twisted my neck round.

It was the first time I'd ever seen even a bit of Monsieur Renoir. And that bit didn't look too good.

His head was stuck between the door and the frame. His eye was blazing, right into me. And his finger was wagging out the door at me.

He moved his lips. He started to open his mouth again.

I pressed my body against the banister and then I ran down. I slipped and landed on my butt. That hurt. I limped into the lift. George was already in, admiring himself in the mirror, trying all his poses. He lifted his sweater and T-shirt to look at his six-pack, just to remind himself how buff he was. He squashed his forehead right up to the glass to take a good look at his zits. Mum said that was not a good idea – the glass was dirty and apparently zits loved dirty glass.

'Did you hear that?' I asked him. I was rubbing my thigh.

'Yeah, bro, dude was loud, and drunk; he couldn't even say the words properly.'

I was now his 'bro', and whenever he said it, he

would beat his chest with his fist as if he was King Kong or Tarzan, King of the Jungle.

George didn't count as an adult but today was an exception; even Mum would understand why I was in the lift. I was injured *and* I was on the run from an ogre. I was *never* going to walk up those stairs again. Ever. I would have to learn how to fly up to the fourth floor, or transform myself into vapour and seep under doors and—

Mum was waiting for us on the landing.

'He said—'

'You were making a lot of noise,' she said.

She had that look in her eyes that meant she was still far far away and was really upset that she had to deal with us now. She was writing a book about vampires. But these were going to be *thinking* vampires. *Literary* vampires, which meant thinking ones. They wouldn't have a thirst for blood. They would have a thirst for knowledge.

George: Seriously, Mum, you're not 'creating' vampires, you're 'creating' nerds.

He used air quotes, which made Mum mad. And then he made her really mad . . .

'Nerd, like my bro here.'

He put his hand out for a fist bump and I fell for it, again. Just as my hand came to knock against his, his floated up into his 'fro and stayed there in the middle, trying to shape his curls into a mohawk.

'Owned,' he said. 'Sizzled and burned.'

Mum shook her head.

'I'm only joking, Mum, right, bro?'

I nodded. Sometimes I felt like helping him out. And I knew that he didn't really think I was a nerd. I could go up to fifteen metres on the zip line; George wouldn't because he said he had to protect his feet, but I knew it was because he hated heights. There were kids in my grade who were macho in class but who wet their pants when we went on the ten-metre line. And I was in the basketball team, even though I spent most of the time on the bench.

In the kitchen I took the repeller that Dad brought back from Azerbaijan, for warding off the evil eye. I held the glass magnet as tightly as I could even though Dad said it was just a superstition and nobody could really give you an evil eye. But I couldn't help thinking that Monsieur Renoir's blazing eye could easily shatter that protector to smithereens.

There he was, standing behind the bench by the water fountain. He had a hat on, but when he was turning his head away, I saw that eye.

That's how I knew it was him.

And I got the chills, just like yesterday.

One hand was on the back of the bench, squeezing it.

This time there was more of him to see. Luckily, he was looking at the people hurrying to the mosque. It was pretty busy because of Friday prayers. He was big and square-shaped and he was wearing a safari suit: khaki, with lots of pockets; it looked like he was in the wrong place. It was a sunny day in October but this wasn't the bush. Grandpa wore his when we went on safari, these last summer holidays.

He raised his hand and took off his panama. It was white with a black band.

I knew it was a panama because there was a *chapellerie* in the old town where a woman made them with straw and Dad tried some on once, just for fun. Mum looked at him and shook her head. Apparently Dad was no Humphrey Bogart (he's this olden-day actor Mum likes). Nor was Monsieur Renoir.

His hair was all squashed up on his head. It looked like a bird's nest.

He fanned himself with the hat and then he put it back on again.

He shuffled round to the front of the bench and sat down, slowly, carefully.

Creak. Creak. Creak.

That's the sound it felt like he was making.

Maybe he had arthritis like Grandma. But I didn't feel sorry for him. He was probably pretending.

He was the only one on the bench. There was no one else in the square now. Everyone was in the mosque. I had to be careful. If he turned round, he would catch me watching.

That wouldn't be good.

He took his hands and grabbed his leg; he lifted it and stretched it out in front of him.

He took his hat off again and put it on his other leg.

He took out a handkerchief from one of his pockets and wiped his forehead. And then he looked up again.

I ducked behind the ticket machine.

It was definitely him.

'Mum, there he is!'

'Robert, don't point.'

'Mer—'

'George!'

He was really Giorgio but everyone called him George. Mum said he was supposed to be Kioko, Key Oh Ko, a Japanese girl's name. Mum found it in a book. It means child born with happiness. The nurse who looked inside Mum's stomach with the special scanner said that George was a girl because there wasn't a penis.

Hmmm, the Curious Case of a Mistaken Identity.

George hated that story and I loved it, so much. When I got really upset with him, I called him Kioko to his face, and once I did it when his friends were around and he begged me not to tell them what it meant. Lucky for him, Katsuo – his name means hero – wasn't there so he couldn't translate.

'His word, not mine. Tell her, bro.'

I stood right against the side of the ticket machine so that Monsieur Renoir wouldn't see me. I poked my head out, very carefully. I didn't want that blazing eye to catch me. His head was bent down again.

George put his headphones on, crossed his arms and leaned against the ticket machine. He looked over Mum's head. He could do that trick, make us all disappear. Just like that. Mum looked up at him. There was so much that she could tell him off about. It was all just so wrong.

1. The headphones.

Those mega-sized things really got on her nerves. He had them on all the time because they were made by some super-cool rapper, Doctor something, not a real doctor, just the Doctor of Rap, I guess. First the headphones and then the hood over them.

2. The jeans.

He was showing his underpants again.

In public.

3. The leaning on the ticket machine so that little old ladies couldn't get to the tickets.

4. The baseball cap, which he had sitting up on his 'fro. He had started growing his hair like that because he wasn't allowed a mohawk like his favourite footballer, Neymar. In Zimbabwe Mum was always arguing with George about his hat. Mum said it was very, VERY rude for a boy to wear a cap like that around adults. People would think he was a tsotsi. Tsotsis were thugs. After that, George posted a picture on Facebook with his cap on and titled it Tsotsi Gangsta.

George was being swag. Swag was what every self-respecting ninth-grader wanted. It was vital to living and breathing. Without it you were . . . ME.

Dad didn't get upset with swag like Mum did. He thought George would soon get bored of all the work swagness required, and at least he had to wear clean underwear.

Even though George was swag and gangsta, he was still sensitive and a good boy. I heard Mum and Dad talking. And I have evidence. He cried when Mufasa,

Simba's dad, died in *The Lion King* 3D, and when Hachiko the dog waited for years and years at the train station for his dead master to come back home, and when I was eight and in hospital because I couldn't breathe properly – I needed oxygen from a tank (I'm all right now, I don't have asthma any more, I don't have to carry around an inhaler; I've grown into my lungs!) – he let me have his iPod and he'd downloaded all the Michael Jackson songs that I liked.

Mum opened her mouth to say something to George, but then she shook her head and looked at her watch. She studied the bus timetable. Dad was always teasing her about how Swiss she had become; if the bus was one minute late, she would start muttering with all the little old ladies. Dad is Italian and nothing runs on time in Italy. And as for Zimbabwe, well, he says, nothing runs there at all. But technically something does run there. Bob the Butternut's motorcade. It runs over anything in its way. When we were in Harare, we saw it. Dad had to drive off the road and stop the car immediately. All the drivers on the road had to do the same otherwise the soldiers in the motorcade with their guns and bazookas would shoot you and then run over your body. Grandpa said they did that all the time and that was the price you had to pay if you got in the president's way. The motorcade was so long. It took ages for it to pass through. There were huge motorbikes, trucks and trucks of soldiers, trucks with men waving sticks in the air, a fire engine, an ambulance, the fancy car with Bob the Butternut in it – though there was another car in the motorcade just like it and maybe that's where the real Bob the Butternut was – helicopters in the sky and more motorbikes, more trucks . . . it made me dizzy.

George: Swag.

He thought Bob the Butternut was a gangsta.

Monsieur Renoir still hadn't moved.

'He swore, Mum.'

'Robert, enough!'

Mum's a writer and she says that sometimes you have to leave things in limbo because life is full of loose ends. I've worked out that means not finishing them.

She took a seat and waited for the bus. I checked on Monsieur Renoir. He was staring at the space between his feet as if there was something there only his eye could see.

Sometimes when I went up the stairs, singing or talking, I stopped just before I reached the *entresol* because I could hear voices above me. The one that was croaky and had lots of coughing between words belonged to Monsieur Badon. He was the concierge and he smoked a lot, even in the lift, which was forbidden, and his fingers were all yellow. He lived next door to Monsieur Renoir with Madame Badon and Fifi, their dog. Madame Badon sometimes let me walk Fifi. I wanted a dog so much but Mum wasn't too keen on the idea. She needed convincing. Their apartment was around the corner from Monsieur Renoir's, near the *sortie de secours*, which was the fire exit; I couldn't see their door from the stairs.

10

Monsieur Badon was always saying, '*Oui* (cough), *oui* (cough), *monsieur* (cough)' or '*Non* (cough), *non* (cough), *monsieur* (cough).' The other voice sounded like a dog growling and snapping; I couldn't tell what it was saying. I would stop singing or talking and go up the stairs slowly, trying not to make a noise, but just as I got to the *entresol* landing, the doors would bang shut; I could feel the blasts of air. It felt like someone had released a thunderbolt and I was trapped.

And there was something in the smell, not just all the smokiness from Monsieur Badon. I was sure it was from Monsieur Renoir's apartment. It came out in a rush when the door slammed. It made me feel like I was back in Zimbabwe with all the animals and the bush, which was very, very strange.

I walked upstairs with Mum once and I asked her what she thought it smelt like. First she said *smoke*, then *musty*, and I said *and* . . . She smelt some more and she said *grass, dry grass and also animal, not just one animal, but animals all mixed together, a bit like a witch doctor's* . . . *a spirit mediu— I mean a fortune-teller's hut.*

In Victoria Falls – it used to be called Mosi-oa-Tunya, which means 'the smoke that thunders', but then this explorer guy called David Livingstone saw it and he named it after the Queen of England like he was giving her a present – anyway, there was a witch doctor in the tourist village.

A witch doctor is usually old and funny-looking because they spend all their time in their huts or they

11

go out looking for special grasses and animal parts at night. They throw bones in the air and can tell you your future or what is wrong with you. They also make brews that can heal you. They have knowledge from the countryside and from the spirit world.

We didn't go inside the hut even though George wanted to ask about his football career.

'Do you think he's one of those *médiums voyants*?' I asked Mum.

'What? Oh, you mean those ones clogging up our mailbox?'

Even though Dad had put up a *pas de publicité* sign, we got junk mail all the time. Mum collected all the flyers that advertised the mediums because she said she was pretty sure she was going to use them one day. Not in real life. In her books.

'Do you, Mum?'

Mum laughed and said of course not, she was just being silly.

Nothing weird or witchy ever happened when I walked up there with Mum.

But when I was alone, sometimes I heard grunting and scraping kinds of noises coming from Monsieur Renoir's apartment, like he was moving heavy things along the floor. I would stand on the landing to see if something would happen, but then I'd get the heebie-jeebies – what if he opened the door and found me *right there*, staring – and I'd scram up the stairs.

I started counting how long I could stay there, listening; my record so far was up to twenty-one. I wrote the numbers in my reporter's notebook; detectives used them too. It was good to flip the pages over the spirals, like I was working on a case and trying to put clues together.

I was just waiting for something to happen.

Well, something *had* happened, and I wasn't even expecting it.

I sneaked another look from behind the ticket machine. Monsieur Renoir's head was all the way down now. It looked like he would topple over at any moment. Was he asleep? Was this a trick so that I would keep staring at him, and then he'd shoot his head up and fix me with that eye? But I couldn't help looking.

There could be two shiny eggs right in the middle of his bird's nest . . .

He lifted his hand and started rubbing his hair, round and round, so the eggs would have cracked and I waited to see egg yolk dripping down his thick beard.

His nose was big and round with lots of little holes in it. It was red . . .

He started rubbing his nose, as if I was controlling his brain.

Maybe I was. I put it to the test. *Your ears, Monsieur Renoir. Your ears.* And then I said it in French. *Vos oreilles, Monsieur Renoir. Vos oreilles.* And look, he was pulling his ears now, left, right, left, right, and then his fingers were inside them, digging . . . gross. I had powers! Magic powers. I could make Monsieur Renoir do anything. *Monsieur Renoir,* I said, *get up from the bench and come and apologize for yelling at me and my brother.* I held my breath. I watched. I waited. Monsieur Renoir shifted his butt, this way and then the other way. *Monsieur Renoir*, I said . . . and there he was, Monsieur Renoir was—

'Bro!'

I was so excited, I had jumped backwards and bumped into George.

'George, look!'

I pointed to the bench, but Monsieur Renoir wasn't there any more. I turned all the way round but he had disappeared. I looked over to Mum. She was reading the *Tribune de Genève*.

Monsieur Renoir had vanished without a trace!

Had I vanished him with my powers?

Was I a murderer?

Should I ask Mum?

'Mum . . .?'

'At last,' she said. She got up. The bus was finally here.

I sat by the window seat, next to Mum. George swagged off to the back even though he was not allowed to sit right at the back because Mum said that was where the real gangsters liked to congregate. Mum turned her head and called, 'George,' but he had his headphones on.

'Mum, can you murder someone by thinking?'

'Yes,' she said.

Oh boy, I was in real trouble.

'Really?'

'It's *fun*,' she said.

'I murdered him!' I shouted.

Everyone was looking at me, the murderer.

'Robert, what's—'

'Monsieur Renoir, I—'

'Robert,' she said, 'I only mean that writers can murder their characters. Now calm down.'

I was happy that George wasn't sitting near us, and that he had his headphones on. He would have said, 'Bro, not cool,' or he would have just looked at me and shaken his head like I was too mental to make any kind of comment about.

But I *had* made Monsieur Renoir vanish, hadn't I?

Or maybe he'd vanished himself.

Maybe he'd been acting, making me think what he wanted me to.

On the bus, I kept thinking about Monsieur Renoir.

Why was he so crabby, so mean, so evil?

Why? Why? Why?

Sometimes Mum got tired of all my questions.

I thought and thought and—

I knew it!

Entresol.

That was it! It was living in the in-between place that had made him that way.

Nonna, my grandma from Rome, said that purgatory was the in-between place where people who hadn't been good enough to go to heaven or bad enough to go to hell went. The people on earth had to pray as hard as they could so that God would make up his mind

15

and take them out of purgatory up into heaven. No one knows exactly what purgatory looks like. Everyone knows that heaven's very beautiful and sunny all the time and that hell's very hot and scary; Nonna says that purgatory is a sad place with *un sacco di pianto*, a lot of crying, but Dad says she's only guessing.

I thought about Monsieur Renoir's in-between place. It was a completely different world in there. When you opened his door and stepped inside, it wasn't like any ordinary apartment, not like ours, it was the Land of In-Between and Monsieur Renoir lived there, dragging his coffin from place to place, looking for children to capture and stuff inside and then, when he needed them for his potions, he—

Or maybe when he got hungry, he just took them out and ate them.

He was, he was . . . *Kronos*! I knew all about the Greek gods because I'd read the Percy Jackson books.

Chapter Two

La Vieille Ville, The Old Town

We got off at Place Neuve. We were going to the park
to play chess with the big chess sets. It was number
3 in my top favourite places in the whole world. We
had epic battles there. Knights duelling to protect the
queen, and pawns being smashed one after the other.
Even George didn't mind coming here. He'd hang back
while we started the game, doing all his swag poses
with his headphones and jeans, hands in the back
pockets, *no*, hands in the front pockets, lean back,
lean forward, cap pushed forward a bit, then back so
some of his curls showed through, phone in pocket
– the one rappers used, apparently – then out . . . it
was exhausting watching him get to the final pose. I
timed him once, eleven minutes, thirty-three seconds;
the pose only lasted for two minutes, nine seconds, and
then he started all over again. The only place where he
doesn't swag is on the football pitch, where everyone
says that watching him is like watching someone dance
with the ball, so maybe it is kind of swagging – he can
do stepovers and snakes and backward snakes and

hocus-pocus and rainbow flicks and roulettes and . . . you get the idea. He plays for FC Lancy Inter-Cantonal, which means that he's in the Super Coca-Cola League and he plays against teams in the three cantons next to Geneva. If he wants, he could try out for Servette under fifteens who are, apparently, like the under-fifteen Manchester United of Geneva. He says when he's pro he'll go and save the Zimbabwean soccer team, which sucks so badly they're not even on FIFA 13; they're just waiting for George to finally get them to qualify for an international competition.

Grandpa said that there was too much political meddling in the national selection. That's why the Zimbabwe team was such a failure.

Grandpa: The selectors are all Shona and they favour their own kind.

Mum: Shhhh, Baba.

Grandpa said it was the truth.

Grandpa: We, Ndebeles, don't count for anything around here, look at the state of this place, they won't even let us bring water from the Zambezi, we are dying of thirst.

The boring thing is that every single Sunday I have to go and watch George's football matches.

I bring my backpack filled with books and DS games.

There was a set free and Mum and I got going. Mum was kinda good except that she forgot where the pieces could move to, in which direction and how many steps, and you had to keep reminding her, and helping her, because otherwise the game was over so quickly which wasn't any fun. I was hoping George would go through his swag poses really fast and take over from Mum, and I was in luck because he couldn't let Mum be checkmated in record time.

'Whoa, Mum,' he said, 'PUT HIM DOWN, DOWN. For the love of all things mortal, put him down.'

Mum dropped her bishop and stepped aside.

And then George swagged on to the board and the game really began.

Even then it didn't last long, because every time I picked up the king he became Monsieur Renoir in my hands and I would drop him and jump and George got really pissed off and stopped playing. He said he had a life, and he went on Facebook to tell his one thousand two hundred 'friends' what a moron his brother was. The really good thing is that George is not allowed to post any pictures of me on his wall so I'm saved from even more humiliation by photographic and video evidence. George's ambition is to have one million hits on a video he posts because then he gets paid by YouTube; he says that posting me singing 'Moves like Jagger' or 'Gangnam Style' and doing my random dance, or him showing off one of his 'skillz' on the football pitch should do it. People would laugh at me and be super awed at him.

George asked if he could go now and Mum said no.

He was our prisoner for the day.

George wanted to hang out with his friends.

'Hanging out' was usually coming to our apartment

and taking over the lounge playing FIFA 13 on PlayStation and writing messages on Facebook and watching videos on YouTube. Sometimes they called girls in their class and made kissing noises over the phone. Mum wanted him to do something useful like read a book, or, 'God forbid', his homework. George said he didn't have to worry about school because he was going to be a football star. He had all the statistics. All the footballers he was sure didn't finish high school and still got PAID.

Dad: Balotelli did, because his parents made sure he did.

It was just after the Euros and everyone was talking about Balotelli hugging and kissing his mamma, Italian style. George didn't have anything smart-alecky to say about that so he just put on his headphones and tuned us all out.

Sometimes his friends brought litre bottles of soda, which were banned in our house. We weren't allowed any sodas because Mum said they were full of sugar and artificial flavours and colours. On our fridge door she's put, under different magnets, lots and lots of articles that she found on the internet about the deadly E numbers in foods, all the gross stuff they do to children's brains and bodies.

But George and his friends would hide the bottles behind the couch and take slugs out of them when Mum was out, and then they forgot the empty bottles and Mum would find them and the crumpled packets of mega-jumbo-size chips. When she showed them to George, he always looked confused, like he had absolutely no idea where they came from.

Mum: We need to go to Zimbabwe more often so that you kids can learn real manners.

But that's not even true – we *have* been to Zimbabwe, three times, and Grandpa let us have sodas when Mum wasn't around. He said Mum and her sisters (Aunty Delphia and Aunty Madeline) used to drink plum-cherry soft drink all the time. It's bright purple and very sweet and you can only find it in Zimbabwe.

Grandpa and Grandma even scolded Mum and Dad for being too strict.

Grandma and Grandpa: Let them be children.

That made Mum cross, because when she was a child Grandpa and Grandma were really strict. I mean, she had to apologize for every single drinking glass she broke and pay for its replacement with her pocket money. Sad.

George: Those were the olden days, Maman.

He puts his arm over Mum's shoulder as if she's a pal of his. Mum hates this because it drags her down, but she always ends up laughing because she can't keep her serious mother face for long.

Mum: Children these days.

And then George bends down and kisses her on top of her head.

Before we went to Zimbabwe, I had to be deprogrammed. I couldn't say random things like 'Bob the Butternut'.

George: You've got Tourette's, bro. You yell out

random things. Bob the Butternut will stick your butt in jail.

Mum got very angry with him and told him to apologize.

George: For what? It's the truth.

Mum: For saying he has Tourette's.

George: I'm speaking truth to power.

I looked up Tourette's in the dictionary, and ever since I did, my head is now filled with random swear words. What happens if I blurt them out? Will I really have Tourette's then? *Questions, questions, questions.*

We're going to Zimbabwe again for the summer holidays if they don't have elections then. People get killed during elections in Zimbabwe because Bob the Butternut wants to rule for ever. It's not a democracy like Switzerland.

Sometimes, when I can't go to sleep, I like to think of all the things I could have in a referendum. All children should be allowed to vote. I told this to George and he looked at me like he couldn't expect anything better from me. First, that I was even thinking about things like referendums, and second, that I would want to do something as boring as vote. But there were so many things to vote for.

Green spaces *(yes)*.

Nuclear power stations *(no)*.

Smoking in restaurants *(no)*.

Smoking anywhere *(no)*.

Music in schools *(hmm, maybe not with a teacher*

22

like Madame Jospin, who raps you on your knuckles when you get the wrong notes on the recorder).

Citizens with guns *(no, imagine Monsieur Renoir with a gun, but then I could imagine Monsieur Renoir with a gun; every Swiss man had a gun, to defend the Republic. Now, I was scared).*

I cared about all these things. Why should adults be the only ones to have a say.

But if George had a say:

Green spaces *(nope, oh wait, football pitches, OK).*

Nuclear power stations *(cool).*

Smoking in restaurants *(cool).*

Smoking anywhere *(slam dunk).*

Music in schools *(rap, gangsta, cool).*

Citizens with guns *(ka pow!).*

So maybe only *some* children. Definitely not teenagers.

Sometimes George called *me* Bob the Butternut. It was humiliating to have the same name as *that* guy. Why couldn't I have had the Italian name, Roberto. You couldn't call a Roberto Bob. I thought of asking Mum and Dad to change my name, but then I tried to imagine me as Roberto and I didn't think I could be a Roberto. No, I was stuck being Robert, and when George wanted, Bob the Butternut.

George was supposed to be hanging out in Paquis, and he was forbidden from hanging out there because there's drugs and stuff like that in the streets. It's just behind the railway station, but only a few blocks from the fancy hotels by the lake.

George (to me only): Mum and Dad need to grow up. They're so lame, they ain't even walking.

I think he put that down in the rap he's always writing.

I wanted to go to the English bookshop but George said no way, he wasn't going to spend hours cramped in there waiting while Mum and me chatted with Catherine and got all hyper. I loved it in there. Catherine sometimes gave me books to review!

George: Sucker! At least get paid, bro!

George didn't get it. Reading wasn't work.

We couldn't go to the flea market in Plainpalais either because of George; he hadn't brought along his skateboard so he couldn't hang around the skate park while Mum and I went up and down looking at all the stuff. Although even if he had his skateboard he probably wasn't going to hang around the skate park anyway, because Mum would have made him put on his helmet and cover every bit of his body with padding.

So we crossed the square, and I made sure to look up at General Dufour in the middle on his beautiful horse. He was riding off to save the Federation of Switzerland from the rebel cantons that wanted to make their own country. I asked him the same question I always did; he nodded his head and said *yes, most definitely*, in French, of course. I waved at Henry Dunant on his plinth and shouted, 'Thank you,' which I always did too; that was for making the Red Cross, where Dad worked. I looked behind me and waved at George, who shook his head and tapped his forehead with his finger – at least he didn't call me 'moron'. We walked up the Rampe de la Treille. Mum couldn't walk so fast because her foot still hurt. She broke it last year ice-skating; she said she was trying too hard to keep up with me. George was lagging far behind. It was difficult for him to keep his swag with the climb. Huffing and puffing was not cool. I ran up the hill and then I waited for them on the Longest Bench in the World; it was even in the *Guinness Book of Records*. A fact: Switzerland has the highest number of benches in the world, because the citizens of the Republic are supposed to sit down on the benches and commune, which Dad says means talk about what referendums they can have next.

I stood on the bench and looked down over the old city wall. The Duke of Savoy and his soldiers climbed over this wall a long time ago, actually in December 1602, to try and capture Geneva, but Mère Royamme, who had fourteen – FOURTEEN – children, saw them from her window and poured a cauldron of boiling soup over their heads and her neighbours followed her example. The Savoyards were defeated. L'Escalade is my favourite holiday in Geneva. We dress up as olden-day Genevois or soldiers, or Savoyards, the little kids as pieces of vegetable, and we come here to have *potage* from huge iron cauldrons, and we walk around the old city watching how olden-day Genevois lived. My favourite is watching the blacksmiths making horseshoes in La Place du Bourg-de-Four. George used to like watching the cannons going off, but now they just annoy him because they're too noisy and he can't listen to his music.

Mum sat down next to me. We waited for George. It was so warm I didn't even need my fleece. Last year, October was very cold and there was snow in Geneva in November. When I spoke to Grandpa on the phone yesterday he said that it was very hot in Bulawayo. Thirty-seven degrees Celsius. Which is hot. And it didn't rain in the rainy season – Bulawayoans don't have any water for four whole days in the week. Grandpa is lucky. He has a borehole and can take water out from the ground. People who live in places like Magwegwe are not as lucky as Grandpa. He took us there in his truck because that's where Grandma and him had their very first house and Mum was born there. I couldn't believe it. It was so small. Another family lived there now. They had six children and there was only one bedroom. Some of the children had to sleep in the kitchen – there wasn't a stove or fridge in there, though – the others with their mum and dad, not on a bed, on the floor. The toilet was outside and they had to share it with other families. They didn't have a bath. They had to use a dish and cold water. Grandpa said that Magwegwe was a township, which was where white people said all black people had to live in the olden days.

Mum: Baba, not all white people, and I think it's better to say people who originally came from Europe, Britain.

Grandpa: And are they not white?

Even though people were really poor in Magwegwe, they were very proud of their houses. Look how clean everything is – Grandpa showed us – and look at the flower gardens and the vegetable patches people tried to grow even though the soil was so dry and full of stones. People tried very hard to make the dirt look pretty.

I tied my fleece around my waist. The leaves of the chestnut trees were crispy on the ground. I jumped on them. A squirrel scrambled up a tree, his cheeks full with *marrons*. Mum took out her notebook and pen. She started writing. Her literary vampires were up to something. I decided to walk all along the bench to the far end. I counted my steps. The last time I did this I counted one hundred and sixty-seven steps. How many this time? One hundred and fifty-nine! I had grown! I stood looking up at the First Chestnut Tree of Geneva. This was the special tree that told us that spring had arrived. There was a Keeper of the Tree who would come and check every single day for the first leaf of the season. When he saw it, he rang the bell to declare that spring had begun. But what if he missed the leaf, or the leaf was hidden? What if he only got the second, third, fourth, even fifth leaf? What if spring began on the wrong day? What would it mean? We were doomed, DOOMED.

There was George. *Finally.* He was leaning back against the old city wall. *Just chilling.*

I ran up to Monsieur Pictet de Rochemont standing

on his plinth with a document rolled up in his hand. I knew what it was. It said that Geneva was now part of Switzerland, or was it the one that said Switzerland would always be a neutral country and never take sides in wars? I walked around the plinth and read out loud what was carved there: *La Traité de Paris 1815; La Traité de Turin 1816; La Traité de Vienna 1815.* We came here on a class visit and we spent ages around Monsieur Pictet de Rochemont, 1755–1824.

Jean: He's in his underwear.

Mr Reynolds: Don't be silly, that's how noblemen dressed in the nineteenth century.

Philip: He looks like a penguin.

Manuel: Someone's pantsed him.

And the whole class went hysterical, and then we ran over to the canons at l'Ancien Arsenal and we pretended to be in a battle, which was fun.

I looked up at Monsieur Pictet. I always did that. I asked him the same question I always did. He thought a bit and then said *hmmm* . . . I waited, but that was it.

In Bulawayo, Grandpa took us to the Natural History Museum. We spent a lot of time in the geology section because Grandpa used to be a mine engineer. First he mined tin, then coal, and he said if he hadn't retired he'd probably be mining diamonds now.

George was so bored in there. He didn't even go in the mine shaft, which was the best bit.

I liked the Hall of Chiefs. Grandpa told us lots of stories of how white people –

Mum: Baba . . .

– tricked the Great Chiefs of Zimbabwe into handing over their land. The chiefs who couldn't read put crosses on pieces of paper and they were given necklaces. And that was that. They lost all their land. George said it served them right for being so dumb. He didn't say it to Grandpa, though. He wasn't that stupid.

Mum got up from the bench and we walked under the arch where one of the gates to the Vieille Ville – which is the Old Town – used to be. In the olden days they used to close and lock the gates – there were three of them – at ten o'clock every night, so if you weren't inside the town's walls by then you had to spend the night outside. Mum says that in the letters she's read by Mary Shelley who wrote *Frankenstein* there was a lot of dashing around to make sure you weren't locked out and left to fend for yourself among the poor who lived outside the walls, because no matter how much you tried to bribe the guards, they would never let you in. Not like in Italy.

We were going to Mum's favourite *crêperie*, just behind Cathédrale Saint-Pierre. Mum liked to hear the bells ringing, George did not. He said it was a human rights infringement on his eardrums. They went on and on. Mum said, well then, so are those headphones. George rolled his eyes and said, how? Mum said because they brought noise from his rap straight into his eardrums, which wasn't any good. Mum refused to call rap music. She was always putting on CDs of jazz, classical music and sometimes African music, even pop like the stuff they sing on *X Factor*, trying to get George into proper music. George just put on his headphones and drowned out all the proper music and flooded his ears with rap. And sometimes it was so loud all the swear words leaked out and Mum got super angry and confiscated his headphones, which was the worst violation of George's rights, ever.

'Yo, Maman,' he said, 'seriously, can we *not* have a crêpe.'

Mum stood by the door, her hand on the handle. She pushed it down and went inside. I looked up at George, who shrugged his shoulders and walked away to one of the benches in the church's big courtyard. He swagged himself down there and started working on his phone. I wondered if this was a situation where bro loyalty was required. My stomach made funny noises. I followed Mum.

She was sitting by the window in the corner, her favourite seat. She was writing very fast.

'Mum—'

She held out her finger.

I waited.

The waiter came and looked at Mum, and then at me. I held out my finger and he went away.

It was very quiet. I waited for the bells but they were quiet too.

Once, I went up all the way inside the cathedral with Dad. Mum couldn't go because she still had her cast on. George was off paintballing. Dad and I had to walk up narrow, winding stairs, one at a time; then we had to go all the way down again before we reached the top

30

because we met a really obese lady trying to move. She was breathing really hard; I thought that she would get stuck and the fire brigade would have to come, but Dad said later that if she'd managed to get all the way up, she could manage to get all the way down. Finally we reached the ceiling of the cathedral. There were wooden beams holding everything together and pictures of how they made the cathedral in the olden days. Then we went even further up to one of the balconies and we looked out at all of Geneva. There was the lake. There was the Jet d'Eau. There was the Russian Orthodox church with its golden domes, their tops covered with snow. I asked Dad what Orthodox meant and he said, 'Traditional, old, and maybe a bit set in its ways.' I watched a pigeon take off and fly over Geneva and I closed my eyes and thought of flying too.

The waiter came again. Mum was ready now. We ordered our specials.

Moitié-moitié for me, which was not a crêpe but an omelette. Half ham, half cheese.

Ham, cheese and spinach for Mum.

And a big bottle of *eau plate*.

The waiter went away.

'Mum, can I *please* have a dog?'

'A dog, no, not that again, I thought we'd decided.'

'You said we'd wait until after a year then we would have this conversation again. It's after a year now.'

'You mean a real dog, not one of those soft toys which look so cute, or those new ones we saw that move and bark.'

'Mum, those are just creepy. A *real* dog.'

'Robert, we live in an apartment.'

'Dogs live in apartments too.'

Mum sighed.

I think she was hoping that I would grow out of wanting to have a dog or that I'd have amnesia and forget that I'd ever wanted one.

'And dogs are not allowed in our park.'

Mum was right. Technically. There were signs all over the park that said *pas de chiens*, but no one paid any attention. The park belonged to our apartment building but wasn't really private because there wasn't a fence or a gate to keep people out. Dad said that was part of the Swiss ethos, the sharing of all green spaces. Our neighbourhood was not like the old town, where rules *had* to be obeyed all the time or people reported you to the police right away. The signs were all rusted and flaking. They had been there for ever.

'Mum . . .'

'Dogs are a big responsibility. They smell. They pick up ticks and fleas. And worms. They're not hygienic, all that hair and who knows what under their feet.'

Mum's usual arguments.

'I'm big now. I'm responsible. We can have a dog with no hair.'

I'd seen those in the park, and to tell the truth, they were scary-looking, but I could get used to them. They were still dogs.

'They take up space.'

'We can get a small one like Fifi.'

32

Fifi was so small you had to be careful not to step on her.

'In winter when it's cold and dark, come rain or snow, you have to take them outside to do their business.'

'I love the cold. I love snow. I love rain.'

I didn't love the dark, but if I had a dog in the dark I wouldn't be afraid.

'And you have to put your hand in a plastic bag and scoop up after it. And then the same dog comes back into the house and sits on the couches. No, Robert. Dogs are animals and animals should be outside.'

'But Aunty Delphia said that we're animals too and *we* live in houses.'

Mum and Aunty Delphia were twins, even though they didn't look alike. They were the opposite of each other, but their bond was deep. Aunty Delphia was a veterinarian and she worked for the National Parks in Zimbabwe. I always made sure to stay close to Aunty Delphia because she knew everything about animals and she was helping me in my mission to convince Mum about a pet.

Mum sighed again.

'How about . . . a cat?' I tried.

'I'm allergic to cats. Remember when that cat got lost on our balcony and we had to bring him inside because it was so cold.'

I did remember. Mum sneezed for weeks. And her eyes got very swollen and red.

'A rabbit?'

'Rabbits hop. They can hop anywhere and break things.'

I was stumped.

Aunty Delphia would have thought of something.

'An imaginary dog! I'll talk to him all the time!'

Mum had Aunty Delphia to thank for that.

Aunty Delphia: Do you remember Didi, Jane?

Mum: Errr, what about him?

Me: Who's Didi?

Mum: Nobody.

Aunty Delphia: Oh, he was somebody, an imaginary somebody.

Me: You had an imaginary friend, Mum?

Mum: Errrr . . .

Aunty Delphia: Yes, neither human nor beast. I think he was an elf.

Me: An elf?

I had never heard of an elf called Didi.

Aunty Delphia: All that time you spent talking to him, Jane, don't you think a pet, a real pet, would be less worrying?

Mum: Good try, sis, still no.

Aunty Delphia winked at me.

Aunty Delphia: We'll get there in the end, Robert.

'He'll still have to stay out of the apartment.'

'You're mean, Mum. I'll be psychologically damaged, for ever.'

Mum didn't seem too worried about that.

The waiter came with our food, and when he left,

Mum leaned in and whispered, 'Robert, what if we make Monsieur Renoir a vampire?'

I jumped out of my seat. Literally.

Mum put her hand on my arm. 'A literary vampire. A Devourer of Knowledge.'

I liked it when Mum talked about her writing, how she made things up and they became real once she put them down on paper. It was magic and I was so proud that I had a magician for a mum. That was pretty cool. Even George didn't mind that she was a writer, because she was semi-famous. Her Amazon rating wasn't anywhere near Dan Brown's or J. K. Rowling's, but her books were in the secondary school library, and according to his friends who *did* read them, they weren't totally lame. Even some older kids at school had friended him on Facebook because of Mum.

'Hmmm . . .'

'Think about it,' she said. 'Inside our very own building, a Devourer of Knowledge. The possibilities. What kind of knowledge? Just think about it.'

I did think about it. Mum could be right. It wasn't children he was putting in the coffin he dragged around his room. It was knowledge. A certain kind of knowledge that was the key to, to . . . LIFE and DEATH.

I jumped out of my chair again and this time it toppled on to the floor.

George walked in right at that moment; I thought that he would walk past us to another table, but he looked at Mum, he looked at me, he looked at the toppled chair, and he just shook his head and sat down on the other chair.

Mum didn't tell him about Monsieur Renoir, the Devourer of Knowledge. She asked him if he wanted to order something. He shrugged. George thought McDonald's was the only place in the universe that should be allowed to make and serve food. Their hamburgers were Epic. Their chips were Epic. Their Cokes were Epic. Their very existence was Epic. The only thing more Epic than a McDonald's in Geneva was a McDonald's in New York. When he was my age, he was banned from McDonald's because Mum said its very existence was a health hazard. He is still technically banned from it, but now that he can go to places all on his own, she can't really enforce the ban. So he hangs out at the McDonald's in Balexert with his friends and eats all the Epicness of McDonald's that there is. I think it's gross to eat there. I saw the documentary about how they make chicken nuggets. They squashed up the whole chicken in one go, beak and claws too. Never, Ever. Ever.

I wanted to tell Mum about the Land of In-Between. *Entresol.* But if I told Mum, then George would know and he would look at me as if I had a highly contagious strain of weirdness. So I zipped my lips and unzipped them only to eat my *moitié-moitié.* George stole half of my chips even though they were zero in their Epicness. He had football practice later so he needed to eat a lot of proteins. Mum wouldn't let him drink raw eggs so he had two *moitié-moitiés.* And then he burped. Mum

36

didn't say anything because she was far far away.

We walked around for a bit. Mum showed me the houses where some famous writers used to live. Her favourite was George Eliot, who wasn't a man; she used a man's name so that she could be taken seriously as a writer. That was in the olden days when there was lots of sexism. It was funny how I felt okay saying *sexism* but it felt really yucky to say *S E X*. Mum said there was still plenty of sexism around and then we played a game trying out boy names for her. Horatio Spartacus was my suggestion, and she said she could live with that. Mum liked looking at the paintings in the galleries. One of them had sculptures in bronze by Salvador Dali by the window. I liked them. There was one of a clock and it looked like it was melting.

George: Swag.

I knew what the name for Salvador's art was: *surrealism*. Madame Vernier made us learn all the schools of art off by heart. Mum said that there were some paintings you could just fall into. The paintings cost a lot of money, even the ones that didn't look so good. I wasn't very good at drawing and there were some pictures that looked like some of mine.

I hoped we'd go into Maison Tavel, because I liked walking into those olden-day rooms where people lived, hundreds and hundreds of years ago; it felt as if the house was still waiting for them to live their olden-day lives in it. But we stopped by the cannons instead; Mum wanted to take a picture to send to Nonna in Rome. She wanted me and George together but George got a phone call right at that moment and it was really important because he took off his headphones and had a proper conversation with the person on the other side. It was a girl. They were in luuuurve. If I said this to George he'd slap me, not really slap me, just fake slap me, just to let me know how moronic I was being. George is too swag to be in luuuurve. He is so swag that girls are in luuuurve with him.

I posed for Nonna. I gave her my cheesy smile. I hugged the cannon. Mum took a picture of George, without his consent.

When we got home I went up the stairs, very quietly. I still had to use the stairs even though I told Mum that my life was in danger *and* I was injured. Mum said to stop being dramatic and that as long as I behaved, everything would be fine; Monsieur Renoir was no ogre. That's what *she* thought. I listened out for him on the *entresol* landing but there wasn't a sound. I beat George to our door; he had to wait for the lift to come down all the way from the ninth floor. Mum was still downstairs talking with Monsieur Badon, who'd been busy smoking. It was Madame Badon who did most of the work, like vacuuming the foyer.

George packed his football bags and went out to training. And then it was just me and Mum. I wanted to talk more about Monsieur Renoir and whether it would be a good idea to break into his apartment. What would we find there? Knowledge? But in what form? A book? That just seemed so obvious. A sword? I couldn't really imagine Monsieur Renoir brandishing a sword. A club? Hmmm. That seemed plausible. The Club of Knowledge. That didn't sound right. What if it was something you put on. A hat? A cloak? Yes, something like that. Or food! Something you ate or drank. Or a stone? There were so many possibilities. What if it was something completely new, something you'd never ever think of? There was so much to talk to Mum about but she'd disappeared into her study and her door was closed, which meant *Do Not Disturb, Unless You're Dying*. I wasn't dying so I did not disturb. I went into the playroom.

George wanted his own room and he wanted the playroom to be it. He kept trying to guilt-trip Dad into handing it over because Dad had his own room in Rome and Nonna hadn't changed a single thing about it. When Dad stepped inside he stepped into his boy self. Mum said that must be uncanny and he said yes, that was the word for it. There were posters of Bob Dylan, Leonard Cohen, Cat Stevens, Janis Joplin in Dad's room. I knew who they were because Dad told me. Dad tried to get George to listen to all of them but he said they literally hurt his ears. I liked the first three because I could hear their words. Janis Joplin screamed a lot and she didn't look too happy in the poster.

George: She's gross.
Mum: Don't be shallow.
Dad: She died very young.
Me: How?
Dad looked at Mum.

39

Mum: She overdosed on drugs.

George: Junkie.

Mum: I don't like that word. She was a drug addict and a very, very talented musician. Sometimes very creative people get trapped in their genius.

George: Three seniors got suspended for spiking drinks at their dance.

Mum looked at Dad.

Mum: Really? I haven't heard anything about that.

George: Oh, they don't want you parents to worry. The school is FULL of junkies, I mean, drug addicts.

Mum and Dad looked really worried.

George: Owned! Seriously, guys, but they did get suspended.

There was a poster of Pelé and the Italian football team who won the World Cup in 1982 right above Dad's bed where there was the crucifix over Nonna's. Dad said that he and his friends walked all the way from Nonna's house to Piazza del Popolo at night to celebrate Italy's victory. The piazza was overflowing and everyone was so happy. George said Pelé was swag; all Brazilians were swag.

There was another with a fist and *Human Rights* above it.

There were football trophies on a shelf, just like George had.

Dad said he had to have his own room; he had sisters. George glared at me. I held my hands up.

'*You* were supposed to be the girl, remember,' I said.

George didn't like people calling it a playroom.

40

When his friends were there it was a 'hanging-out zone'. He didn't *play* any more and he thought I was getting too old to play, too. I didn't really play there. I read. Sometimes I worked on Lego (*George: That's playing*) or used the computer.

I looked at the computer.

I wonder, I thought, if I google Monsieur Renoir, is that stalking? If I google him once, that isn't stalking. I typed *Monsieur Renoir*. There were hundreds of them. I clicked on images and there were all the Monsieur Renoirs that the computer knew. And none of them were mine.

The internet was a World Wide Web and it captured people. Even *I* was in it. When you typed my name and clicked on images there was a picture of me holding the cup I won for the science quiz at the Musée des Sciences last year.

George was in it because he was in Lancy FC. Lancy FC had a website and there were images of all their football matches and videos. And there was Facebook and YouTube, and even though Dad and Mum tried to keep up with what George was up to in the World Wide Web, they just got tangled up in it. It was too sticky.

Dad was in it because there were articles he'd written about how to help refugees. We had learnt about refugees in our Peace and Conflict unit; Dad came and gave a talk to the class. Refugees fled wars. They went to another country and asked for help. Refugees didn't have much money. Einstein was a refugee.

Mum was a writer so she needed the internet.

But not Monsieur Renoir. He was nowhere. He had escaped the World Wide Web. But what if he was in disguise? What if he was wearing a fat suit? What if he was really skinny? I looked at the computer screen thinking, should I type in *Monsieur Renoir in a fat suit*, but what if Monsieur Renoir had the most advanced technology in the *entresol* and he could hack into our computer and what if he found my search *Monsieur Renoir in a fat suit*? I jumped from my chair. I stood up, my heart beating so fast I had to press my hand on it to calm it down. I tried to remember the yoga breathing we had learnt at school from Miss Davies, our gym teacher.

Ooooom, I said. *Ooooom*.

I was oooooming so loud I didn't hear Mum.

'Robert . . .'

She touched my elbow.

'Ooooom, ooo—'

'What are you doing?'

'Yoga.'

'Oh, yoga, good. I'll get dinner started.'

I sat down again and opened my creative journal. We had a homework assignment for the mid-term break. We could write anything we wanted. It could be a story or a poem, even a song. Monsieur Renoir loomed over the pages. Did he have something to tell me? I was afraid but I tried to pay attention. What was it?

'Robert,' he said, 'I know where you live.'

'I know where *you* live, Monsieur Renoir.'

Monsieur Renoir smiled. I think it was a smile. He opened his mouth and all his teeth showed. They were the whitest teeth I'd ever seen. Teeth that didn't belong to Monsieur Renoir. Where did he get them from?

I waited for him to say something more, but that was it.

I had my shower, put on my pyjamas and when George and Dad came home we all had dinner.

Dad had a *lavoretto*, which was a business trip; he was leaving on Sunday to go to Turkmenistan and he was only coming back on Friday. I loved the names that Dad travelled to: Kazakhstan, Tajikistan, Kyrgyzstan, Uzbekistan, Azerbaijan, Ararat. He said that in Turkmenistan there was a ginormous statue of the president in gold which turned around so that it always faced the sun.

Then George told us his news. There was a selector at training and he took down George's name. We all toasted him with glasses of water.

I tried to read a bit in bed – *Warriors* Book 4, *Eclipse*. At night I was reading these and in the mornings Young Sherlock Holmes, because I needed to be bright and fresh to keep up with the Young Sherlock Holmes.

But I just couldn't concentrate.

Monsieur Renoir wouldn't leave me alone.

I hoped that he wouldn't visit me in my dreams. He was awful enough in real life.

'Robert . . .'

I jumped.

Phew, it was Mum. She sat on the edge of my bed.

43

'Robert,' she said, 'I've been making some enquiries about Monsieur Renoir.'

Enquiries? Mum? What was going on? Did Mum think she was Sherlock Holmes?

'He's not Swiss.'

What was she talking about?

'He's English. British.'

'Mum, he yelled at us in French.'

But then I remembered what George had said about how his words sounded. Maybe he wasn't drunk. Maybe he was just British.

'Monsieur Badon has known Monsieur Renoir for over fifteen years. He says Monsieur Renoir was a pilot in the British Royal Air Force.'

Our concierge was Mum's informant. Concierges knew everything about everyone.

'He's in his eighties. He fought against the Mau Mau in Kenya.'

'What's the Mau Mau?'

'They were the black . . . I mean the local people who lived in Kenya who fought against the British for independence. It happened a long time ago, in the 1950s, I think, way before you were even born.'

This was so confusing.

'And he isn't really Monsieur Renoir, you know.'

I shivered. Literally.

What did Mum mean? Was this a case of mistaken identity after all? Nothing ever was what it first appeared.

'He's just never bothered to remove the name plate

next to the buzzer. I suspect the real Monsieur Renoir is long dead.'

If he wasn't Monsieur Renoir, then who was he?

'Jack Montgomery Clift. That's his name.'

Jack Montgomery Clift?

And suddenly Monsieur Renoir wasn't Monsieur Renoir any more. He was someone completely different. He was Jack Montgomery Clift. English. British.

'Anyway,' said Mum, 'he can still be a vampire. A literary vampire with a heroic and troubled past. Perfect.'

'Why, why did he shout at us?'

'You were making a noise.'

'Mum, he used a swear—'

'I know he did. There's a whole story in there. Maybe something in his history. He lives shut up in that room, who knows what . . .'

Mum narrowed her eyes.

'You know, when you were small, a young woman with a baby was stuck in the lift, the old one, for a couple of hours, and if I remember correctly, they were visiting him – yes, I think that's right. I remember the woman because she was incredibly skinny and she reeked of—'

Mum got up.

'Hey, it's late, good night, sweetheart.'

I guess she was going to say the woman reeked of garlic.

'Don't let the bed bugs—'

'Bite!'

That's our routine, our tradition every night. And Dad says *sogni*, and I shout *d'oro*, which means *golden sleep*. George just throws himself on the top bunk bed and sleeps. One minute he's awake, the next, gone.

The phone rang and Mum picked it up in the bedroom. She was silent for a while and then I heard her say *oh*, and then she started crying.

Chapter Three

Aunty Delphia and Bob the Butternut

Aunty Delphia was in jail because she said something about the president. Some men came to Grandpa's house and took Aunty Delphia away in her pyjamas. They didn't even let her put on her slippers. Grandma and Grandpa couldn't find out where she was. The police said that she was under arrest for plotting to overthrow the government.

Aunty Delphia was shorter than Mum, who was one metre and fifty-nine centimetres tall. She always had a smile on her face. And dimples, just like me. Sometimes she wore beads of different colours in her hair. She said a monkey tried to snatch them off once and so now she always wore a bush hat when she had them on.

Aunty Delphia's office was in the National Park, in the biggest tree house ever. It took us three hours to get there from Bulawayo and Aunty Delphia had to stop lots of times to let goats and cows cross the road and then we drove right into the bush on a bumpy dirt road and there were signs that said *Mind the Elephants*. Cynthia, Aunty Delphia's daughter, was there too. She was only one and a half years old and she usually stayed with Grandma and Grandpa in Bulawayo when Aunty Delphia was working. This was a special treat for her. George wasn't around because he was playing football in Bulawayo. Grandpa had organized for him to train with the under-fifteen Highlanders team. Dad and Grandpa were watching him.

Aunty Delphia operated on the animals downstairs, but she usually did that in the bush, because you couldn't drag an injured elephant all the way back to the tree house and he definitely wouldn't fit.

When I stood outside on the veranda I got dizzy from looking up at the blue sky; it stretched on for ever, and from looking out at the grass and trees; it didn't seem to end. Animals came and went as they liked. The grass rustled and waved, guinea fowl and antelopes and buffaloes just wandering about. There was a huge tree that looked as though it was the wrong way up: its roots stuck up in the air. It was called a baobab. Apparently the gods got really upset with this tree because it was so vain – it was always tossing its branches and leaves about and saying how beautiful and majestic it was – so they uprooted it and planted it upside down just so that it would shut up.

Aunty Delphia went up to an elephant to give it an injection behind its ear; that's where the skin is the thinnest and you can easily see the vein and that's where you have to stick the needle.

Don't ever go up to an elephant when its ears are lying back or folded and if it rolls up its trunk, because that means it's not happy and it's going to charge for real; or from behind, because elephants definitely don't like surprises. And if you meet an elephant and its ears are spread out and they're flapping about and it's waving its trunk about, it's trying to give you a warning by getting all dramatic, a chance to scram. That's called a mock charge.

The elephant had eaten something that had given it a really bad stomach ache and he was losing a lot of water and getting really low on vitamins. Aunty Delphia had to make sure he didn't get dehydrated.

A fact: elephant skin is very sensitive; wounds take a very long time to heal so they have to be disinfected really well otherwise they will get infections.

When Mum heard this she said, *see, what's good enough for an elephant is good enough for you guys.* Mum is kind of obsessed about germs and infections.

It's hard to think of elephant skin being sensitive, it looks so tough and leathery. But they can feel a *fly* landing on them.

On another day, Aunty Delphia put drops in a baby elephant's eyes because they had an infection. The elephant – Aunty Delphia called her Thandi – liked Aunty Delphia and it looked like she was trying to kiss her with her trunk.

A fact: the elephant's trunk is its nose, arm, hand, voice, drinking straw, hose to spray itself with when it is too hot, and lots of other things besides.

Aunty Delphia's very worst experience was seeing a rhinoceros who'd been shot and his horn hacked off.

49

The rhino wasn't dead but there was nothing she could do to make it better, it had lost too much blood. A ranger had to shoot it again to end its pain.

There are almost no rhinos left in Zimbabwe.

A ranger came in the tree house and he said they had found another seven dead elephants in the park, their tusks were gone and they had captured two poachers.

Poachers were people who went into National Parks and hunted animals illegally. They hunted elephants for their tusks to sell to people who made necklaces out of them or ground them up to make potions they thought had magic powers.

Aunty Delphia said poachers were really bad because they killed as many animals as they felt like and they didn't care about the ecosystem and how nature had to be looked after otherwise we would all suffer in the end because the environment we all depended on would be destroyed.

'You can hunt, *legally*?' I asked Aunty Delphia.

'Yes, Robert,' she said. 'Unfortunately, that's the case.'

She told me that the National Parks gave out permits which were like permission slips to kill animals.

'Why would you even want to kill them?' I asked her. I could see giraffes chewing leaves off trees.

'Good question, Robert,' she said. 'The only reason you should kill an animal is for food, or if they are an immediate threat to you.'

She said that some people thought killing was a

big game, that it was fun to put a bullet into a living creature, and hunters paid the National Parks lots of money to be allowed to hunt and that money was supposed to go to protect the animals they were killing.

'No offence, Aunty Delphia, but that doesn't make any sense.'

Poachers were bad and hunters were good but they were both doing the same thing.

Aunty Delphia smiled. It wasn't a happy smile. Her dimples didn't show so much.

'Human beings are very illogical animals, Robert,' she said.

She picked up Cynthia, who was running around, and gave her a cuddle and then she put her down again.

'Do you know what culling is?' she asked me.

I shook my head.

'Well, it's a very controversial practice we do here in Zimbabwe,' she said.

Every year, the National Parks decided on a number of elephants that could be killed by hunters.

That was just so wrong!

I loved the elephants even though they could really bear a grudge so you had to be extra careful not to upset them. On safari we stopped at a watering hole and watched the elephants taking turns to drink; everyone had to wait for the bull elephant who was the leader of the herd to drink first. Two baby elephants were playing with each other in the water, twisting their trunks together and wrestling, and there were other elephants having mud baths – that looked like fun. We were so close that if I reached out my hand and waved my fleece about I could touch one. When the ranger started the car, the elephants got surprised and they all surrounded the baby elephants and made loud screeching cries which frightened even me. I was really hoping that just this once the elephants wouldn't remember us just in case we met them again.

'Too many elephants in one place can do a lot of damage,' said Aunty Delphia. 'They can uproot whole trees.'

On safari, I watched them tugging and pulling at tree branches. They curled their trunks over the branches and stripped off the leaves. Then they stuffed the leaves into their mouths. There was a baby elephant who was only a few weeks old; he grabbed tiny branches and he tried very hard to do what the big elephants were doing. He was very cute.

Aunty Delphia pointed outside.

Elephants liked baobabs because they stored lots of water and when there was a drought they attacked the bark; even though the baobab looked so strong and had been there for years and years, it could end up dying.

'Now imagine hundreds and hundreds of elephants in a small space and also villagers trying to live and survive in the same land. It's a balancing act. We have to make choices. And one of them is to cull.'

It sounded so cruel. People were hunting, poaching

and culling. How could the elephants have a chance? But Aunty Delphia was looking after them too.

When I woke up, Mum was still talking on the phone. It felt like maybe she had been doing that the whole night. I sat on the couch in the playroom and then I lay down, listening to Mum's voice in the lounge. She hadn't closed the door.

'She can't have just disappeared, how is that possible? I know, Baba, but she must be in a police station, if not Bulawayo Central, Ross Camp, all the others.'

Mum was quiet for a while.

'They can't make someone disappear like that. It's not the eighties, Baba. What is the lawyer's number? Yes, bye. Yes. I'll phone.'

There was silence and I was just about to go into the lounge when I heard Mum tapping a number on the phone.

Dad came into the playroom. He gave me a kiss on my forehead and ruffled my hair and then he went into the lounge. He closed the door behind him.

Aunty Delphia had disappeared.

I got up from the couch and went to my desk.

Aunty Delphia and I would go off together, before everyone else woke up. We would walk along the trail to the hide, where we could sit under the thatched roof and watch the animals come to the watering hole. There were buffaloes and warthogs, and peacocks and elephants. Aunty Delphia would hold my hand and it felt like we were sharing a secret.

I pulled open the drawer and I took out my reporter's notebook.

In Bulawayo, we went for long walks at the Hillside Dams and in the Matopos National Park. She told me lots of stories about the animals that lived there.

On the mighty boulders and hills of the Matopos leopards used to roam free, and even now, one or two still wander about.

I stood on top of the grave of the man who found Zimbabwe, except he didn't call it Zimbabwe. He called it after himself, Rhodesia.

George: Swag.

I imagined leopards leaping from all the huge rocks until they came to where I was. There were big lizards on the rocks and they would get a fright when they heard us and dart away.

Aunty Delphia and I would lie on flat slabs of rock. We were two gigantic lizards looking up at the sky. She made stories out of the changing shapes of the fluffy white clouds.

And now, Bob the Butternut had put her in jail.

Aunty Delphia needs help, I wrote in my reporter's notebook.

And then I wrote some more:

Monsieur Renoir is not Monsieur Renoir.

Monsieur Renoir is Jack Montgomery Clift.

Monsieur Renoir is a Royal Air Force pilot.

Monsieur Renoir fought the Mau Mau.

Monsieur Renoir has Knowledge.

It looked like a puzzle, a riddle. I doodled around the points, making circles and spirals, and I thought it looked like a plane flying, doing acrobatic stunts and then going round and round looking for something. There was something in all that information.

The Mau Mau lived in Kenya.

Kenya is in Africa.

I went to the shelf and took out the atlas. I turned the pages until I found the map of Africa. There was Kenya. It was in the east, near the Horn of Africa. It had a coastline, so there were places with beaches. To get to Zimbabwe I had to go over Tanzania, Malawi and Zambia. Zimbabwe looked like a teapot and it had no coastline. I went back up to Kenya. Somewhere in there Monsieur Renoir flew his plane and fought the Mau Mau.

And then I remembered what Mum had said about the smell outside Monsieur Renoir's apartment, how it made her think of a witch doctor's hut.

Monsieur Renoir has a blazing eye. What if he could cast spells? What if he could make potions? What if he could solve problems, like the *médium voyants* promised in their flyers? *Travail garantie, 100%.*

I knew how the pieces of the puzzle fitted. Monsieur Renoir had Knowledge. He had been in battles. He was a Royal Air Force pilot. He was a hero. He would know how to find Aunty Delphia and how to free her. I was sure that was part of his Knowledge.

I had an idea!

Dear Monsieur Renoir,

My Aunty Delphia has been put in jail in Zimbabwe by the president. I know that you have special powers. You have Knowledge. You will know the right thing to do. Please help her. Please write back and tell me what we have to do to save her.

I looked at what I'd written and then I wrote it down again on a separate piece of paper. I couldn't rip out the page from the reporter's notebook.

It felt like I should write more. Maybe I should tell him that I knew he wasn't really Monsieur Renoir but Jack Montgomery Clift, Royal Air Force pilot, and that's why I knew he would know what to do. I looked at the paper. I put my pen over it to write some more but I couldn't think of the right words to say. I don't know why, but I felt strange. What if he thought I'd been spying on him? What if Monsieur Renoir got really mad when he saw the letter? What if he thought I was invading his privacy? But then I thought about Aunty Delphia and I had to try.

And then I knew what else I could write.

I'm sorry that we made so much noise the other day.

I had to be brave.

I went downstairs and stood in front of Monsieur Renoir's door. I took a deep breath. I slid the letter under the door and then I ran like mad up the stairs.

It was only when I was home that I remembered something.

I forgot to sign my name.

Chapter Four

The Tennis Match

Dad drove me to the tennis centre, Les Evaux, for my class. I still sat in the back seat behind him. At least I wasn't on the booster seat any more. George always used to Laugh Out Loud when I got on it. Luckily Mum found a study on the internet that said booster seats were not very safe because they made you put the seat belt on all wrong.

Mum was always finding studies on the internet.

Mum was on the phone again when we left. She was talking to Aunty Madeline, her older sister who lived in Plymouth.

I just kept thinking of Mum and Aunty Delphia's stories about when they were kids. They were mostly stories about Aunty Delphia because Mum said she was the one who used to get up to lots of mischief and who got away with murder (not literally). When they were telling the stories, Mum called Aunty Delphia Dee.

Once, Aunty Delphia climbed on to the roof and came down with a snake in her hands. A big one, said Grandpa. Aunty Delphia was holding it like it was just a plastic toy. She wouldn't let Grandpa kill it. He had to drive all the way to Matopos National Park. She freed it in the bush.

Another time, their dog, Maxine, was having puppies and one got stuck. Aunty Delphia pulled the puppy out from her. Aunty Delphia was only eleven years old. Everyone else was so scared in case Maxine became really angry. Aunty Delphia went up to Maxine like she was a veterinarian already and saved the puppy.

Aunty Delphia laughed at some of the stories, and I loved Aunty Delphia's laugh because it sounded like tinkling piano keys.

On Sundays, when Aunty Delphia was supposed to be resting, she drove around villages and treated all the dogs there, for free. I went along with her. We spent a lot of time together.

I rubbed my eyes.

Dad kept glancing at me in his mirror.

'*Allora, Robert, che si dice?*'

Dad used our drives to Les Evaux as my 'sprucing up Italian' time.

'*Niente,*' I said, which means 'nothing'. I hoped Dad would give up.

'*Niente? Non è possibile!*'

'*Si, è possibile.*'

Of course, it wasn't the truth. There was lots going on but I couldn't explain it all in Italian. How could I say that Monsieur Renoir who isn't really Monsieur Renoir, the Devourer of Knowledge, Royal Air Force pilot, who lives in the Land of In-Between, possesses the knowledge to find Aunty Delphia and to set her free from Bob the Butternut? And that I'd already asked for his help – but maybe I'd leave that bit out. It was too much. Would George be able to say it in Chinese? This was his third year doing Chinese and it was the only subject he always passed. His teacher said he spoke well, too. And if he read any book, it was the Chinese ones his teacher gave him, especially the comics. Sometimes, when Mum or Dad shouted at him, he would say something in Chinese and Mum or Dad would get really mad because they thought he was swearing at them and he would put on his really innocent, offended face and say, 'I only said "I love you my mother, my dear father, and I bow to your hard-earned, superior wisdom".' I thought it sounded a lot like sarcasm, Chinese style.

'*Sei preoccupato per Zia Delphia?*'

'*Sì.*' I *was* worried about her.

'We'll find her,' he said in English.

Maybe I should tell Dad about Monsieur Renoir, that *he* was part of the *we* too.

'Dad, did she really try to overthrow the government?'

'No, she didn't.'

Aunty Delphia was sitting on a rocking chair and feeding a baby monkey with milk from a bottle. The monkey's mother didn't like this baby monkey and wouldn't feed her. Aunty Delphia said some people thought that the mother monkey must know best, that maybe she wasn't feeding the baby monkey because she knew it was weak and wouldn't survive anyway, but

Aunty Delphia said sometimes nature needed a helping hand. When we left Zimbabwe, I saw the baby monkey swinging from a tree branch.

Dad turned to me when we were at a traffic light.

'She gave an interview about poaching. Aunty Delphia explained that to you, didn't she?'

I nodded.

'Well, she named names.'

'What do you mean?'

The traffic light went green and someone hooted right away. It was usually cars with French number plates that did that. French people were so impatient. Or people from Zurich. Dad said that people from Zurich were bankers – Mum wasn't around so she couldn't tell Dad that that was a stereotype, but I did and he said that he was making a generalization – and that they believed *time is money* and thought that the Genevois were too relaxed and kinda lazy and that they lived off all the money Zurich people made. He said it was the age-old story of the north–south divide; for instance, in Italy it's Milan versus Rome and in Zimbabwe it's Harare versus Bulawayo. In England it's Plymouth versus Manchester.

Dad didn't say anything until we were stuck at another traffic light.

'She gave a journalist the names of these important people who were paying other people to go into the National Parks to kill the animals for their fur, their skin, their tusks, their horns, or just for recreation. She made those important people very angry and so they accused her of plotting against the Zimbabwean president.'

In Zimbabwe, I heard Aunty Delphia tell Mum that her job was getting harder because of the lawlessness. Gangs of people were turning up with guns and saying this game park was theirs and then going around and shooting anything in it and chopping down the trees. The police wouldn't do anything to help because they were afraid of the gangsters.

'Are they . . . are they going to torture her?'

Dad looked at me. I gave him a little wave.

'I don't know, Robert,' he said.

We had finished the unit on Peace and Conflict. We had learnt about 9/11 and the terrorists who hijacked the planes and crashed them into buildings in New York. I knew all about Osama Bin Laden. I knew all about war and terror and torture, all the stuff the bad guys did. I was happy that I lived in Switzerland. There was no war. There were no terrorists. There was no torture.

There were cellars.

I liked the French word for cellar: *cave*. You say it like this: *c ah ve*.

Every apartment in our building has a cellar, which is really a nuclear bomb shelter. If some evil person *does* detonate a nuclear bomb, we can all squeeze into the cellar and stay there till we hear the sirens give the all clear. Every February, on a Wednesday, round about lunchtime, the practice 'evacuate' siren goes off all over Switzerland just to make sure it's still working.

After our unit I begged Dad to take me down to the cellar. The door was heavy and hard to open, and inside Dad had put all our old clothes and toys. What if someone dropped a bomb right this minute, how could we hide in there? We'd all be killed and our clothes and toys saved. Dad said that no one was going to drop a bomb, and I asked him how he could be so sure and he didn't have any answer so we stayed down there and cleared it up together. Dad took the boxes upstairs and when Mum asked what was going on, he said, don't ask. Then we went to Migros and bought a box of canned food and all the other stuff the Swiss survival book said we needed, and we put them in the cellar, and now I know that we can always hide there, no matter what.

A fact: there are hundreds and hundreds of tunnels under Switzerland (built by Italians!), just in case the enemy attacks and citizens have to hide and move unseen from one place to another. And there are forts and towers that look like shacks and boulders up in the mountains, ready and waiting for Swiss soldiers to use.

'Do you think she's scared, Dad?'

After I asked the question, I felt very sad.

'I don't know, Robert. Your aunt is a very brave woman.'

I knew she was.

'I don't think she's scared,' I said. And I believed that. She wasn't scared when we sat in the hide and the elephants got really close or when the buffaloes started running about because they'd seen a lion. She wasn't scared when a cow came charging at her on a farm and she stared it down.

And Monsieur Renoir was going to work things out. *Please, Monsieur Renoir, help her, help her.*

Great. My nemesis was at the tennis court. Claude Leboeuf. Yes, he'd signed up just to torture me for the week with his serves aimed right at my penis. I couldn't concentrate when he served. I just jumped out of his way and he won all the points. And it didn't help if he was my partner. His racket was a lethal weapon. He would poach my balls, and if I got in his way, he would whack me right there, and George told me that if you get hit more than three times there your penis will just snap off and you have to pee like a GIRL, all the time and not just after ten o'clock at night.

A fact: you are not allowed to pee standing up after ten o'clock at night in Switzerland. You have to do it sitting down, because apparently that doesn't make as much noise. *And* you're not supposed to flush the toilet. Eeeew. We don't obey these two rules in our apartment. Dad says that our household has the democratic and enduring union of the Roman spirit of anarchy and the Zimbabwean spirit of *next time*.

George watched one session during the summer holidays and afterwards he said, 'Yo, bro, he's *smaller* than you.' I said, 'He's *stronger*.' George thought about that and then he said, 'Man up.' I think he means I need to get buff, but I don't think a ten-year-old can get a

64

six-pack, can they? My best friend, Jin, when we were fighting, called me F A T.

Mum: You're not fat.

Dad: You have a boxer's body.

George: Extra heavyweight.

Ha ha ha.

Mum: You're bigger-boned.

Dad: Wait till you reach puberty, you'll be more buff than your brother.

George: Yeah, right.

Me: Jin's T H I N, even though he eats a lot.

Mum: Jin's small-boned.

George: There're no fat Korean people; they're all Gangnam style.

Gangnam was a rich people's area in Korea, Jin told me that.

Mum: George, that's a stereotype and stereotypes lead dangerously into xenophobic statements, and those things are not allowed here.

George: Yo, Maman, I'm half black, I can't be racist.

Mum: You're not half anything, you're black and white.

And then she thought about that.

Mum: And race is a social construct, it doesn't exist.

George put on his headphones.

I told Mum about Michael Jackson's song 'Black or White', and sang some of it to her.

'That's nice, Robert,' Mum said, and went off to her bookshelf. She was looking at the book *How to Tell Your Child about Racism* and I wanted to tell her

65

Michael Jackson had done it already and she shouldn't worry.

At the end of the tennis class I was promoted to *avancé* and Claude remained behind in *moyen*. Dad and I went to the *buvette*. We were clinking our glasses of orange juice when Dad's phone rang. It was Mum. He stood up and walked towards the swimming pool. When he came back, he said we had to go.

'Did they find Aunty Delphia, Dad?'

Dad didn't hear. He put the francs for our snack on the table and started walking. I ran after him.

'Did they find he—'

'Not now, Robert,' he said.

I knew that something bad had happened then. Dad was really very, very patient and he didn't raise his voice often.

He stopped walking and waited for me.

'Yes, they found her, Robert,' he said.

That was good. Monsieur Renoir's powers were starting to work already! We knew where Aunty Delphia was. But Dad wasn't happy. He wasn't excited. What was wrong?

'Was she tortured, Dad?'

That just came out of me.

Dad looked at me. He looked around me, and then he looked at me again.

'Yes, Robert,' he said. 'She was tortured.'

We got in the car.

I didn't want to think of Aunty Delphia that way.

I opened my backpack. I wanted to do something. I started rummaging around like I was looking for something. There was always stuff in my backpack for me to find because I never really emptied it out, only when noxious smells started coming out of it which usually turned out to be mouldy sandwiches. I fished out a catapult. Grandpa and I made it in Zimbabwe. We made it from a tree branch and strips of rubber Grandpa cut from an old bicycle tyre. He showed me how to shoot stones against the gum tree; I hadn't used it in Geneva because it was a weapon.

Grandpa kept a catapult and stones in the pockets of his safari suit, in case he had to defend us against rámpaging lions; he was a herd boy when he was young and he had a very good shot.

Aunty Delphia said that it would take more than a stone to stop a rampaging lion and that a rampaging lion would rampage even more if a stone hit him on the nose; the best thing to do if you came across a lion was to pray and just hope there was some juicy impala nearby, because lions only ate humans as a last resort. Apparently we don't make a tasty snack.

If a lion does decide it wants to eat you, Aunty Delphia said that the last thing you should do is turn your back and run, because the lion is a predator and it loves to chase things. You should try and make yourself as big as possible by waving your arms around and you should shout your head off so that the lion maybe thinks you're some dangerous and crazy animal and becomes afraid of you!

Aunty Delphia tickled me when she said that.

But even the bravest deer would still be hurt and killed by a lion. Lions were so strong. They would pounce on the deer and tear him apart.

I sniffed and wiped my nose with my hand. I hit my hand with the rubber of the catapult. My eyes were watery.

Dad looked at me through his mirror.

'Can you help her, Dad?'

Dad helped people who'd been hurt by their governments or who didn't have a home any more because of wars. That was what the Red Cross was for. He helped them find new homes and places where they were safe.

'Robert . . .'

'Yes, Dad?'

But he didn't say anything else.

Dad never lied. He could have said, 'Yes, Robert, *certo*, I can help her.' He could have said it to make everything better, but he didn't.

Aunty Delphia was all alone. What if Bob the Butternut's men came back? Grandma and Grandpa were too old, and even though Grandpa had his catapult, it wasn't enough.

Aunty Delphia needed help.

Dad looked at me again in his mirror.

We were both quiet all the way home.

Chapter Five

Boy

I was in the hallway when I heard Mum. She was on the phone. Dad was outside; he was going over some bills he'd just taken from the letter box.

'. . . can't a doctor come to the house? Are you sure she can't go to the hospi— How can they drag— Yes, Baba, I know, I know.'

I took off my shoes.

'I will call that friend of mine – yes, we were classmates, she is still around. I'll ask her if she can come to the house, she has contacts. Okay, bye bye.'

I put my coat away and went into the lounge.

Mum had the phone in her hands; she was just looking at it. And then she made this choking sound – she looked up and saw me and she put her fist in her mouth. Her body was rocking, back and forth.

'Mum—'

'Robert, go outside.'

It was Dad.

'What's wrong with—'

'Robert, outside, please.'

I went down the stairs. I took a deep breath and tiptoed down the *entresol* stairs and then I stopped. I listened. *Monsieur Renoir*, I said in my head, *if you're in there, they found Aunty Delphia, but I'm sure you know that already. Thank you for finding her.* I couldn't say the next things. There wasn't a single sound. Nothing. So I walked all the way down and then I stood in the foyer, thinking of something to do. I opened the door and went into the park. I stood in the middle of the grass and looked up. I found our windows and I counted down until I reached *entresol*, Monsieur Renoir's windows. There they were! I waited for a long time, looking up. But nothing happened. Monsieur Renoir didn't draw the curtains. He didn't open the windows. The only thing that happened was that I got a sore neck and I felt kind of dizzy. I rubbed my neck and looked slowly down, which was a good thing because there was a dog poo right there. A big one.

And there was a *caninette*, right there, with hundreds of plastic bags waiting to be torn out from the dispenser and used. And a dustbin too, right next to it! In the poster on the *caninette* a dog who kinda looked like Tom, the cat in *Tom and Jerry*, was yapping away in a cartoon bubble: *Un super chien, c'est un super maître!* Which basically means a super dog has a super master. which is a polite way of saying . . . A MASTER THAT USES THE BAG TO PICK UP AFTER THEIR DOG!

I stepped back from the poo.

If *I* had a dog, I would be a *super maître*.

What could I do now?

Sometimes I *did* miss my brother. He was hanging out with friends. I wasn't old enough to hang out. I had to organize play dates with Jin, and Jin was stuck in a French village somewhere getting mega bored. He wasn't allowed to bring any electronic games with him because his mum and dad said that they had bought the house there so that they could 'commune with nature'. Jin said, it sucks. I couldn't even talk to him because I wasn't allowed a cell phone until I turned twelve.

Mum: Look what happens when you give a child a phone.

She was looking at George, who was scrolling down his like a maniac. She had also read all kinds of studies about how they sizzled and burned your brain cells; she didn't say, just look at your brother, but I did anyway.

Me: What if I'm in an emergency?

Mum: What emergency?

I thought about this. All the kinds of emergencies I could ever be in.

Me: What if, what if you forget me at school?

Mum: That's not an emergency. You're allowed to use the school phone.

I thought again.

Me: I could be kidnapped, in this very park.

Mum: I don't think so. I, and everyone else, would hear you screaming, and I can see you from the balcony.

Which was Mum's rule. I wasn't allowed to wander off to areas where she couldn't see me from the balcony. I couldn't disappear into bushes or go up the path to the shops. I had to be visible at all times.

71

The problem was, every single minute of my day was accounted for, and I was never alone. Mum or Dad took me everywhere.

The usual old ladies were walking their dogs. I tried to X-ray into their heads to see if they were the ones who'd left the poo. Nope. Nothing. Anyway, I knew which dog it was. The big black dog that the man with the tattoo on his head always brought into the park at around about four o'clock. I looked at my watch. Quarter to four. Maybe he was early today. The man always let his dog loose from the leash. You weren't allowed dogs in the park so *obviously* you weren't allowed to set them free from their leashes to terrorize other dogs. Duh. He brought terror to the little dogs that were on their leashes. One of the old ladies was going to call the police, one day.

There was Madame Badon. She gave me a tiny wave. I waved back.

'*Bonjour, Madame,*' I said.

'*Bonjour, Robert,*' she said. '*Comment allez-vous?*'

'*Bien, merci.*'

I bent down to give Fifi a pat on the head. I knew she wasn't the culprit. She was way too small to have poo that big.

Madame Badon was once very rich and beautiful and lived in the old town, but hers was a tale of woe (Mum's words). She was married five times and each husband ran off with a big chunk of her fortune and her good looks until all she could do was marry her sixth husband, Monsieur Badon, and move in with him. I didn't think it was woeful that Madame Badon lived with Monsieur Badon. She could have moved in with Monsieur Renoir, who yelled at innocent kids. But then I remembered. Monsieur Renoir was a hero. Monsieur Badon just smoked a lot.

'*Madame Badon,*' I said, '*Monsieur Renoir est-il un pilote?*'

I guess that's what Sherlock Holmes would call a leading question.

'*Oui, oui, en Afrique*, many, many years ago.'

I nodded.

'Ummm . . .'

I didn't know how to ask her what evidence she had.

'But he has a terrible, terrible family history, poor man. An estrangement with the granddaughter. He has seen his great-grandson only once, when he was a baby, they came here and it was a very bad visit. They are living in England.'

Maybe he scared away his granddaughter and his great-grandson with all his shouting. He scared them so much with his blazing eye they never came back to visit.

'I have to go now. Fifi is very impatient if I stay still – look at her, the naughty girl.'

Fifi was jumping about and twisting the leash around her body.

'Robert, something else . . .'

She stepped closer to me. She bent her head towards mine.

'You know what he has in his apartment?' she whispered.

I felt a cold, cold shiver down my spine.

'Monsieur Badon, he has seen it.'

I looked up at Monsieur Renoir's balcony. I guess I wanted to make sure he wasn't watching.

'*Un crocodile.*'

Fifi yelped. So did I.

Madame Badon smiled, and that was when I noticed she had red on her teeth.

'*Au revoir, Robert,*' she said.

'*Au revoir, Madame Badon.*'

I decided to head back home.

Monsieur Renoir's door was closed like it always was.

But there was a piece of paper on the doormat.

It said *BOY*.

My heart bumped and banged. I snatched the paper.

And then the door handle moved down. I jerked away. I hit my back against the wall. The handle moved up again. I shot up the stairs.

I stood by our door. At first all I could hear was my heart thumping and my breathing, but then I heard the lift. I heard it stop, the bell ringing. Someone was getting in down below. The lift door closed. It didn't come up. I held on to the banister and made myself go down again as quietly as I could. And then I stopped. I looked down the stairs. There was a man in the foyer. It was Monsieur Renoir. This was my chance. I *had* to go to him. I *had* to ask him to help Aunty Delphia some more. To use his Knowledge.

I went down the stairs with his note in my hand.

'Monsieur Renoir?'

Something fell on the floor. It made a tinkling sound but all I saw was a small blue box. Monsieur Renoir bent down to pick it up; he raised his head and saw my feet and then the rest of me and he opened his mouth.

'Yes?' he said. 'What is it, BOY?'

He said every word like it belonged to its own growling universe.

This time, bits of his hair were standing on end as if he'd walked through an electrical field. His eye was fixed on me, blazing right into every bit of me again. And then he reached out his arm and that finger was pointing at me.

I shot up the stairs and back into our apartment.

I stood with my back against the door, breathing hard.

Mum and Dad were having an argument.

'I'm going, Claudio,' Mum said.

My stomach was making funny noises. I went into the kitchen. I had a glass of milk.

'Jane, come on, listen to me, *Jane* . . .' Their voices disappeared into the bathroom and then they came back again into their bedroom.

'I have to do something,' Mum said. 'She's my sister.'

'Jane, it's not safe, your father—'

'She's my sister. I have to . . .'

George was my brother. If George was tortured by some evil guy I would go there and try and save him. Even though he could be highly irritating, he *was* my brother. My only brother. I would *have* to save him. And he wasn't even my twin. Our bond wasn't as strong as a twin bond. It was just an ordinary brother bond. But I would still have to save him.

'Robert . . .'

I jumped and almost dropped the milk.

'Is Mum going to Zimbabwe?'

Dad looked at his watch and then ran his hand through his imaginary hair. Dad sometimes forgot that he didn't have hair any more. When he was young, he had lots and lots of hair on his head. It was thick and black and curly and it reached his shoulders. Then, one day, it just disappeared. He woke up and most of it was on his pillow. Some more fell into the sink when he washed his face. By the end of the day, it had all vanished. Ever since George had heard this story, he'd become obsessed with his hair.

'I'm not sure,' he said.

'Do you want some milk, Dad?'

'No, *grazie*, Robert. Is George back?'

I wanted to help my brother but I had to tell the truth. I couldn't wave a wand and say *abracadabra* and bring him into being.

'No.'

Dad looked at his watch again.

George still had some time. Six o'clock was the latest he could be out on his own. If he started walking from Balexert now, he'd make it. If he was still at Grand Saconnex football pitch and he hadn't taken his bicycle or scooter, he was busted. If he was in town and he stepped on to a bus right now, he was busted.

'What's that in your hand?' Dad asked.

I was still holding Monsieur Renoir's note. I hadn't read it.

'Paper,' I said to Dad. Luckily Dad wasn't really listening. He went back to Mum.

I went to the playroom. I sat down on the couch. I opened the paper. I read:

BOY

You are brave and that is a good thing. The tyrant will fall. Evil shall be avenged. The good set free. It is only a matter of time. One evil deed a man does festers and grows and consumes a man's soul until he is no longer who he was, and the time comes for him to make amends before he meets his Holy Maker, and he looks for the Instrument of his atonement, and Boy, perhaps it is You.

I felt chills all over my body.

The note made me feel very afraid, as if Monsieur Renoir was breathing on me. What did it mean?

I heard the front door opening. I put the note under the couch seat. George was home, with time to spare. Raj, his friend who lived in the building next to ours, was behind him.

'Good evening, sir,' Raj said to Dad.

George rolled his eyes.

'Good evening, Raj.'

Raj had just started at the international school. He

was from India and very respectful, like all children used to be in the olden days. George said he was so funny; he was always jumping up in class whenever he had to ask or answer a question. Taresh, George's other friend, was also from India and was swag like George. He didn't hitch his jeans right up to his waist like Raj or wear his shirts and T-shirts tucked into them. The difference, Mum said, was that Raj grew up in India and Taresh grew up in Europe. Mum also liked Raj because he read books, not just stuff on Facebook walls. Raj was allowed to come to our place any time he liked, even when George didn't want him around. George used Raj as cover. Raj did his homework and George pretended to be doing his too but as soon as Mum was out of the way he went straight back to Facebook.

Raj had a backpack full of books.

'We're doing homework,' said George and went into the play— *hangout* room.

'Good,' said Dad.

'Hello, Raj.' That was Mum. There were too many people in the hallway. Raj couldn't even see Mum, who was behind Dad, but he still said, 'Good evening, ma'am.'

Dad looked back at Mum, then he went into the lounge. Mum followed. I went into the playroom even though I really wanted to watch *Doctor Who*. I knew that Mum and Dad needed time alone.

'They've found Aunty Delphia,' I said to George, who had his headphones on. He was listening to Lil Wayne and watching him on his computer.

'Was she missing?' asked Raj.

I was mad with George. Mum was right. He could be *so* self-absorbed. I stood right in front of him and yelled at him.

'THEY FOUND AUNTY DELPHIA!'

George took his headphones off. He glared at me.

'I know,' he said. 'Calm down.'

He sounded really mad. What was *wrong* with him?

'Was she missing?' asked Raj again.

'Yes,' I said.

'That's good they found her,' Raj said.

He cared. He didn't even know Aunty Delphia and he cared. George had his headphones back on. Lil Wayne was still rapping.

I gave up on him. I turned to Raj.

'She was tortured,' I said.

Raj shook his head.

'She was. My dad said so.'

'I believe you.'

'Maybe, she was . . . waterboarded.'

I had a funny feeling when I said that.

'What is wrong with you?!' shouted George. His headphones were off again. 'You can't just blab about her to any—'

And then he stormed out of the room.

What was wrong with *him*? And I wasn't blabbing to anyone. I was talking to Raj, his friend, kind of friend.

'No, only Americans do that to terrorists,' said Raj.

'She's not a terrorist.'

'To Americans, any Indian or Pakistani is a terrorist.

When my dad went there on a business trip, he was taken to a cubicle and kept there for six hours. Can you imagine? He's the chief executive of an American company in India and they wanted to know where he got the money from to travel all the way to America. He was on a business trip! Americans are so ignorant sometimes.'

Raj said 'Mericans' instead of 'Americans' and sometimes when he talked it was hard to understand him. When Taresh comes over he talks 'Raj style' and all George's friends collapse laughing. He's so country, Taresh says. Mum caught Taresh doing it once and said that this was not acceptable behaviour and then Taresh said, 'I'm very sorry, ma'am,' Raj style, and Mum stared at him so hard that he said, 'I'm sorry, Mrs Sartori,' and as soon as Mum was out of the room they all burst out laughing at Taresh and mimicked him.

'Evan got swirled,' I said. Evan was a seventh-grader.

'What's swirled?' asked Raj. 'Is it when they pick you up and swing you from your leg? That can really damage your brain.'

'No, someone pushed his head down the toilet and then they flushed. And the bowl wasn't even clean.'

'That's bad,' said Raj. 'You can die.'

Was waterboarding worse than swirling? I wanted to ask Raj but I wasn't sure if I really wanted to know, so I didn't.

I started telling him about Monsieur Renoir and the Land of In-Between, but as I got to the Devouring of

Knowledge he said he had to do his homework. I said okay.

I began work on my creative journal.

I wrote about the safari trip we took with Aunty Delphia, and when I finished, I started crying for no reason.

I didn't want Raj or George to see me so I went to my room and lay down on my bed. I got up again and took all my soft toys from the top of the cupboard and put them on top of me. Every time the tooth fairy brings a new soft toy, George says, 'Mum, he's TEN, seriously.' And then, 'It's *my* bedroom too.'

Soft toys are definitely not swag.

Aunty Delphia has soft toys too. Two teddy bears on her bed. One's yellow and doesn't have eyes any more, and the other one's brown and his hand's been sewn back on back to front. She was six when she got the yellow one, seven the brown one. When I went to Zimbabwe, I left Mr Fred the lion on her bed, between the two bears.

I breathed into the toys and they breathed back. I cried into the toys and they cried back. We comforted each other. It's okay, I said. It's okay, they said back.

Chapter Six

Movie Night

I must have fallen asleep under the soft toys, because when I opened my eyes again, I screamed.

'I'm blind!' I shouted.

Mum and Dad came rushing into the room.

'Robert—'

'What's the—'

It was too late. Now I knew I wasn't blind. I'd just woken up in the dark room.

'Dork,' said George.

It was eight o'clock and Dad had ordered pizza. Raj had gone home.

'Are you going to Zimbabwe?' I asked Mum.

'No,' she said.

'Aunty Madeline is coming over on Monday,' Dad said.

If Aunty Madeline was coming, my cousin Gregory was coming too. Gregory worshipped George. Gregory was happy to be George's *slave*. I'm thirsty, George would say and Gregory would, *snap*, appear with a glass of cold water. Hmmm, maybe an iced tea (that was the only soda-like drink Mum allowed in the house), and *snap*, Gregory would get it. *Snap snap snap.* Even Mum saw it. 'George, *enough*,' she would say. And George, 'What?' And Gregory, standing there waiting to fulfil the next wish. It was annoying, because Gregory was *my* age and we should have been friends, but he was in luuurve with my brother, as if he was a girl. I was hoping he would grow out of it soon. Maybe he *had* grown out of it. I hadn't seen him since July.

'Did you speak to Gregory?' I asked.

'No. He asked to speak to George.'

I groaned.

'George was too busy with his homework.'

I waited. Nope. He hadn't asked to speak to me. I did not exist. I was just the *not* George.

The TV was on BBC.

Mum kept switching from BBC World to Sky News to CNN International to Al Jazeera English and then back again to BBC World. Finally she got something on Al Jazeera English.

The newsreader said that elections were scheduled for March next year, and that tension was rising in Zimbabwe. There were reports of fresh attacks by youth militia. The camera left the newsreader and went into Zimbabwe. There was Bob the Butternut shaking his fist and women with big butts with his face on them jumping up and down. Mum switched off the TV.

Usually on Saturday evenings we all watched a movie together, but today was a different kind of Saturday. I didn't think Mum wanted to watch a movie, but then Dad said, okay guys, who's choosing today? Mum said she was tired and was going to bed. She said good night. I didn't remind her that she had forgotten to say something, like I did every night.

Dad said we could watch a movie without Mum.

We always watched the movie together.

'Just us boys tonight,' Dad said.

Dad was trying to make it okay that Mum wasn't with us.

'Two and a half men,' said George. He was stroking his abs.

He wasn't even original. That was from an American TV show.

I wanted to watch *The Sandlot* again, because I was thinking of learning to play baseball. I found a baseball mitt and ball at the flea market in Nyon and I liked putting my hand in the mitt and throwing the ball into it. George said baseball was lame and I wasn't American. 'Two strikes and you're out,' he said like he was a ninja assassin. Dad said baseball was played in Japan and Cuba, and probably other countries. 'Dude,' George said, 'do you even see what they wear? Tightie whities, and cups to stop their balls from getting whacked.'

'What cups? What balls?' I asked.

Dad gave George a look.

'Dad, what cups, what balls?'

'He means you have to wear a protective covering over your testicles.'

Ouch.

'I told you it was lame.'

'And what about the baseball cap you wear all the time?' said Dad.

Ouch! Sizzled and burned.

'For the hundredth time, it's not a *baseball* cap, it's an *American football* cap, snapback.'

Snapback just meant that it had that plastic thing at the back with holes so that you could change the size of the cap, but the way George said it, it was as if it was the most amazing thing ever invented. He also wore his cap with a sticker still attached to it. The sticker was VERY IMPORTANT because it told all his Facebook friends that the cap was AUTHENTIC and was therefore swag. You could get rich making all those shiny stickers and sticking them on any old cap.

George asked if he really needed to watch a family movie. He was way tired and he had a match tomorrow.

'In that case, straight to bed,' said Dad.

'It's nine o'clock,' wailed George.

'You're tired.'

'I'll read a book.'

The room became very quiet.

'Show me this book.'

Dad winked at me while George went looking for the book he was suddenly so eager to read. We heard him rummaging around in the playroom and then he came back holding a heavy book.

'Here, happy?'

'Really? You're reading *that* book? I'm impressed.'

It was *Conversations with Myself* by Nelson

Mandela. It wasn't even George's book. It was Mum's and she gave it to George because *he shouldn't only get stuff from Wikipedia for his school projects*; she had five bookshelves groaning with books, and here was one for his project on people who had changed the world. George loved the Nelson Mandela T-shirt that Mum bought for him at the airport in Johannesburg. It had a picture of Nelson Mandela's head and the words *History depends on who wrote it*. Nelson Mandela was swag.

'Okay, then. *Leggere*. But leave your phone here and no switching on the computer.'

George glared and Dad pretended not to notice.

'I'll watch the movie,' George said. '*I'm* choosing.'

It was my turn to choose, but it was getting late and I was afraid that Dad might notice.

'*Terminator.*'

'A *family* movie,' said Dad.

'It *is* a family movie.'

Dad ignored him again. I went to the DVDs that Mum bought on sale at Manor. There was one with Will Smith. Will Smith had swag.

'How about this one?' I said, holding it up. '*The Poo*—'

George laughed out loud.

'*Pursuit*, you dork.'

'*Of Happyness*,' I said.

'It's spelt wrong,' said George.

'Ahhh, the school fees have been worth it after all,' said Dad.

Sizzled and burned #2.

'Are you dissing me, Dad?'

'*Credo proprio di sì.*'

'Cool,' said George, and he flung himself on to the sofa. His long body hogged every single bit of it. Dad and I had to squeeze together on the other smaller one.

'*Happyness* it is,' said Dad.

'Maybe we should save it for when Mum wants to—'

'Can we watch it already? I have a football match tomorrow.'

I put the DVD in.

'Mum's so ancient, hasn't she heard of streaming movies online?' said George when I couldn't find the remote for the DVD player. 'Are we there yet?' he yawned.

I mean, he could help me look.

Dad found the remote under the couch and we finally watched the movie. Even George liked it. The movie made me sad, especially the part where Will Smith had to sleep in the toilet with his son because his wife had left him because he had no money because he couldn't sell any of his medical machines. What if *we* didn't have a place to live and Mum went to Zimbabwe and Dad didn't work any more and we had to sleep in the toilets at Cornavin railway station?

'Are we poor, Dad?'

'Dork,' said George.

'No, Robert, we're not poor.'

'We're not rich,' said George. 'Mikhail's father owns

a football team in Russia and he lives in a mansion on the lake. They have servants. You know what Mikhail got for his birthday, bro? A football pitch. Epic. And he says if I ever want to play football in Russia, I should just tell him, and he'll tell his dad.'

'And we're not going to get poor,' said Dad. 'We have savings. We have money put aside for you guys.'

'Mikhail's dad is the four hundredth richest person in the world, and you, Dad, maybe the one billionth . . .'

'I'm not a millionaire, but we're doing just fine. Your mother's books sell really well.'

'Cool. Can I have a credit card? Mikhail has one and—'

'No.' Dad got up. 'It's time for bed, guys. Come on.'

'We're going to thrash La Sallaz. They're *nul*.'

He got away with saying *nul* in that way because Mum wasn't around. She hates that word. That's what Hitler thought of the Jews, gypsies, gay people. They were *nul*. Nothing. Rubbish. Disposable. Relax, Mum, George says. It's just an expression. But Mum believes in words. They have power and we have to be careful with them.

'I'm going to score a hat-trick, bro, how much do you bet?'

'Nothing.'

'That's right, bro, be scared.'

'Bed. And brush your teeth properly, George, like how the orthodontist showed you.'

'Chillax, old man,' said George, but not loud enough for Dad to hear him.

George had braces, and first they were definitely not swag and then they were maybe swag and now they're definitely swag. They're grillz for teenagers. Grillz are the metal things rappers and gangstas wear over their teeth. Don't ask me why. They just do. I think they're supposed to be knuckledusters for teeth. If someones smashes their fist into your mouth, they get crushed knuckles. But what if that person is wearing a knuckleduster? SHOWDOWN – Grillz versus Knuckledusters. For a while George kept a toothpick in his mouth and turned it round because gangstas do that, but Dad told him to stop because he just looked like a *maleducado*, which I think basically was the point. My teeth were perfect. The dentist said she had never seen such perfect teeth on a ten-year-old. Not a single cavity. George said that proved what a dork I was: the dentist loved me, sad.

Great, the kid upstairs had decided to play his piano. It was eleven o'clock! And double great, he was banging out Beethoven's Fifth Symphony, again.

There was a whole poster in the foyer with drawings showing you all the things you could and could not do in an apartment in Geneva, day, night, or day *and* night. And YOU COULD NOT BANG OUT BEETHOVEN'S FIFTH SYMPHONY AT ELEVEN O'CLOCK AT NIGHT.

George was on the top bunk. He hit the ceiling with his fist. The kid stopped.

I waited. Sometimes he stopped for a full five minutes and then started up again, and then Dad had to use the broom. Not today. All clear.

89

I closed my eyes.

'Robert,' said George.

'Huh?'

George and I didn't really chit-chat when we were in our beds.

'Aunty Delphia's cool.'

His voice sounded funny.

'Yes, she is,' I said.

'Remember those two lions?'

Something was wrong if George was reminding me about them.

'Yes.'

On safari, we bumped into (not literally *bumped*) these lions having S E X. George lost all his swag. He was very, very scared when the male lion stood up and walked on top of a boulder very near our jeep and looked straight at us like the Lion King. George wanted the ranger to start the car and get away. But the ranger just stood up in the jeep and beamed a strong torch at the Lion King, who glared at us even more. The female lion had gone off to hunt. Finally the ranger turned off the light and we drove away. George said he never wanted to go on a safari ever again. He said they were lame.

'Remember what she said?'

I did.

Aunty Delphia said that it was healthy to be frightened and humble of nature; that way we would respect it and not go trampling all over it as if everything in life existed solely for our own benefit.

'She didn't think I was a douchebag.'

'Do you think she's okay, George?'

'She better be,' he said.

He sounded really angry, like if anything happened to Aunty Delphia, he was going to make someone pay.

I thought of Aunty Delphia. She had to be okay. She just had to be. And then I thought of Monsieur Renoir's note. I crept out of bed and went to the playroom. I took it out from under the seat cushion. I put it in the Young Sherlock Holmes book I was reading.

I closed my eyes and tried to think of Monsieur Renoir as Jack Montgomery Clift. Someone good and noble. But Monsieur Renoir said that perhaps I was the instrument of his atonement. I didn't know exactly what that meant, but it made me feel that he wanted me to help him. How could I? I had no special powers. And I didn't even know what he needed help with. Maybe I had read the note wrong. Maybe I didn't understand it. I opened my eyes and my lids drooped over them again.

'Good night, Dad!' I shouted.

'Good night, Robert,' Dad answered.

'Didn't you forget something?' I shouted.

'*Sogni—*'

'*D'ORO!*'

Except it wasn't a golden asleep. I woke up crying because in my sleep Aunty Delphia had woken me up and we were taking a walk in the moonlight in the bush and the moonlight was shining on both of us like a spotlight, and then all of a sudden it was gone and we were in the dark, the darkest dark ever, and I shouted *Aunty Delphia!* but she wasn't there any more.

Chapter Seven

The Football Match

Mum went to the match, because she hadn't missed any of George's matches at home. George was number 9. He had some fans. Three girls who kept waving at him and calling his name, *George, George, George*, except they said it the French way, *Joerje, Jeorje, Jeorje*. If George was me and he heard them, he'd say, 'Hilarious,' but he wasn't me so he just jumped up and down on the spot and then touched the ground and did the sign of the cross because ALL FOOTBALLERS DO THAT. Hilarious. Mum didn't like him doing it. We didn't go to church and George was an *atheist*, but first Mum had to explain what that was exactly, so he was sure that was what he meant. He didn't believe in anything. He believed in nothing. No supreme being. We were scientific facts. George was proud of being an atheist. I wasn't sure what I was. I think I believed in God.

George: Sure, bro, the old man in the sky, just like the tooth fairy.

Mum told George that if he wanted us to respect

his belief – *I don't believe, Mum, that's the point* – he should respect other people's. She found a book on one of her shelves about all the world's religions.

Mum said that we were lucky because we weren't born into a religion. We could choose for ourselves.

Me: What do you and Dad believe in?

She thought about that.

Mum: I believe in God, sometimes.

Me: When? Do you believe in him now?

Mum: Yes.

Me: Why?

Mum: Because you're standing here, and your brother too, and when I look at both of you, I have to believe in God, you're so perfect and beautiful.

George made a puking noise.

Mum went to a Catholic school in Bulawayo and her teachers were very strict nuns from Germany. Every day, at twelve o'clock, when the cathedral bells rang, they stopped whatever they were doing, stood up, and said the Angelus, which is a prayer to Mary who is the Mother of God.

George: Seriously, God has a mother?

Dad was spiritual, not religious. He believed in something greater than ourselves. What it was he didn't know; maybe it was just love.

A fact: under Geneva (and some of France) there is a really long, circle-shaped tunnel where scientists are doing experiments to find the God Particle; I think that's the particle that will explain *everything*.

*

94

The match started and number 2 in George's team got a yellow card for pushing in the first five minutes (I had to watch at least thirty minutes of the game before I could do my own stuff). He was timed out for ten minutes and in those ten minutes George scored his hat-trick. Two headers and one solo goal. Mum did not like him doing headers. Duck, when those come, *duck*, she told him. Mum had read an article in the *New York Times* that said pubescent boys should avoid headers because they interfered with brain development.

Me (in my head): What brain?

George told Mum to *chillax*.

But Mum couldn't *chillax* because there were so many things that could go wrong. When a British football player had a heart attack on the pitch and died, literally, for seventy-six whole minutes, Mum made George go to the doctor to check his heart. Dr Legrand said his heart was in perfect working order. Apparently George thumped his chest really hard and roared.

But at least now George had his 'fro to cushion the headers.

By my thirty minutes the score was 7–0. George had scored another two goals. A penalty and a free kick. I felt sorry for La Sallaz. They looked so small and puny. They had travelled all the way from Lausanne to be humiliated.

I took out my Young Sherlock Holmes. Mum said that in the original series Sherlock Holmes had a catch phrase: 'Elementary, my dear Watson, elementary.' Watson was Sherlock Holmes' assistant. I don't think that Mum approved that Sherlock Holmes and Watson in the new TV series could now use the internet to help them solve crimes.

I looked at Monsieur Renoir's note. I read it, slowly.

Brave tyrant Evil avenged festers consumes a man's soul amends Instrument of his atonement You.

And then I thought of the crocodile in Monsieur Renoir's apartment opening his mouth and snapping away at the words . . . at me—

I slammed the book shut.

George took forever to come out of the changing rooms. Dad was losing his patience. He had to be at the airport in forty minutes or he would miss his flight.

Finally the 'hero' appeared.

'Did you video it?' he asked Dad.

Lie, Dad, lie, I begged him.

'Yes.'

'Cool.' He was already on his Facebook page.

Mum and I dropped Dad off at the airport. George stayed at home to upload his video footage and seven of the ten goals Dad had captured. Mum and I went to the lake. She parked the car in the underground parking of the President Wilson hotel. We crossed the street and walked on the promenade towards the park. There were so many people out and there were boats sailing in the water. Someone was even water-skiing. I wanted to ask Mum how Aunty Delphia was, but I didn't want her to feel sad, so we walked quietly, thinking our own thoughts.

'Mum, your phone's ringing.'

Mum took it out from her bag.

'Hello, Maddy, have you heard anything?'

Mum listened to Aunty Madeline.

'Is she on antiretrovirals – can they get them? Good. I'll call them when I get home.'

When Mum was finished, I didn't ask her what antiretrovirals were. I would google it.

It was too late to ask her if I could speak to Gregory. I wanted to have a heads-up with him. I wanted to entice him with the new Skylanders game I had on the Wii. I needed someone to play it with. It was boring to play it alone. Curse Jin's parents and their French cottage in the middle of nowhere. Why would you do that to a child, during half-term break when he needed to be with his friends! I knew what was going to happen when Gregory came. He was going to be sucked into FIFA 13 and he'd be worse than La Sallaz. George was going to win 50–0 and then his slave was going to mop his brow with his loser's T-shirt. I knew all about it. The gods did it all the time to the mortals.

'How's Aunty Delphia?' I asked.

'She's better, much better.' But Mum sounded sad and her words came out like her nose was blocked. I wanted to tell her that we should let Monsieur Renoir know about Aunty Delphia; even if she was safe again with Grandma and Grandpa, Monsieur Renoir – *Royal Air Force man Jack Montgomery Clift* – would know what to do with Bob the Butternut and his men. He would fix things, I was sure of it.

'Mum—'

Her phone clucked. She had a message. It was a long one, because she kept scrolling down.

When it was Cynthia's bedtime sometimes I sat on the edge of her bed and I listened to Aunty Delphia's stories. She didn't read from a book. She made them up. Sometimes they were so exciting and funny that Cynthia wouldn't go to sleep even though she was yawning away and rubbing her eyes and then Grandpa would come and do one of his whistling tunes until she closed her eyes. My favourite story was the one about the mouse who thought he was an elephant and who tried to hang out with the elephants until the elephants told him that they thought being a mouse must be the best thing ever because he could go to all these places that they couldn't because they were too big and clumsy, and they would really appreciate it if the kind mouse would be their story-teller and tell them tales from other lands. Aunty Delphia drew while telling the story and she was really good; you could see how a mouse might really think they were an elephant.

Elephant 1: Listen, you're not an elephant. You don't have a tusk.

Mouse: Oh, but I do.

He wriggled his whiskers.

Elephant 2: Those aren't tusks.

Mouse: Yes they are, that's what yours looked like when you were my size.

Elephant 3: Humph. And your trunk, where's that?
The mouse tapped his nose.
Mouse: Right here, growing day by day.

When Mum was finished reading, she stood there looking down at the phone.

'Mum . . .'

I wanted to ask her if she'd started putting all of Aunty Delphia's stories into a book like she said she would. They would be like that guy Aesop's fables, I guess.

'I've been invited to a book festival in Jamaica, of all places, in Negril, on the beach. Dad and I stayed there for a week when he was on a mission with the Colombia office. It's very beautiful.'

'Can I come?'

I love the beach. The real beach, with sand and palm trees and huge coconuts. During the summer holidays on our way to Zimbabwe we stopped in Cape Town. The sand was great but we couldn't really go in the water because it was too cold and there were sharks. Three days before, a shark had chomped a man's hand off. George showed me the pictures on his phone.

From Zimbabwe we drove up into Mozambique and we could swim in the water there but then George told me that there were landmines all over Mozambique put there during the war, even on the beaches, and if I stamped on one it would be as good as a shark ripping my legs off. He was about to show me some pictures in the hotel foyer but Dad grabbed his phone and confiscated it for the whole time we were in Mozambique. Dad said there weren't any landmines on the beach.

'Are there sharks there?'

'I don't think so. I've never heard of a shark attack near Jamaica.'

'What about landmines?'

'No, Robert. There aren't any landmines in Jamaica. In fact, I don't think Jamaica has ever been at war.'

Jamaica sounded just like Switzerland, and I loved Switzerland. Even better, it had the sea and real beaches.

Switzerland had beaches along the lake. Some of them were made of pebbles, some of them had sand, but it wasn't sea sand. It wasn't soft and pink. Dad, George and I swam in the lake water. It was always cold, even in July when the sun was blazing. Mum never swam in the lake. She had a phobia about lake water. In Zimbabwe, you can't swim in lakes or dams because of a worm called bilharzia which is really gross. Basically, it's in the water and if it gets into you it takes over your body and you pee blood. There isn't any bilharzia in Swiss lakes but Mum just thinks: lake – bilharzia. I liked jumping off the jetty in Nyon at the Plage des Trois Jetées.

'So can I come, Mum?'

'I don't think I'll be going, Robert. Your aunt—'

'But if you *are* going, can I come?'

'It's in August, during school holidays, so yes, you

could *theoretically* come. One of my favourite writers is going to be there.'

We went to the Edinburgh Book Festival with Mum. That was fun. George said it was lame. He liked the street performers though, the ones who swallowed swords when they were high up on stilts; later he said those were lame too because they weren't really *swallowing* the swords, it was all tricks. He liked the street footballers, but then he said he could do all those tricks if he wasn't playing, like, real football on a real football pitch in a real league.

Mum: It's not cool to be so cynical; you have a lifetime ahead of you for that.

George: Whatever, Maman. I can't get all hyper like a ten-year-old loser.

I was the ten-year-old loser.

Mum spent a lot of time on the phone talking to Grandma and Grandpa in Bulawayo. She closed the door of the lounge so I couldn't hear what she was saying and whether she sounded sad or if she was crying. George was sleeping on the couch in the playroom with his headphones on.

I helped Mum make dinner: Wiener schnitzels. Usually when we cooked together Mum would ask me about my projects or what I was reading, but this time she didn't say anything. We ate in the kitchen like we always did when Dad was on a *lavoretto*. George had uploaded his video and he had two hundred and three likes. If I was George I would be thinking that the vast majority of my one thousand and whatever 'friends' didn't like it or just didn't care.

George went to get a glass of water and he left the tap running.

'There is no water in Bulawayo. Stop wasting water,' Mum said.

George talked back.

'Mum, it all goes into the lake, so—'

'Turn off the tap and go to bed, now!'

George looked down at her and opened his mouth.

'Now!'

I had never seen Mum so mad. Ever. And she was shaking. Even George was scared.

Please, George, don't say something stupid like 'Okay, okay, take a chill pill, Ma.'

But he just turned the tap off. He brushed his teeth and went to bed, even though it was only nine o'clock.

We could hear Mum clearing up the dishes and loading them into the dishwasher.

She came into our room and stood there for a bit.

'Are you awake, George?'

George grunted. 'I'm awake.'

'I'm sorry, guys.'

'It's okay, Mum,' I said.

George grunted again.

'I'm going through—'

'Menopause!' I shouted.

'Calm down.' said George. 'What the hell is menopause?'

'Don't swear,' said Mum.

'*Where,* where was the swearing?'

'Hell.'

'Seriously, *hell*?'

'In *that* context.'

'Menopause is when women can't have babies and they go all crazy, sorry, Mum. I saw it on *The Simpsons*. Can you still have babies, Mum?'

'Seriously, bro, stop.'

'Can you, Mum?'

'Yes, I can still have babies. I'm not going through menopause. I'm going through a rather stressful period at the moment but I shouldn't have shouted, I apologize. Good night, guys.'

'Do you want more babies?' I asked.

'Jesus, stop!'

'Don't use the Lord's name in vain, George.'

'Don't *what*?'

'Good night, boys.'

'Mum?'

'Yes, Robert?'

'What does atonement mean?'

'Atonement? To make amends.'

Mum didn't ask me why I was asking. I was always asking her to explain words to me.

I waited for her to say 'Don't let the bed bugs—' but she went into the lounge and I could hear the BBC World News music. This was the second time Mum hadn't said it. I felt sad; a tradition was being bro—

'Don't let the bed bugs—'

It wasn't Mum.
It was George.
'Bite,' I said.
George grunted.
Sometimes he was the best brother, ever.

Chapter Eight

Aunty Madeline and the Slave

The slave was arriving in three hours and George, his master, was still asleep.

It was eleven o'clock, and when we were in Zimbabwe Grandpa just shook his head at how much George slept. Sometimes he was still asleep at one o'clock. Even the rooster who crowed his head off at twelve o'clock couldn't wake him up. Dad called it the sleep of the dead. Mum tried to tell Grandpa about all the studies she'd read saying how teenagers needed this sleep during their growth spurts, but Grandpa just shook his head.

Look at me, didn't I grow up fine.

When Grandpa was a boy he had to wake up every day before sunrise, which is like five o'clock, and go off to the hills with the cows, and then he had to walk *three* hours to school, without shoes.

And during the school holidays he had to stay with the cows up in the hills until sunset. He couldn't fall asleep in case the cows wandered off and ended up on the road and got run over, and when he finally got home he just ate some porridge and maybe a piece of cow entrails, which are all the left-over bits of stomach, and he slept on the floor, which was made of cow dung (which is cow poo), with all his other brothers and sisters, in one hut.

This thing of sleeping so much, it is a modern thing, perhaps you should take him to the doctor.

George would finally wander in yawning and fiddling with his phone, like maybe Grandpa would take the hint and Wi-Fi the house. Grandpa would take a look at George and shake his head again.

And this thing of these gadgets, it cannot be good for these young ones.

Mum and Dad agreed with him completely about the gadget bit.

We had to tidy up the playroom because that was where Aunty Madeline was going to sleep. Gregory was going to be in our bedroom. Being the guest, he was going to sleep in my bed; I would sleep on a mattress on the floor. I was helping Mum make up the mattress.

'Robert, Grandpa's got a donkey now,' Mum said.

'A donkey, really, why?'

'Someone wasn't treating him well so your aunt brought him home before she—'

Mum shook her head.

'What's his name?'

'I . . . I didn't ask.'

'Is he all right now?'

'Yes, Grandpa's looking after him. He's taken up residence with the chickens.'

I loved Grandpa's house. I loved helping him feed

the chickens. I loved helping him wash the dogs with the hosepipe. I loved helping him fix TVs and radios in his workshop while Pastor Haig was on one of the TVs talking about God and the Chosen who would leave the wickedness of the world to dine in the heavenly banquet of Our Father. It was FUN. Grandpa showed me how to whistle to call the cows back to you.

Grandpa's house didn't have a swimming pool, a tennis court or a football pitch so George couldn't take photos of himself posing and post them (eventually) on Facebook. The only thing he took pictures of was him driving Grandpa's truck in the back yard, but even then he didn't take a picture of the whole truck because it was really old and rusty.

'Aunty Delphia will fix him.'

Mum patted the pillow she was holding.

'Yes, yes she will, Robert. Next time I'll ask what his name is.'

'Ah, the good life comes tomorrow.' George was rubbing his hands.

'He's your cousin,' I said. 'Family.'

Family is everything, is what Nonna says. Without it you are nothing.

'Family *slave*.'

'George, stop with this slave business, don't just throw that word around,' said Mum.

There they were! Gregory came running right past me and Mum, straight into George.

'Yo, man, what's up?' said George, detaching himself from Gregory's hug. Boy, was it embarrassing to watch a ten-year-old boy make a fool of himself. I felt I owed it to family honour to help Gregory out.

'Gregory,' I said, 'I've got Skylanders—'

But no, Gregory was a sucker for punishment. He was telling my brother, who had his headphones on, how happy he was to be here in Geneva . . . *I watched that video where you scored that goal, fifteen times . . . blah, blah, blah* . . . I thought he was going to pee in his pants, he was that excited. *And I showed it to my class and . . . blah, blah, blah* . . .

I gave up. I needed adult company.

Usually, when Mum and Aunty Madeline met at the airport, they giggled and kissed each other; they were like two little girls. This time they just hugged, quietly. Aunty Madeline gave me a hug too and said, 'My, what a big boy you are, Robert, and look at that brother of yours, he's a man now.'

Aunty Madeline met Uncle Stewart on the internet on a dating site for the mature person, then Uncle Stewart travelled all the way to Zimbabwe and found Aunty Madeline, and then they were married and Aunty Madeline flew all the way back to England with Uncle Stewart and then they had a baby (Gregory) and I guess this is the bit where you say 'and they lived happily ever after', although looking over at Gregory now, who was carrying George's sweater, I don't think it would be a totally accurate ending.

In the car Gregory completely ignored me and

jabbered on and on to George, who completely ignored him. I needed a break from my life. When we got home I asked Mum if I could go down to the park. Mum said that was a good idea and that Gregory and George should come with me.

George: I have plans.
Mum: What plans?
George: A hangout.
Mum: Where?
George: I don't know.
Mum: Out, all of you, stay in the park, and that means you too, George.

'This is lame,' said George when we were all standing outside. 'I didn't even bring my ball.' He looked at me and then at Gregory. 'Go and get my ball, Gregory.' And like a good dog Gregory went back up to the apartment and came panting down with the Wayne Rooney ball. He was all shiny and hyper when he handed it over to his master.

'What,' said the master, 'do you want a biscuit?'

Gregory didn't understand sarcasm and he actually said, 'Oh yes, that would be nice, George.'

I slapped my forehead. How could we even be related?

Lucky for him, George hadn't heard him; he was already in the middle of the park practising his free kicks.

'He wasn't really asking you if you wanted a biscuit,' I said. I don't know why, but I kept trying to help

Gregory. I guess it was Nonna's fault. You had to help the weak in every family. Nonna came from Naples, and even though she had lived in Rome since she was six years old, Naples was still in her blood (Nonna's own words).

'Yes he was. He said do you—'

'He says that to me all the time. He says it when *you* think you've done something amazing and he just thinks you're being a dork.'

'What's a dork?'

Okay, he was obviously way too sheltered. There was nothing I could do to help him. He was on his own.

'Never mind,' I said.

Gregory ran up to George. George put him between two trees and the last I saw of him he was jumping up and down like a mad monkey trying to save George's goals. Fat chance, slave.

I looked up at Monsieur Renoir's apartment. The windows were open. The curtains were drawn back. I don't know why but I waved one hand, then the other, and then I criss-crossed my arms over my head. I could have shouted 'Monsieur Renoir!' but Mum might have heard me, and anyway I wasn't really sure what I was doing. And then I decided I'd just go and knock on his door and see what would happen. I wasn't supposed to talk to strangers but he wasn't a stranger any more. He lived in our building. And now I knew who he really was. He had written me a note. And he had asked me a question – *What is it, BOY?* – and I had chickened out. What was wrong with me? I was such a scaredy-cat. I was supposed to be helping Aunty Delphia. I needed to do something.

I went back inside the building and climbed the steps slowly until I was in *entresol*. I took a step towards his door, and then another. This was it. My face was right against the door. I raised my hand. I could ring the bell or knock. My hand went to the bell and then I snatched it back and my fingers crooked themselves and I knocked, gently. I didn't wait. I dashed up the stairs, fell once, twice, three times, and pressed myself against the wall because I heard a door open below me and I heard steps, and then more steps back, and then a door banging shut, and I ran up the stairs again and dashed into our apartment.

I was mad. Mad. MAD.

I waited behind the door, and then I dragged over Mum's fancy-schmancy chair which we were not allowed to sit on and definitely not to stand on because it was an 'antique', but this was an emergency. I peeked into the peephole.

Nothing.

I jumped from the chair because I heard footsteps behind me.

'Robert,' Mum said, 'what are you doing here? Where's George? Where's Gregory? Has something happened?'

Something *had* happened but I didn't know what it was.

I shook my head.

'They're still downstairs playing.'

'Are you all right?' Mum asked.

I didn't know. *Was* I all right?

I nodded.

'I'm going to do my project homework,' I said.

I brought all my books to the dining room table.

My Hero. I couldn't do it on Aunty Delphia. I couldn't ask Mum too many questions. We weren't allowed to do it on Nelson Mandela because he was everyone's hero.

Me: Is he a cliché?

Mr Reynolds: That's not what I meant, Robert. We've already done him in class. Some originality, please. Put your thinking caps on. There are heroes out there, folks. Go find them and bring them back here.

I went over to George's desk because he had a bookshelf with all these encyclopedias that Mum bought for him. I tried to get one. I leaned over the desk; I lost balance and banged my hand on the keyboard. I looked up at the screen.

The Zimbabwe Situation.

That was what he had on his Google search.

I don't know why, but I held my breath.

Was George working on a project?

Was he doing some research?

I looked down at his desk and then I saw the picture on his pinboard.

He was wearing the Highlanders kit and he was standing next to Aunty Delphia; he was way taller than her. She was looking up at him, her hand raised and his going down; they were giving each other a high five.

I remembered that football match. George was really excited because they were playing at Barbourfields Stadium, which is famous all over Zimbabwe, and not in the usual dusty field where the goals didn't even have any netting. Aunty Delphia kept blowing on a vuvuzela, which is a plastic horn, every time George touched the ball and did his tricks. And later she gave him a statue made of wire and red, white and black beads of a boy with a football at his feet. The statue was leaning against the computer screen.

The screen was dark again. I didn't press any key.

I wanted to give my brother a hug.

I decided to make Nonno, who wasn't alive any more, my hero. I was going to have to ask Dad a whole lot of questions. I'd have to read all about the Second World War. I knew stuff already from Horrible Histories. I got to work and I was so busy that I didn't even notice that Mum was standing right next to me.

'Robert—'

I jumped in my chair.

'Can you go down and call George and Gregory. I can't see them from the balcony.'

I put on my shoes and my coat and I opened the door.

'Take your hat,' said Mum.

I grabbed it from the coat stand; it fell down on the doormat and that's when I saw it.

I banged the door shut.

'Mum!' I yelled.

Mum came running.

'Robert, what is it?'

'Don't open the door, Mum. Don't.'

Mum opened the door.

There wasn't anyone by the door, but someone had left a box. A blue box. It was lying on the mat.

I had seen that box before.

'Don't touch it, Mum, don't.'

Mum touched it. She picked it up.

'Don't open it, Mum, it could be a bomb.'

'It's too small to be a bomb, Robert.'

'It could be—'

Mum lifted the lid.

'Look,' she said.

She stretched out her hand. I looked inside.

'It's a medal,' I said.

It was a cross with a purple ribbon.

'I think it's bronze,' Mum said. She brought it closer to her face. 'You know what, it looks like a Victoria Cross. The highest honour for bravery in battle. Look what it says there. *For Valour*.'

Mum always knew random facts. It was all the research she did for her books. She had boxes and boxes of information, a whole cupboard of it, because she didn't throw any of it away even if her story had gone somewhere else and she didn't need the information any more. She had magazine articles, newspaper clippings, and pages and pages of printouts from the internet.

'It must be an imitation or a replica.'

Aunty Madeline looked inside the box.

'So, who's been exceptionally valiant, and in what field of combat, and where's Gregory?' she asked. 'I hope this cross hasn't got anything to do with him.'

I shook my head. 'He's outside, with George. They're playing football.'

Aunty Madeline smiled. Gregory was an only child and I don't think he was Mr Popular at school. He was just one of those kids who tried too hard and got on everyone's nerves with all their eager beaverness. Probably the teacher's *chouchou*. The problem was, Aunty Madeline thought that George and Gregory were friends.

'Do you think it's his?' I asked Mum. Mum was still holding out the box as if she wanted me to take it. But I was too scared to touch it. It wasn't a bomb; it wasn't going to explode in my hands or anything, but it just felt wrong to even touch it.

'Whose?'

'Monsieur Renoir's. He was in the Royal Air Force, you said.'

I don't know why, but I didn't tell Mum about Monsieur Renoir dropping a box that looked exactly like this one, and the tinkling sound I had heard. I didn't tell her about writing to him. Or about his letter. Or his question. There were secrets I was keeping and I didn't know why I was keeping them.

'That could make sense,' said Mum.

I looked at the cross.

'Why's he left it here?'

Mum thought about that.

'Well . . . maybe he means it for you, Robert. A peace offering?'

'For shouting at us?'

'I don't know, but you . . . we have to give it back to him. I'll go down with—'

But just then the phone rang. Mum gave me the box and hurried to the lounge. Aunty Madeline followed her.

The box felt warm in my hand.

'Yes, Baba,' I heard Mum say. 'How is she? Is she . . . is she talking, at least? Did my friend see her?'

I looked at the medal. I thought of Monsieur Renoir – *Jack Montgomery Clift*; it was no use, he *was* Monsieur Renoir – with the medal pinned on a jacket, on his uniform. It wouldn't be this Monsieur Renoir. It would be the young and gallant Monsieur Renoir. Monsieur Renoir before he became Monsieur Renoir. When he was just Jack, I suppose. I couldn't leave it lying around for Gregory to start poking his nose in, so I looked for somewhere to keep it safe. In the end I put it in my backpack.

'Can you bring her on the phone, just try, maybe she'll talk to us.'

Mum and Aunty Madeline waited a long time.

Please, Aunty Delphia, come to the phone. I want to say hello to you. I want to tell you about Monsieur Renoir. Please, Aunty Delphia.

'It's all right, Baba. Let her rest.'

George and Gregory came back in. George went off to football practice and then it was just Gregory and me, but, tough luck, I'd given him my FULL ATTENTION before and he'd dissed me; now I had things to do. I needed to think. He was sitting on the couch in the playroom looking forlorn. *Oh George, oh George, where art thou?* Mum and Aunty Madeline were talking in the lounge. I took my backpack to my room. I shoved the backpack under my bed and I sat down and thought. *A peace offering.* Monsieur Renoir didn't know me. Not really. He didn't like me. I thought Mum had it all wrong. We didn't even know if he *had* left the box there. What if he had dropped it right there on the mat and now it was lost and he was busy hunting everywhere for it, and he was going to keep a lookout by the stairs, ready to open his door and grab me inside his *entresol* kingdom and torture me until—

I pulled my backpack out and took out the box. I opened it. I pressed my finger on the metal. It felt real. It was cold. It looked old. In the middle of the cross there was a crown, and on top of it a lion. FOR VALOUR was written under the crown. My heart beat really fast when I read that. This was serious. Something important was happening and it was happening to me. It felt as if I was in the middle of a story and I was too scared to do anything; I didn't know what to do to make the story go the right way. I looked at the cross; if I just stayed here looking at it maybe the story would take care of itself and I would just go along with it. I wouldn't have to *do* anything. But my eyes got tired of looking at the one thing, and my hand was tired too. I knew what I had to do next. The story wanted me to, so I put my finger under the medal to take it out of the box, but then I heard a dog yelping and I jumped. The yelping was getting louder.

'Gregory, Gregory, what's—'

That was Aunty Madeline in full panic mode.

I closed the box and shoved it in my backpack. I pushed my backpack as far under the bed as I could get it.

It wasn't a dog doing all that yelping, but Gregory, who was sitting on Aunty Madeline's lap, now sniffing.

'What happened?'

'What *happened*,' said Mum, 'is that you are *supposed* to be here with Gregory playing and now he's had an accident.'

I couldn't see any blood, so I was sure it wasn't anything serious. He wasn't missing any body parts, was he?

It turned out he was.

'He swallowed his loose tooth,' said Aunty Madeline, stroking his hair.

Oh tragedy!

No tooth fairy.

'Why don't you show him the medal?' Aunty Madeline said.

Double tragedy.

'Medal,' sniffed Gregory.

'Let's play here,' I said. 'Come on, Gregory, I can show you—'

'I want to see the medal, Mummy,' cried Gregory.

Gregory had a British accent. He called his mum 'Mummy' and when he said it, no offence, but it sounded really childish even when he wasn't sitting on her lap and crying. But Mum said that even Prince Charles, who was like fifty-something, called the Queen, who was his mum, Mummy.

'Robert,' said Aunty Madeline, 'can you—'

'I don't have it,' I said.

'Robert,' said Mum, in her 'I'm giving you a warning' voice.

'I don't,' I said.

'Robert!' shouted Mum.

'I gave it back,' I said.

'You gave it back,' said Mum, very slowly. 'Are you sure?'

'Yes.'

Mum looked at me. Aunty Madeline looked at me. Gregory looked at me. I looked at me.

Liar, liar, pants on fire, all the eyes said.

'We can play a board game,' I said. And I went all hyper showing Gregory *all* the games on the shelves, but he didn't know any board game whatsoever. He was hopeless. What did he do with his life?

'I need to go to the toilet,' he said.

'Number one or number two?' asked Aunty Madeline.

He was TEN YEARS OLD, THREE WHOLE MONTHS OLDER THAN ME.

'Number two,' he said.

Uh-huh . . . thanks for sharing.

119

'That's good,' said Aunty Madeline.

Do you want a biscuit?

I felt bad about lying to Mum. But I couldn't show the medal to Gregory. He would spoil it. I'd tell Mum later when they were gone and face the consequences for dishonourable behaviour. And maybe it wasn't really lying. Maybe I *would* give the medal back to Monsieur Renoir. Maybe I was just telling the truth earlier than actually doing it.

Number 5's dad gave George a lift home. He'd had an epic training session. He'd dribbled past five players to score an epic goal. Gregory was the only one really listening. Mum and I had heard this tale before. Aunty Madeline was having a bath. I wanted to use the computer. I wanted to google 'Victoria Cross', but maybe I should leave that for now.

Dad skyped us. George hogged the computer because he'd saved The Most Important Information Of His Life for Dad. The Swiss Under-Fifteen coach had watched him train and had written his name down. George wasn't even Swiss. Was he going to become Swiss? Would he have to join the army when he left school? Would he have a gun? Would he kill people?

Then Dad told me that he had something really special to give me when he got back. I asked him what it was and when he said I would have to wait I asked him to please give me a clue and he said it was TOP SECRET. Then Mum told us she wanted to speak with Dad in private. And could we please set the table.

I set the table because George was 'tired'.

Gregory was 'tired' because George was tired and he'd done his poo, and to be quite honest, I really didn't want him touching any plates or forks. I laid everything out and then I sat by the table thinking of Dad's surprise. Dad always brought me something from his *lavorettos*. Turkish delight, from Turkey, duh, and that was great because I had just finished reading *The Lion, the Witch and the Wardrobe* and I tasted the very sweets that the White Witch tempted Edmund with. Okay, I kinda understood why Edmund acted like such a jerk – Turkish delight was delicious. He brought an Aladdin lamp from Kyrgyzstan that would grant you one wish, your heart's desire, if you were *pure of heart*; I hadn't made a wish yet because I didn't know what my heart's desire was, and thinking about the lamp made me feel even more guilty about lying to Mum. Dad brought back football jerseys for George. But George only wore three in broad daylight: Manchester United, Italy, Lancy FC. All the others were his pyjamas. When Barcelona had 'UNICEF' on the front of their jersey, George wore it on the pitch too; Barcelona had *paid* UNICEF one million dollars to have their logo there – that was epic swag. But when 'UNICEF' disappeared to the butt of the jersey, George didn't even use it as pyjamas; he said Barcelona were lame, overrated and boring, though Messi was okay. Grandpa bought him a Highlanders jersey. The symbol for Highlanders is a shield over a spear and a knobkerrie, which is like a stick with a big knob on. Grandpa said that's to remind people all over Zimbabwe, especially in Harare, that Ndebele people are warriors. Their motto is *We are a Fortress*, which is in Ndebele and I can't really say it properly because your tongue has to move around your mouth in a special way.

Grandpa took us to the townships. There were children playing with a football made of rags and plastic bags in the street. I thought George would say that was lame, but he didn't. He just watched and then played a bit with them. And later, back home, he said some of the boys were pretty skilled. George has lots of footballs; he has three real match ones: Jabulani, the South Africa World Cup football, and two UEFA ones; he hasn't even taken them out of the box yet.

I would have to google *Turkmenistan: images* just to see what was there. There were so many things I had to find out. All the stuff about the medal, and there was the other thing I'd heard Mum say to Aunty Madeline on the phone. *Antiretrosomething*. Mum said we relied too much on Google. What if Google ceased to exist. What would we do for knowledge then? We'd be completely lost.

George: Seriously, Mum, Google is like the biggest company in the world, how are they going to cease to exist?

Mum: Someone could just pull the plug on them.

George (and me too, in my head): What plug?

Mum: The metaphorical plug. Okay, what if someone

spread a bug and it infected Google and destroyed its whole operating system and all that knowledge that people had stored with Google was lost, just gone, and there was no way to bring it back, and because no one had physically written it down on paper, it was just these discrete pieces of learning, very small pieces, in people's heads: can you imagine the enormity of the loss . . . science, medicine, literature, GONE.

George: No school.

Mum: George! That's why it's important you learn to use reference books, things that you can pick up and hold in your hands.

George: Books burn, Maman. Remember the Dark Ages. Sizzled and burned, literally.

I had to admit that George had a point. Google could cease to exist but there were backups and backups of backups. Mum didn't really understand the internet. I mean, she didn't have *any* apps on her smartphone. How could you *not* have apps on a smartphone? That made it a *dumb*phone. Sad.

Mum made George clear the table and load the dishwasher. She didn't stand there and watch him, so Gregory did most of the work.

I went in the bedroom and took the backpack out again. I was going to give the medal back to Monsieur Renoir. I didn't like having it stashed in my backpack, hidden under the bed. I wanted to be pure of heart, and lying was very bad. I looked up at the Aladdin lamp. When Dad gave it to me, George rubbed his hand on it, 'Oh magic lamp, from Kyr . . . whatever, I wish to be a famous footballer and to earn six hundred million dollars, to win the Ballon d'Or five times, the World Cup four times, the Champions League six times and the Euro three times, the Africa Cup of Nations eleven times, anything else, *I'll be back*.' He said the last bit like the Terminator, in the movie he wasn't allowed to watch at home but which he'd watched lots of times at his friends' houses.

Mum *was* right, he was so self-absorbed.

'You only get one wish,' I said. 'And the lamp has to belong to you and you have to be pure of heart.'

Dad wasn't in the room any more, so he said, 'It's a teapot, you dork.'

I was lying on the mattress, looking under my bed, feeling the medal there in the dark. Gregory was already asleep. How could a ten-year-old boy drool and fart so much in his sleep? I didn't know how I was ever going to sleep in that bed again. Never mind the bed bugs.

I was hoping that Mum didn't have any plans for tomorrow. I wanted to look up things on the internet. I hoped she didn't want me to entertain Gregory. Please, George, have no plans, Gregory will *luuurve* you for it. I closed my eyes. I thought of airplanes, and Monsieur Renoir in one of them. I thought and thought until Monsieur Renoir wasn't Monsieur Renoir any more but someone young and strong with a moustache and his hands on the joystick, diving and zigzagging through the air, and then his plane was spiralling round and round, getting closer to the ground . . . I saw Monsieur

Renoir floating in the air with his parachute until he landed on the ground, where the enemy was waiting for him. *FOR VALOUR*, I whispered.

Chapter Nine

For Valour

Aunty Madeline cut George's hair; she was a hairdresser. It took two hours. Goodbye, afro, hello, kind of mohawk. George spent another two hours posing in front of the mirror and then he took some photographs and posted them on Facebook. *With the cap. Without the cap.* In two minutes he had one hundred and six likes for 'without the cap' and ninety likes for 'with the cap'. Did teenagers have no lives? The haircut was a success and George threw his cap on his desk. He could have swag without it. What a discovery.

Mum and Aunty Madeline were going to town because they wanted to send money to Grandpa with Western Union. They were dragging me along with them because I was only ten years old and I couldn't be left on my own. George was fourteen and *he* was the one who definitely should never be left on his own. Anyway, he had a hangout.

Gregory and I sat together on the bus. Mum and Aunty Madeline were four seats back. I had Gregory all to myself and we didn't say a single word to one another. Gregory had his forehead stuck to the window and his tongue out on it. I was starting to wonder about him, whether he was mentally challenged, just weird, or if it was a phase he was going through, like early-onset puberty.

Mum made the payment and then we went over to Manor. The only thing I liked about Manor was the pizza, upstairs at the restaurant. You put your own ingredients on a plate and gave them to the pizza guy, who spread them out on the dough and then put your pizza in the oven. He gave you a wooden disc that lit up blue and vibrated when your pizza was ready.

Finally we got to the fifth floor, but then Gregory got fixated with the PlayStation console in the tech station which was just in front of the restaurant entrance. There were some teenagers playing FIFA 13. Was he trying to learn some moves? We wasted twenty minutes waiting for Gregory to blink, and move on.

I stuffed my pizza with salmon and anchovies, capers and mushrooms; I even managed to sneak in some pancetta, which are small bacon pieces I'm not allowed to have.

I was walking out to the terrace with my pizza when I saw him.

I saw his hat first. It was on the table.

He was sitting down. This time he had sunglasses on.

I couldn't run. I was trapped behind Gregory, whose tray kept tilting because he'd overloaded it with two giant glasses of soda, and some people behind me.

Luckily, he wasn't looking at the door. He was looking over the roofs, at the Jet d'Eau, I guess.

I was right by his table.

There wasn't any food on it.

There was a leather book next to the hat, tied up with a string. It looked a bit like the fancy books Mum got when we went to Florence; she was so excited because she bought them from a special shop where a girl was making them the traditional way, by hand.

But this book was different. It didn't have all those watery swirls on the parts of its cover which were paper.

It had a square patch of animal skin.

It gave me chills looking at it.

The animal skin was white and greyish and furry.

I couldn't help thinking it looked like a cat's or a dog's or a hamster's.

I got even more chills.

Maybe it was a goat. It could be a goat. Or a cow.

He took off his glasses. He rubbed his eye.

There was a bit of paper sticking out of the book.

LAST, I read—

And then he started turning round.

I gave Gregory a shove. I ducked my head and pushed my way over to Mum and Aunty Madeline, who'd found a seat at the back.

But I could feel his eye blazing into my back.

I felt like I'd stolen the medal even though he'd left it on the doorstep.

But Mum had told me to give it back. I'd lied to her.

Maybe he had made a mistake. Maybe he never meant to leave it there. Maybe he was confused. Maybe he had that sickness that made you forget things when you grew old. Al . . . Al . . . Alzheimer's.

I felt really, really bad.

But maybe he did mean to give it to me. Maybe it was how I was paying him for helping Aunty Delphia. Maybe keeping the medal meant he was going to help keep Aunty Delphia safe. Maybe this was our deal.

Maybe that was what he meant by atonement. I was the instrument of his atonement.

I shivered.

It was all so mixed up.

Mum asked me if I was okay, because I wasn't eating much of the pizza even though I'd put a lot of salmon on it.

I knew what I had.

A guilty conscience.

But how could I have a guilty conscience if I didn't know what the right thing to do was?

What if this was all a riddle and the medal was a clue? And the medal and Monsieur Renoir's note went together?

What if Aunty Delphia needed me to—

I told Mum I wanted to get some water.

I *had* to see him. But I didn't know what I was going to do when I got to his table.

My heart was beating really, really fast. It hurt but I guess I deserved it.

What if he shouted swear words at me?

What if he yelled I was a thief and called for the police?

What if he fixed that eye on me for so long that I shrivelled up and di—

But he wasn't there any more. He had disappeared.

Mum and I went to the Payot bookshop across the street. We left Aunty Madeline and Gregory behind. We were going to pick them up in forty-five minutes. Gregory was stationed like a zombie in front of the console.

I went straight over to the children's section. I looked for a book on the Mau Mau but I couldn't find anything. Not even a Horrible Histories.

There was a whole shelf on World War II books with planes zooming about on their covers. I looked at those in case they had medals in them or some clue. I looked at the other books too. There was a book about a girl who hid from the Nazis in an attic. I already knew a bit about her. There was a book about a boy who got mistaken for a prisoner in a concentration camp because he was wearing pyjamas. George was reading that one for his English class. But there wasn't anything about the Victoria Cross or fighter pilots. And then I saw a book with a boy on the cover who looked just like me, *and* he was hugging a dog just like Grandpa's. *A Medal for Leroy.* I opened it, and in the corner of some of the pages was a drawing of a medal; it looked like a Victoria Cross. It was about something happening in

1915, in World War I. I'd get it. I walked over to Mum, and right in front of her was a book about objects from the Second World War. I lifted it. It was heavy. I put it down again and turned the pages. It was a non-fiction book so I turned to the back pages, to the index. There it was: *Victoria Cross*. I found the page. There was a photograph of the cross. It looked just like the medal in my backpack. It was real. There was just something so wrong that the medal was in my backpack, under my bed. I wanted to get out of the bookshop right now and give Monsieur Renoir his medal back. I shut the book and turned round. I bumped into a leg.

'Mum—'

But it wasn't Mum.

'*Excusez-moi,*' I said.

The leg went up and up.

'You're excused,' boomed the voice.

It was Mike, my basketball coach!

'What's up, Robert?' he asked.

'Hmmm, nothing,' I said.

'Well, you see anything around here an eight-year-old girl might like to read?'

'Hmmm, no. The children's section's over there.' I pointed to the corner. 'They have lots of pink books. I don't know what's inside them. I never touch them.'

Mike laughed. It was a loud laugh that shook his whole body and made everyone at the bookshop stop what they were doing and look for that laugh.

'Okay then, Robert, show me where they're hiding.'

*

131

Mike had played for the NBA and he was the only teacher on campus who had swag. Just being a black American meant you had swag. Mum said that was another example of George's dangerous stereotypes. Not all black Americans had swag. Some, many of them, had zero swag.

George: Okay. Name one, just one.

Mum: Barack Obama.

George: Barack Obama! Oh God, Mum, he's like the PRESIDENT of AMERICA, what are you talking about. He is swag.

So it wasn't just about wearing droopy jeans, or wearing a cap the right way, or walking funny; swag was – swag was just swag.

Mum said George was in the process of finding and defining his identity and this black-consciousness hyper-awareness was all part of it.

The only part of his Italian identity George was interested in was Balotelli.

'You have to help me, my man. I'm in a fix. If I don't get something for my little niece, I'm dead.'

I took him to the children's section and showed him the pink books. He picked one up.

'What do you think?' he asked.

The Girls' Activity Book. It was *very* pink.

'Hmmm,' I said.

'Hmmm,' Mike said. 'Yes, let's do this. Thanks, Robert.'

'Mike?'

'Yes, my man.'

132

I looked round to see where Mum was. I couldn't find her. She was probably downstairs, looking at the travel books.

'Can I show you something, Mike?'

Mike looked at his watch and said, 'Sure, why not.'

I took him to the book about objects and the Second World War. I found the page on the Victoria Cross.

'Sweet,' he said. But he sounded sad.

After the NBA Mike told us he went to war. In Iraq. He joined the army because he was bored and he wanted an adventure.

'Mike, if you had a Victoria Cross, I mean if the Queen gave it to you, would you give it away?'

Mike thought about it.

'That's an interesting question, Robert. I guess there are reasons why a recipient of an honour like this *might* give it away.'

I waited.

Mike looked at his watch again.

'Say if you thought you didn't deserve it, or if it brought back too many memories of the war.'

He looked at me.

'Shame or fear, guilt. But sometimes people give things that they treasure as gifts. You never know. We're strange beasts.'

'Hmmm,' I said.

'Okay, Robert, have to get going. You doing your drills?'

I hadn't started them yet, but Mike was already at the counter so I didn't have to lie, again.

I was pretty good at basketball; the problem was that I didn't like pushing and shoving people around – there were some kids who thought they were Michael Jordan or Kobe Bryant and that they should always have the ball and you should always pass it to them even if you were right by the hoops and were the best shooter. Mike was always telling me to stand my ground; apparently, I had game.

I stood there waiting for Mum, thinking about Mike's words. And then I thought about Monsieur Renoir's letter. *Atonement*. To make amends. For what?

When we got home, I took the box out from the backpack and locked myself in the toilet. I opened the box. I picked up the medal and put the box on my lap. I looked at the medal. 'FOR VALOUR,' I said. I put it in my palm. It gave me goose bumps. I turned the medal over. There was supposed to be a name in the circle, but it was covered in green gunk. It was strange that it was only that side of the medal that was damaged. I rubbed the gunk and some of it came off on my fingers, and then I got worried that I would damage the medal even more. I thought about Mike's words. *Shame or fear, guilt*. Or a gift. And I thought of Monsieur Renoir doing something in Kenya against the Mau Mau that had won him a medal. Did you say 'win a medal' when it was a war one? It wasn't like the Olympics. It didn't seem right to say 'win'. It wasn't a competition.

'Robert!' It was Mum.

'I'm in the toilet.'

'Jin's on the phone!'

I jumped from the seat. The box fell.

'I'm coming,' I yelled.

The cushiony bit that the medal lay on had fallen out. And something else, which must have been underneath the cushiony bit. I picked it up. It was a little, tiny piece of newspaper, yellow, folded over and over.

'Robert!'

'I'm coming, Mum,' I yelled.

I pushed the cushiony, satiny bit and the piece of paper back in the box, and then the medal.

I rushed out.

'I'm taking it in your bedroom,' I yelled, picking up the phone.

'Jin!'

'What took you so long?'

'I was in the toilet.'

'TMI.'

I guess it *was* too much information.

'My mum's coming to Geneva tomorrow and she can bring you back for a sleepover.'

'Really?!'

'I'm so bored here. All we ever do is walk.'

'My cousin's here. He's weird.'

'My mum wants to speak to your mum.'

'Okay, hold on . . . Mum!' I yelled. 'Jin's mum wants to speak to you and please say YES, I can go for a sleepover. See you, Jin,' I yelled one last time into the phone.

I dashed to my room and put the medal back in my bag.

I could hear Mum saying that my cousin was around, but finally she said yes, just for the one night.

I couldn't wait for tomorrow.

In bed, I opened *A Medal for Leroy* and I started reading. I didn't stop till the very last page. And then I read the first page again.

Chapter Ten

Shame or Fear, Guilt

I left the medal at the bottom of my backpack, then shoved in my pyjamas, a change of clothes and my toothbrush, some DS games and my DS – I was sneaking them in. I packed the *Young Sherlock Holmes*. Jin arrived at ten o'clock with his mum. I couldn't wait to tell him about Monsieur Renoir and the medal, but I couldn't tell him in the car while his mum was driving. The drive took forever and there was nothing to see outside the window except trees and grass. No wonder Jin was bored.

'The end of the world is on the twenty-first of December 2012, that's this year,' said Jin.

'Jin, don't start with that. I told you it's a hoax,' said his mum.

'But it's been predicted—'

'By lunatics.'

This was the first I'd heard about this.

'What do you mean?'

'This guy, Nostra— what's his name, Mum?'

'Nostradamus, and I told you it's nonsense.'

'So this guy, Nostradamus, he worked it out a long time ago. The world is going to come to an end on the twenty-first of December, so you better not ask Father Christmas for anything.'

'*Jin*, stop it now.'

Jin knew I still believed in Father Christmas. He was always trying to show me how he couldn't really exist.

Jin: Okay, how can Father Christmas get a present for EVERY SINGLE CHILD in the WHOLE WORLD? ONE PERSON? It's just your parents, same with the tooth fairy.

Sometimes Jin sounded just like George.

I didn't quite know how Father Christmas did it, but I knew he did do it. It was something to do with different time zones and his helpers, and some magic. It worked. I knew it did. I refused to believe it wasn't him. I heard Mum whisper to Dad that that was my blind spot.

Dad had told me all about the Millennium Bug which was supposed to happen on 1 January 2000, when all the computers in the entire world would crash and everything on earth would go completely black and life would just be full of chaos and might even stop. Everyone had gone to sleep in 1999 thinking that when they woke up, *if* they did, the world would be changed for ever. But everyone woke up and the world was pretty much the same. The Millennium Bug was one big scam (Dad's words).

But this was THE END OF THE WORLD Jin was talking about.

'How?'

'It's going to blow up, or maybe the sun will disappear, or maybe we'll get hit by a mega asteroid.'

How come Mum or Dad or even George hadn't told me anything about this? The end of the world was coming in EIGHT WEEKS!

Maybe those scientists under Geneva were going to find the God Particle and then it would blow up the universe because it was supposed to be a secret.

I closed my eyes. I squeezed them tight.

Giordano Bruno was up there on his plinth. He was in my favourite square in Rome, Campo de' Fiori. He was in the very same spot where he was burned at the stake because he said that there were other intelligent beings in the galaxy and that the sun was just a star and not the centre of the universe and the Church said he was a liar and had to pay so they set him on fire.

He was wearing a cape with a hood; he looked like he could be in *Star Wars*, but if he was in *Star Wars* he would have to be a Sith Lord because they were the ones that dressed like that and Sith Lords were just evil.

I asked him about the end of the world, was it really going to happen, would it be the end of the other worlds too.

He lifted his head. He—

'Robert, hey, Robert, we've arrived.'

I opened my eyes.

I looked outside.

Jin lived at the edge of the world.

139

Jin's mum said, 'This is great, isn't it, we're right in the middle of a National Park. Can you smell all this clean air, Robert?'

I sneezed.

'We'll have some lunch and then we'll go for a walk up the stream.'

Jin clapped his forehead.

'Mum, we've done that TEN times already.'

'Robert hasn't done it.'

'I'm okay,' I said.

'We're going for a walk,' said Jin's mum.

While she made lunch, Jin took me up to his room. It was right under the roof.

'Cool,' I said. 'Hey, Jin, look.' I took out all my clothes from the backpack and showed him the box. I opened it.

'Wow, where did you find it?'

I told him about Monsieur Renoir.

'It's a Victoria Cross. The highest honour. FOR VALOUR.'

Jin picked it up and turned it over on his palm.

'What's this green furry stuff?'

'I don't know.'

'I think its eating away the metal – look, there's a tiny hole there.' Jin lifted up the medal. There *was* a hole.

'I'll get a magnifying glass,' he said.

We took turns with the magnifying glass; there were seven more tiny holes.

'Do you think he damaged it on purpose?' Jin said.

Why would he want to do that? Mike's words flashed in my head: *shame or fear, guilt*. And then I remembered Monsieur Renoir's letter. I fished out the *Young Sherlock Holmes* book and took out the letter. I showed it to Jin.

'That's creepy,' he said.

'I know.'

'Do you think he killed people?' Jin asked.

'They don't give you medals for killing people,' I said.

'Yes they do. Soldiers kill people. That's their job.'

'He was a fighter pilot. He fought the Mau Mau.'

Jin started running around his room shouting, 'Mau Mau, Mau Mau,' and flapping his arms about, for no apparent reason. Sometimes, even if he was my best friend, he was a bit silly.

'Fighter pilots drop bombs. Bombs kill people. Maybe he dropped the nuclear bomb,' Jin said.

'He wouldn't be a hero.'

'Yes he would. If you kill lots of bad people you're a hero.'

'The nuclear bomb killed ordinary people, not just bad people, and anyway, the nuclear bomb was in the Second World War.'

'In North Korea, the soldiers kill ordinary people trying to go to South Korea and they're heroes. They get medals and food.'

Jin was from South Korea. The leader of North Korea was a dictator and he was good friends with Bob the Butternut.

Maybe Monsieur Renoir *did* feel bad about being a pilot and dropping bombs. Even if he had received a medal. But maybe it wasn't for killing people. Maybe he had *saved* people. Maybe he had never really wanted to go to war.

Mr Reynolds, our humanities teacher, made us go round the room and say which countries we came from. There were twenty-two children in our class and we came from seventeen different countries. In every single country there had been a war. No one was Swiss (Switzerland had only had wars in the olden days before it was Switzerland). Most important of all was the War on Terror, which was a war against all the terrorists of the world.

Jin's mum called us down for lunch. It was sushi, which I loved. Mum said you had to be careful with sushi because she'd read an article on the internet about tapeworms in raw fish that could live in your body and brain and which ate up all your nutrients and made you basically stupid and then you died, but I had almost finished the sushi before I remembered all that. Jin's dad and his older sister Su joined us. Su was in the same grade as George but in a different homeroom. After lunch we had to walk to 'digest' our food. It wasn't too bad. Jin and I walked far ahead and we talked about the medal and Monsieur Renoir. And then I remembered the piece of paper in the box. I told Jin about it.

We had to walk all the way back to the house. There wasn't a bus or anything to take you back, which sucked.

We looked at the medal again, and then I lifted the cushiony bit and took out the crumbling paper underneath. I unfolded it, carefully. It was hard to read anything, even with the magnifying glass, but we figured out how many missing letters there were. We saw INFA-TRY, FRANC-, 1916, -R-VATE, --WA--. All the other letters had been smudged and had disappeared.

I put the magnifying glass even closer.

'I think that's an N between the A and the T.' I said. 'INFANTRY.'

'What does infantry mean?' Jin asked.

'Soldier, I guess.' I didn't think it meant 'pilot' too.

'FRANCE,' Jin said, pointing at the FRANC-.

I nodded.

'-R-VATE,' I said.

We looked at it for a long time.

We went through the alphabet, but it was only when we got to P that it was obvious: PRIVATE.

'Does private mean that it's a secret or something?'

'I suppose so,' said Jin.

'Hey, do you think it's like in Doodle Army?'

'In Boot Camp?'

'Yes, remember, the guy has to say "Yes, Sarge!" all the time and the sarge tells him to hit the deck, *Private*, and do push-ups, remember?'

'We need a computer,' Jin said. 'Mum's got one but I'm not allowed on it. She says it's cooking my brains.'

'--WA--,' I said. 'Hmmm, this one's harder.'

We were both quiet for a while.

'I'm tired,' said Jin.

'Okay, we'll come back to it later.'

We took turns playing on the DS. We got busted by Su, who just barged in the room without knocking.

'I'm going to tell Mum,' she said. She was such a tittle-tattle.

'No, pleeese, no, Su,' begged Jin.

She sat down on his bed and started twirling her hair around her finger.

I sneezed. She wore so much perfume.

'Okay, if you do one thing for me, I won't.'

'What?'

She was looking at me and I thought, 'A-uh a-uh a-uh, no ways.'

'If you give me your brother's phone number.'

NO WAYS. George would literally kill me.

'I don't know it.'

'Okay.' She stood up. 'Mum!'

'Okay, okay it's . . .'

I was *so* busted.

'Don't tell him I told you.'

Su wasn't a cool girl. George had ignored her Facebook Friend requests a million times. George said that her homeroom class was full of the most annoying people ever. They were so hyper about school.

I was doomed, *doomed*.

We were camping out in Jin's room. We looked at the medal under torchlight. We counted the holes again.

Eight. Jin had written the words down from the newspaper. We read them out aloud. Mum said every word told a story and a writer had to be careful about not just the words but how she put them together. The same words could mean different things depending on the situation.

'Do you think the medal belongs to the private?' Jin asked, pointing at the paper.

I nodded.

'We can't give it back to him, though,' I said. 'I think he's dead.'

'Really?'

'It says 1916. That means the First World War.'

'Smarty-pants.'

'Peace and Conflict. Horrible Histories,' I said. 'He'd be one hundred and something if he was still alive.'

Monsieur Renoir couldn't be the private.

'My great-grandmother's ninety-nine.'

'That's old.'

'I know. Maybe the private had children, and grandchildren. They would like it. I would.'

I nodded.

'Monsieur Renoir would know,' Jin said.

I guess that made sense, but Monsieur Renoir gave me the medal. Why didn't he give it to the private's family?

'Uhhh, Jin, maybe Monsieur Renoir—'

'No more talking, guys,' shouted Jin's mum.

'What?' whispered Jin.

'Uhhh, nothing.'

I didn't finish what I wanted to say to Jin because it made me all jumpy even just thinking about it.

I put the medal away. Jin turned off the torch. I couldn't sleep for a long time because when I closed my eyes I saw soldiers squeezed together in muddy trenches, trying to hide from the enemy, tanks crawling, machine guns firing, aeroplanes buzzing in the sky, bombs dropping in the trenches, battles raging, poisonous gases.

Dead soldiers on the battlefield, lying in no-man's-land.

A medal.

I started thinking about the words again and I wondered what kind of story they told and how the medal belonged to them. And how Monsieur Renoir belonged to them all.

When I came home, George had already received a hundred texts from Su. He was *not* talking to me. Gregory was leaving tomorrow and so I had to be a super-friendly host. It was too cold outside, so Mum had the great idea that we go swimming at Varembé. Gregory didn't have any trunks and he had to wear one of mine – there was no way I was ever going to use that pair again. Aunty Madeline didn't like swimming because it messed up her hair, so only Mum went with us. She tried to bribe George to come with twenty francs but he said no thanks, he wasn't *that* desperate.

Mum said Gregory and I had to share a changing room in the men's section.

'Mum, *privacy*.'

'You either share or you change in the women's section.'

'Eeeeeew.'

Mum made me do embarrassing things when we went out without Dad or George. For example, I had to use the women's toilets. When I asked why I couldn't use the men's, she said for safety reasons.

Me: MUM! IT'S THE TOILET!

I was allowed to go in the men's with George and he had to promise that he wouldn't leave me alone in there.

George: Seriously, Mum, should I flush the toilet for him too.

George said Mum was afraid of paedophiles, men who touched your penis and balls (Mum didn't like that word – 'testicles', she said).

Me: Dr Legrand does.

George (shaking his head): He's a doctor, doofus. And Mum is STILL with you when he touches them.

I let Gregory go in the cubicle first and I waited outside. He took ages.

'Gregory,' I said, 'are you finished?'

A funny sound came out like he was choking.

I took a breath and pushed the cubicle door open.

'Gregory . . .'

His T-shirt and sweater were all over his head. He was trying to set his arms free. He was going to kill himself.

'Gregory, stay still.' He was thrashing and gurgling. 'Stay still!'

I grabbed his clothes and yanked them over his head, then I rushed out; there was way too much of him to see.

Finally he came out. Why had Mum given him my favourite trunks? Why?

I changed and threw our stuff in a locker.

'What have you been doing?' asked Mum.

'Gregory was fighting with his clothes.'

Mum looked at Gregory. 'Are you all right?' she asked him.

'Yes, Aunty,' but his voice was all shaky and he was trembling.

We had to stay in the baby pool because Gregory was a beginner. I really hoped that no one from school would see me. My reputation would be ruined, RUINED.

I was getting out of the pool when I saw him.

Monsieur Renoir.

He was in the middle-sized pool, leaning against the edge, just standing in the water. He looked kinda funny. There were other old people around him.

'Come on, Robert, let's go.'

I didn't point him out to Mum this time.

I turned to follow Mum but I turned back one more time to take a last look at Monsieur Renoir.

He was still in the pool.

Then he looked up from the water and he saw me.

I stood like a statue. I couldn't move.

It must be his eye, I thought.

His lips split open. His perfect white teeth were lined up in his mouth. His hair was matted down on his head; this time it looked like someone had sat on the bird's nest. No, it looked like a crown of THORNS pressing down on his head, and very soon the thorns would dig into his skin and blood would start trickling down and—

Monsieur Renoir was smiling. At me.

He looked like a crocodile before he opens his mouth and, SNAP, you're dead.

I ran. And not all ziggyzaggy like how Aunty Delphia says you should if a crocodile decides it wants to eat you.

I just scrammed away from there.

Chapter Eleven

Google

FREE AT LAST!

Gregory was gone. George was off to football practice. Mum was in her study. I had the computer to myself. My investigation could begin. Step aside, Young Sherlock Holmes.

Google: Victoria Cross.

Google: Lost Victoria Crosses.

Google: Stolen Victorian Crosses.

Google: Mau Mau.

Google: Infantry.

Google: Private.

Google: Jack Montgomery Clift.

The first search result from Google was Wikipedia for every single one of them (except Jack Montgomery Clift. Nothing. He wasn't on Google; there was a Montgomery Clift but he was an actor who died a long time ago).

Mum was always saying that we depended way too much on Wikipedia.

Mum: It's not the gospel truth; every entry on

Wikipedia is a set of opinions. You have to check these opinions against others and not be lazy and do all your research from one source.

George (mumbling): Yeah, yeah, whatever, Wikipedia's the boss of me.

But Wikipedia was a start. I needed a start.

I printed pages and pages of information, recycling Mum's printouts. Sometimes, when I was bored, I would take one of her printouts and read a random bit. Mum said I shouldn't do that and she always checked what printouts she put out in our recycling tray because she didn't want anything 'inappropriate' there. Once, I forgot to use new printing paper for an essay and I handed it in with all of Mum's story on the other side, the one about the gay man who lives in Paris with his lover and has the 'f' word in it. Mum was mortified, that was her exact word. *Mortified.*

I knew definitely what infantry meant now (soldiers who fought on foot, not on horses or ships or planes).

I knew what a private was in the army. It was the lowest rank.

I knew about the Mau Mau (even though I had to skip lots of the Wikipedia entry because I couldn't really understand it). I underlined the bit on the use of air power by the Royal Air Force to destroy the Mau Mau in their hideouts in the bush in Kenya. They killed hundreds of them.

And I knew lots about Victoria Crosses.

But I knew *nothing* about Jack Montgomery Clift.

And I had a headache.

151

I slumped down on the couch. I got up and went to the kitchen and drank two glasses of water. Liquids were good for headaches. Mum read that in a study. I went back to the playroom. I sat down on the couch. I went over everything I knew.

The Victoria Cross 'is the highest military decoration awarded for valour in the face of the enemy to members of the armed forces of various Commonwealth countries and previous British Empire territories'. I would look up 'British Commonwealth' and 'British Empire territories' later, or I'd ask Mum.

Victoria Crosses had been stolen all over the world. When I read this I started feeling really strange and jumpy, like I was making something bad happen; it was kinda like the same feeling I had at Jin's house when I was about to tell him what I thought might have happened. I closed my eyes and counted up to ten. I opened them and made myself read.

They were stolen in England, in Canada, in India, in Burma which is in Asia, in New Zealand, even in South Africa which is underneath Zimbabwe; the soldier who got it was a captain. I looked to see if there were any that had been stolen in Kenya and that weird feeling came again. But there were none.

Victoria Crosses vanished in other ways. Someone traded one for a beer in England. Somewhere else in England, some kids thought it was a toy and lost it in a field while playing a battle game.

There were Victoria Crosses destroyed in fires and

air raids and a Victoria Cross was buried with a soldier somewhere in India.

None of them had disappeared in Kenya.

I cut out the parts on the missing Victoria Crosses and I stuck them in my reporter's notebook. I highlighted the stolen ones and when I saw them sticking out in bright yellow I became nervous all over again. I don't know why I kept going back to that.

I mean, Monsieur Renoir could have just found the medal, couldn't he; he could have been walking in a field somewhere with his dog and the dog ran off and started digging away at some bushes and . . . there was the long-lost medal lying on the ground! But then why hadn't he tried to give it back. It just didn't make any sense.

Or maybe . . . he'd bought it from the flea market in Nyon! At that stall where there were all kinds of books, badges and medals. Dad and I stopped there once; the market was only on the last Sunday of every month. There were medals in wooden trays, just thrown there as if they weren't anything special. But there were other ones in cabinets that were locked. You could see them through the glass window.

Me: Why would you buy one, Dad? You haven't earned it.

Dad said people collected things. Some did it for pleasure, some to be surrounded by what they thought were beautiful and valuable things. It made them feel good about themselves, maybe even more important and special. ·

153

Me: To show off.
Dad: Yes, that's a reasonable assumption.

And some did it to make a profit. They bought something that they thought would be more valuable later on, waited and then sold it off and sometimes they had guessed right and they made zillions more money. It was just so wrong to do it with medals. Any medal. Why would you buy someone else's Olympic gold medal? What was the meaning of that? Why would you collect medals and sell them? Shouldn't you find their owners, give the medals back? Dad said it was complicated. The stall owner had to make a living, just like everyone else. And besides, some of the medals probably had been sold to him by the relatives of the people who'd received them. 'Why?' I asked. 'Don't they care?' Dad said sometimes people needed the money or the medals didn't mean as much to them as before. Sometimes, he said, the medals may have been found in garages or cellars that old people let be cleared for a very small price. In that case, Dad said, that was a moral *and* ethical question: should you tell the old person what you had found? How much more valuable was the medal than anything else that might be in the cellar? You should, I said.

Maybe I was just being dramatic and thinking mean things about Monsieur Renoir because he was so scary.

That crocodile smile kept gnashing away at me.

There were people who collected Victoria Crosses. They sold them in auctions for a lot of money. This just seemed so wrong, even when I thought about all of Dad's explanations.

I read about the acts of valour that the soldiers had done.

Sometimes it was saving other soldiers from the enemy.

Sometimes it was killing the enemy.

Sometimes soldiers rushed into enemy trenches.

Sometimes they rushed into the battlefield to help an injured soldier.

Acts of valour had happened all over the world but mostly in France in World War I.

There was a lot of blood.

There was a link to 'bronze disease' and I clicked on it. There were pictures of coins with it and they looked exactly like the medal.

'After casting and cooling down, any bronze artefact begins to corrode as soon as it comes into contact with air.'

AIR! That was everywhere!

Other things corroded bronze: acid and salt. There were pages on how to stop the corrosion, but you had to be a scientist to understand them.

There were pages and pages of *references* after the Mau Mau entry. Those were the other sources I was supposed to check on, but I was only ten years old! Everyone had an opinion! I only read the first bit and my eyes got tired and my brain started hurting.

Dad said that this happened to him with some of the documents he had to read for work. The only cure was fresh air. Immediately. I stuck my head out of the window. I counted to ten and stuck it back inside. My cheeks were cold. I sat down on the couch. I started reading again.

'The Mau Mau uprising was a military conflict that took place in Kenya between 1952 and 1960. It involved a Kikuyu-dominated anti-colonial group called Mau Mau and elements of the British army . . .'

Who were the Kikuyu? Mum was right. Once you started on Google, it never ended. You could get lost in the internet.

I read about why they were called the Mau Mau.

'The origin of the term Mau Mau is uncertain. According to some members of the Mau Mau, they never referred to themselves as such, instead preferring the military title Kenya Land and Freedom Army (KLFA). Some publications, such as Fred Majdalany's *State of Emergency: The Full Story of Mau Mau*, claim that it was an anagram of *uma uma*, which means "get out get out".'

I knew what an anagram was: it was when you could scramble the letters of a word and they still made a proper word.

Like the Young Sherlock Holmes, I asked myself some logical, penetrating questions. Who did the Mau Mau want to *get out get out*? The British army, I guessed. And who was in the British army? Monsieur Renoir! The Mau Mau wanted Monsieur Renoir to *get out get out* of Kenya and Monsieur Renoir, the British Royal Air Force pilot, had . . .

I turned the pages.

'Air power: for an extended period the chief British weapon against the forest fighters was air power. It was the only service capable of both psychologically influencing and inflicting considerable casualties on the Mau Mau fighters operating in the dense forests. Lack of timely and accurate intelligence meant bombing was rather haphazard, but almost 900 insurgents had been killed or wounded by air attack in June 1954. Lincoln bombers flew their first mission on 18 November and remained in Kenya until 28 June 1955, conducting over 900 sorties and dropping six million bombs.'

SIX MILLION BOMBS!

What did a Lincoln bomber look like?

I went back to the computer and googled 'Lincoln bomber' and clicked on images. There it was. It looked pretty cool. I tried to imagine Monsieur Renoir sitting in it and I just couldn't imagine it, and then I tried to imagine him standing next to one with his arm on a wing like in some of the pictures with his cool jacket and bomber hat and I still couldn't imagine it. Then I tried to imagine him under a plane, fixing something. Hmmmm . . . I could kind of imagine that. I thought of the plane flying high above the forest dropping bombs. SIX MILLION BOMBS! I thought of all the trees that were burned in the forest. All the birds that fell from the trees. What animals lived in forests?

Snakes. Snakes, sizzling and burning. And deer. There must be deer. I thought of all the animals we had seen on safari – lions and giraffes and elephants – trapped in the forest, the fire getting closer and closer. And the Mau Mau hiding there and the bombs (SIX MILLION) finding them. Did children live in the forest?

And Monsieur Renoir, did he drop a bomb, lots of bombs? Did he watch the forest go up in flames? Did he feel it getting hot in his plane? Did he feel sorry or was he happy that he was bombing the Mau Mau, the enemy who wanted him to *get out get out*?

I thought about all this knowledge I had now and what I could do with it, how I could use it.

And then I did something else.

I googled Aunty Delphia.

She was in the *News*. I clicked on that. I read. Aunty Delphia had been nominated for an award for her courageous conservation work in Zimbabwe.

'Robert, what are you doing?' Mum was calling from the lounge.

'Homework.' Which was kind of the truth. I was researching.

'How about taking a break?'

Mum's breaks usually meant she wanted us to go somewhere.

'I need to go to the post office to collect my proof, then we can go and get a snack at the *boulangerie*.'

YES!

'Okay, Mum, coming.'

*

I pressed the green button on the ticket machine. We were number 269. That seemed like a lot of people. We were the 269th person to come into the post office today. Maybe even more people had been in, because look at Mum and me, there were two of us. And it wasn't even near the end of the day yet. I was busy trying to do all these mathematical problems when I heard:

'*Oui, en Angleterre.*'

I looked up.

I moved away from the machine and looked at the counters.

Right at the last one, he was there.

He had a brown box on the counter. It was pretty long.

The window opened and he pushed the box to the lady.

What was in there?

'*Oui, Jack,*' he said. '*Il n'y a rien de nouveau à l'intérieur.*'

And then he coughed and stuck his hand in his pocket and took out a handkerchief to cover his mouth.

He rubbed his hand over his eye.

He paid the lady and then he turned round.

I went round the machine and watched him walk out of the post office in his funny, stiff way.

Yes, in England.

Yes, Jack.

There is nothing new inside.

*

I just had this feeling that Monsieur Renoir was stalking me.

I was pretty spooked out and I kept looking backwards to check that he wasn't following me. And then I thought maybe he'd leap out from the hedges. *And* my head was full of all the knowledge from Google.

Mum noticed.

'You're very serious, Robert.'

'Hmmm,' I said.

A huge cat always jumped out right in front of us on this bit of the pavement, opposite the church, and we had to ask it permission to go on ahead. Yes, there it was.

'Your turn,' said Mum. She sneezed.

I didn't really feel like it, but I didn't want Mum to start getting worried about me.

'Oh Great One, Mistress of the Universe, we ask that you grant us passage to the *boulangerie*.'

'That's good,' said Mum. She sneezed again.

We waited.

The cat looked at us and licked its lips, miaowed and stepped aside.

'Oh thank you, Blessed One,' I said.

'Impressive,' said Mum. She sneezed thank you to the cat.

'Mum, do you think she really understands?'

'I believe she does.'

Maybe this was a good time to continue my campaign.

'Can I have a guinea pig?'

160

'A guinea pig, what for? Is it a school project?'

I almost said yes.

'For a pet.'

'Oh, Robert.' She shook her head. 'And the clue's in the word "pig".'

'*Mum*, it's not a real pig.'

It was actually a rodent, but I definitely wasn't going to tell Mum that. I knew Mum didn't like pigs. When we passed the farm at the old people's house, I liked to watch the pigs rolling about in the mud and Mum would always say, ugh, pigs are so dirty.

'I know. A bad joke.'

'A hamster?'

'Definitely not. Hamsters are rodents.'

And rodents were rats.

And Mum wasn't thinking about Geronimo Stilton when she said rodents.

I don't know if it was because we were passing the fountain but I shouted, 'A FISH!'

A fish wasn't really a pet but I was DESPERATE.

Mum said *maybe* to the fish.

We sat at a table outside.

Mum didn't open her parcel. The proof is like a rough copy of a book, the book before it becomes the book you can buy in shops, and Mum was usually really excited when she got it. But I guess she was thinking of Aunty Delphia.

'Mum, who are the Kikuyu?'

'A tribe in Kenya. Why do you ask?'

'Nothing.'

'Oh,' she said. 'You're still thinking about Monsieur Renoir. What did he say when you gave him the medal?'

'Err . . .'

Luckily the waitress came over.

I ordered a chocolate milk and butterfly wings, not real ones, duh, a pastry that's shaped like butterfly wings and has sugar sprinkled all over it.

Mum ordered a green tea and an apple strudel.

When the waitress left, I waited for Mum to bust me.

'It's funny how in Africa they're called tribes and in Europe ethnic groups. Tribal conflicts in Africa and ethnic conflicts in Europe. One sounds more civilized than the other. Or maybe I'm just paranoid.'

Mum did that a lot, talk to herself.

We ate our snack and then we went into the newsagent. Mum usually bought fashion magazines, which she liked looking at in the bath, but this time she just waited for me. I chose a *Pokémon World*.

When we were walking back to our apartment, I asked Mum how Aunty Delphia was.

Mum took my hand, squeezed it.

'If everything goes well she'll be in Botswana by this evening.'

I knew where Botswana was. It was one of Zimbabwe's neighbours and it wasn't ruled by a dictator.

'But it's a secret,' she said. 'No one outside the family must know.'

She held my hand a little longer and then she let go.

I wanted to know how Aunty Delphia was getting to Botswana and what she was going to do when she got there. Was she still going to be a veterinarian? And what about Bob the Butternut, was he going to go after her there?

'What about Cynthia, Grandma and Grandpa?'

'They're still in Zimbabwe.'

'Is she going to stay in Botswana for ever?'

'She'll be safe there for the time being, that's the most important thing. I don't know how long she'll stay. We just have to wait and see.'

I remembered then that I hadn't googled that word . . . *antiretro* . . . There were so many things in my head, it was hard to keep track.

Mum stopped walking. She was looking over at the church. She crossed the road. And then she stepped up on to the lawn.

'I'm going in for a moment,' she said.

I followed her. We had never been inside this church. In Rome, Dad liked taking pictures of churches because of the 'architectural details'. I liked looking at the confession boxes. They were tall and dark and, I don't know why, they made me think of Doctor Who's phone box, the Tardis. If you stepped inside, you'd get teleported into another dimension. When you came out of a confession box you were supposed to be a new person, without sin; I guess that's almost a new dimension.

Mum walked up to the front and stopped by the

163

trestle of candles. Above them was the Holy Mother of God. She was wearing a long white dress with blue on the edges.

You were supposed to pray to ask Mary for help because she was a mother and mothers were kind and patient and she would tell Jesus and God to help you and they would listen to her because she was their mother and they didn't want to disappoint her. I didn't really understand how it all worked and Grandma and Grandpa and Pastor Haig believed that you had to pray straight to God otherwise you were praying to idols.

Only four of the candles were lit up. They weren't real candles that you had to light with matches but electric ones, lined up one after the other in three rows, and there was a box with a slot where you had to put your donation in, to light a candle. Mum put a coin in and a candle in the third row lit up.

'Can I do one?' I asked.

Mum gave me a coin and I put it in the slot. A candle in the second row lit up. Mum stood there for a bit with her head bowed, her eyes closed. I wondered if she was praying. And then I knew she was praying for Aunty Delphia. So I closed my eyes too. I had never prayed before so I just talked to God. I told him about Aunty Delphia and how much I loved her and what a great person she was, and then I asked him to look after Grandpa and Grandma and Cynthia because Bob the Butternut might be angry that Aunty Delphia had got away, and I told him that I loved them all, and then

I thought, God knows this already and I didn't want him to get bored and stop listening and move on to someone else. So I said, Amen.

Dad was coming home in four more hours. I couldn't wait to see what his surprise was.

Chapter Twelve

The Surprise

A carpet. It wasn't a very big carpet. It fitted, rolled up, in Dad's carry-on bag. It was just any old carpet.

'It's a Turkmen rug,' said Dad.

I nodded.

'Not just a rug, though; what it *really* is is a flying carpet.'

'Yeah, right,' said George. 'Aladdin, Aladdin, where are you?'

'It's exactly your size, Robert. You sit on it and your mind flies.'

George said LOL. And Dad said, '*Basta con queste stupidaggini.*' which basically means shut up.

'I found it in a village, and a boy – your age, Robert – told me all about its magical powers, how you can travel the world just by sitting on it in a quiet place and closing your eyes.'

'Yeah, Dad, where's he been then?'

He just couldn't shut up.

'And it stinks, Dad, what the heck?'

'It's been on a camel.'

'A camel!' I said.

'Yes. The boy – his name was Aziz – he took it off the camel's back and gave it to me.'

'For free?' George rolled his eyes.

'I insisted on giving him some money just to show my gratitude for the gift.'

'SUCKER.'

Dad ignored him.

'Do you want to give it a try, Robert?'

'Seriously, Dad, he'll catch a bug or something. Anyway, I think I made it into Servette. If I get into Servette, it's easier to be selected for the Swiss under fifteens.'

Dad and George started talking about football.

When Dad was a teenager he was a goalkeeper and captain. He was selected for Roma but he got tired of all the football practices; he said that he wasn't as dedicated and talented as George. There is a picture of Dad in his football jersey. George says it's hard to believe, but Dad was pretty buff back then.

George wanted to be Swiss. He wanted to be Swiss right now. Dad said he didn't think that was possible.

'Geneva sucks. I can't play for Zimbabwe because I'm here. I can't play for Italy because I'm here. I can't play for Switzerland because I'm here.'

He kind of made sense. But Mum was always saying that we were lucky. We had an international upbringing, which meant that we had choices. But, I thought, sometimes too many choices weren't so good;

maybe sometimes all the choices cancelled each other out so you were left with nothing, like George.

'How can I be a pro football player if I can't even play under-fifteen INTERNATIONAL football!'

By international, I guess George meant playing against some French kids across the border.

'Don't shout.'

Dad was pretty tired from his trip. I was standing listening to them, the carpet rolled up under my arm. It felt good to have it there.

'It's not fair. It's my dream.'

It *was* his dream. Football was his passion. It was his life.

Dad sighed.

'Okay, if you're serious about it, find out what you need to become Swiss.'

George went straight to work. Google was his best friend. He had the information in two minutes. He printed it out and gave it to Dad.

'It says here you have to be resident in Switzerland for twelve years; we've only been here for ten . . . oh, wait a minute – time spent in Switzerland between the ages of ten and twenty counts as double.'

'Yes!' said George. 'I've been here for twenty years. I'm Swiss!'

He had the maths wrong, but Dad just read on.

Dad held out his hand.

'Wait a minute. There are other requirements.'

'What?'

'Are you well integrated in the Swiss community?

168

That would be a yes, I suppose. You speak passable French, you play for the local team; the only down side, you don't go to the local school. Are you accustomed to the Swiss way of life? Well, you tell me, George, are you?'

'Fondue, skiing, boules, ice hockey, Roger Federer, chocolate.'

'And you think clichés are going to impress the Swiss cantonal and federal authorities? You know, I think Robert has a better chance; he knows the Swiss anthem.'

'Yes, he does,' said Mum. 'Note perfect.'

I started singing with my hand on my heart.

'Sur nos monts, quand le soleil, Annonce un brill—'

'Stop,' said George.

'Well sung,' said Dad. He looked down at the paper again. 'Do you comply with the Swiss legal system? Do you compromise the internal and external security of Switzerland?'

'Dad, they want *me* to play for the Swiss under fifteens. *They* want *me*.'

Mum said it was harder to become Swiss now than before because of the right-wing party that was really popular in the German-speaking part. Last year there were posters showing lots of white sheep on the map of Switzerland and a black sheep being kicked out by one of the white sheep. There was another poster that showed lots of black hands grabbing Swiss passports. Mum said that it was the first time she felt really sad in Switzerland and I heard her tell

Dad that it made her sick to have us kids see that kind of ugliness.

'So, I *can* be Swiss.' He was looking at Dad like he was expecting a high five or something.

'Maybe you should wait till the summer camp with Manchester United before you decide.'

What if he got scouted by Manchester United? By *the* Manchester United.

The problem was, if George waited till next summer, he wouldn't be under fifteen any more. He'd be under sixteen. He told all this to Dad, really slowly in case Dad needed help working it out.

'You can't just become Swiss, George. It's a process. I think it might take a year, so you'd still not be able to play for the under fifteens anyway.'

George looked like he was going to have a tantrum, so I stepped aside.

I thought about Monsieur Renoir. Was he Swiss? It was funny how you could be so many things. You could be English and British and you could go fly a plane in Kenya and then come and live in Switzerland. Dad said this was globalization, which for the most part was a good thing. You didn't have to live in your little village and think that was the centre of the universe. Globalization should make people less selfish because they saw how other people lived, but actually it made a lot of people even more selfish because they wanted the best things of the world for themselves.

Did Monsieur Renoir know the Swiss national anthem? Did he know the Escalade song?

170

And then I remembered something the new kid, Blake, said to me at school.

'Am I black, Mum?'

'You're brown, moron,' said George.

'Blake said I was black. He said even if I'm brown, I'm black, like him.'

Mum sighed.

'Where's he from?'

'America.'

'Well, in America, that's how you would be class— That's how people . . . In Geneva, and anywhere else in the world, for that matter, you're Robert Sartori.'

'You're black, Mum. Grandma's blacker than you.'

'Yes, but—'

'I'm black *and* white.'

'Yes, but I really don't like people dividing everything into colour and race; you know we are all people, and if you believe in God, he just made us all different for a bit of variety; it would be boring if he made just green people.'

George slapped his forehead. 'Seriously, Mum, *God*? *Green* people?'

'I said *if* you believe.'

'I'm black,' said George. 'Black's dope.'

'Huh?' I said. That was a new word. *Dope.*

George made the 'it's way over your head' sign with his hand.

'You know, that's why I like Geneva,' said Mum. 'There's the Swiss and then lots of people who come from different places, and in the international school you don't just learn one particular history, you learn about the world; you learn what's happening to people all over the world and no one is a minority, everyone's equal. It makes things harder sometimes, because you can't just accept something automatically, like, oh, we're fighting against this country, that's okay because I'm from that country; you can't do that because you have classmates who come from those *other* countries . . .'

George yawned. So did Dad, but he had an excuse.

'I think your generation will be more tolerant, less hysterical about going to war, and that will be a very good thing.'

I took the carpet into my bedroom. I rolled it out. I sat down next to it. I looked at the patterns. I didn't mind the smell. I put my hands on it. Even though it was warm, I felt a shiver go along my arm. I thought of a camel, the carpet on its back, a boy sitting on the carpet travelling through deserts, and then I *was* that boy travelling far, far away.

When George came into the room he said, 'You're not sleeping in here with that. You can sit on it and fly out the window; it stinks.'

HA HA HA.

I rolled the carpet up and put it outside on the balcony. When I needed it, I would use it.

Later, when Mum and Dad thought I was sleeping (George was already dreaming of all his new girlfriends

172

in Servette – *Jeorje, Jeorje, Jeorje, I luuurve you, Jeorje*), I heard them talking in the kitchen.

Dad said, 'You should have seen the boy, Jane, he had this light in his eyes, so full of life, intelligent, he made me think so much of Robert. I mean, he could be anything, a doctor, engineer, writer, but he's stuck in the backwaters of Turkmenistan, using all that charm, intelligence to persuade a tourist to buy a carpet so he can help feed his family. It's too much sometimes.'

I lay in bed thinking of the boy, Aziz, and then I thought, Dad thinks I'm intelligent, and I fell asleep.

Chapter Thirteen

School

Dad woke us late, so everything was a mad rush. I hated it when he didn't wake me up thirty minutes early so that I could do my morning reading. I stuffed my backpack with everything I could think of that I needed and dashed out. Luckily Mum was there to give me my snack and water. I was pretty grumpy in the car. George was his normal self with his headphones on.

I'd finished my project on Nonno. Dad helped me interview Nonna, on the phone. She liked to talk about Nonno. I liked listening to Nonna's stories about the war. Nonno was a Partisan and he fought against Hitler and Mussolini. His picture was next to Nonna's bedside. It was the only picture of him in the house. He died before I was born and George doesn't remember him. In the picture, Nonno has very thick black hair that's slicked high, back from his forehead, and he has a fur scarf wrapped around his throat. He has a Roman nose like Dad's, which means that it's straight and pointing a bit down. He looks like a hero. He looks like one of those pilots in the images that I looked up with those planes that flew over the forest in Kenya bombing the Mau Mau. He wasn't a pilot, though. When the war started he was working in Tuscany in his grandfather's hotel and then he went off to the mountains and he joined the Partisans there; they fought with the Americans and defeated the Germans who had come to Italy to turn it into Germany.

I asked Nonna if Nonno had received a medal.

'*Niente*,' she said. '*Sono tutti ladri.*'

Nothing. They are all thieves.

Dad told me later that Nonna was probably talking about politicians.

'*Tutto bene?*' asked Dad.

I gave him a thumbs-up, even though it wasn't really all okay.

School was okay, I guess. I'd already counted in my Dilbert calendar how many days left till the Christmas holidays. SEVEN WHOLE WEEKS! I kept counting and counting. I was hoping that I'd added some extra days by mistake.

'*Tutto a posto?*' said Dad, looking at me in his mirror.

I shrugged.

'Come on, Robert. School's not that bad, not like in my day. You don't have a sadistic teacher like Scarciolla who beats you up.'

'What's sadistic?'

'To enjoy hurting someone.'

Dad went to a school just for boys in Rome. His teachers were priests. Dad has told George and me the story of Scarciolla, his class teacher, hundreds of times.

Dad was afraid of school so much that in the first grade he would wake up with a temperature that would go away as soon as his mum said he could stay at home.

'Philip's sadistic. Tanya's sadistic. Jean is sadistic. Manuel is sadistic. To—'

'Are you sure? All of them?'

'Trust me, Dad. They *enjoy* giving pain.'

'But not to you?'

'Hmmm . . .'

I was the youngest in the class and those wise guys called me 'baby' to my face.

'Robert—'

'Don't worry, Dad. I can defend myself. With Jin's help. We're very good at dodging.'

'The school has a zero tolerance on bullying, Robert.'

'I don't think they care, Dad. They're kids.'

But Dad was right. School wasn't so bad.

Good points	Bad points	So-so
Jin	Manuel, Jean, Philip, Tanya, Tomm	Mr Reynolds
Basketball (Mike)	Music	Art
Library	Swimming (changing in the communal changing room)	French class
Computer class	Assemblies	School trips
Break times	Mrs Drake (principal) aka Dracula	Tests
		Reports

If I added the 'Good points' and the 'So-so points', school was more than okay. George thought I had it way too easy: 'Just wait till you get to middle school, dude, you have ten teachers and you have to dash from one class to another two floors down in, like, two seconds, and if you're late, detention.'

Dad put on the radio, the English station WRS.

Everyone was happy. Obama was the president of the United States of America. There he was on the radio, '. . . *and an end to a decade of war. . . blah blah blah*.' I heard people clapping and cheering when he said that.

'Does he mean the War on Terror?' I asked.

Dad didn't give an answer right away.

'Dad?'

'I guess so. The war in Afghanistan and in Iraq . . . no, there is no war in Iraq, I don't think. And I suppose you can call what is happening in Pakistan along the border with Afghanistan part of that war. It's hard to tell these days what exactly *is* a war.'

I remembered something I wanted to ask Dad from our Peace and Conflict unit.

'Dad, what are drones?'

'Drones?'

'Drones, not like in *Star Wars*, but the things that fly over places and drop bombs.'

'Oh, *those* drones. They're like remote-controlled planes. They take pictures like satellites.'

'And drop bombs in Pakistan. That's what Omar said in class. So nobody's in them?'

'No,' said Dad.

'That's not fair.'

And then we listened to the next bit of news:

'*Over to local news now. There has been some unusual seismic activity located near the shores of Lake Geneva. Scientists from the University of Geneva are calling these mini earthquakes, and are monitoring them because of a possible tsunami risk, which is not as implausible as it sounds. In the sixth century, rocks falling in the lake did indeed result in an eight-metre wave crashing over the city's walls. The shoreline was devastated; bridges, villages and mills were destroyed and many people perished. Rockfall, earthquakes or a very large storm could cause a tsunami.*'

A TSUNAMI! IN GENEVA!

George showed me a video on YouTube of the tsunami in Thailand. The waves were huge. They swallowed everything up. Geneva could be swallowed up too! It could be smashed to smithereens!

'Dad, do you think—'

'It's a very, very faint probability, Robert, don't worry about it.'

But it was still a probability.

I *was* worried.

I loved Geneva. All of it. I didn't want any of it to disappear. Was this the beginning of the END OF THE WORLD? Was this how it was going to happen?

'Dad—'

'We should tell your mother about this. I'm sure she can use it.'

What did Dad mean? What was Mum going to do with a tsunami in Geneva?

'Her vampires,' said Dad.

'Hmmm?'

'She's not letting me read any of it this time. She says she's trying something new.'

'Do you think a tsunami would destroy vampires?'

'That's what your mother might be able to tell us.' Dad was smiling at me. I tried to smile back, but I couldn't.

'She could make it into a vampire *dystopian* thing, you know, what she calls those the-world-is-coming-to-an-end books.'

Dad wasn't being helpful.

'The man said *mini earthquakes*, Dad.'

'Robert, there's not going to be a tsunami in Geneva, I promise. It's just the case that there is no news in Geneva so they have to come up with this stuff.'

Usually Dad didn't put the news on when we drove to school. He said that I took the news to heart. Unlike George, who didn't even hear it.

What was happening to Geneva?

There was an ice storm in February when the lake froze up and waves crashed over boats and froze. It was because of the *bise*; that's the very, very cold wind that blows over from the Alps. When it rained, the wind blew the water over the railings and trees and buildings and the water froze so that there were icicles everywhere and ice statues, even hanging from trees and the tramlines. Mum said it was like a winter

179

wonderland. I thought about Mum's vampires, the icy wind blowing the water from the lake and the rain over them, freezing them. What would happen? Would they hibernate in the ice? Would they die like the dinosaurs and the mammoths? Maybe Mum could use the ice storm too. If THE END OF THE WORLD didn't come first.

Everything seemed so wrong.

2012.

Tsunami.

Aunty Delphia.

Monsieur Renoir . . . the medal . . .

King Arthur and the Holy Grail! That just flashed in my head.

I knew about the Holy Grail because we went on a road trip all over England with Aunty Madeline and Uncle Stewart (*and* Gregory) and we visited lots of abbeys, which were churches. Most of them were in ruins because Henry the Eighth destroyed them all because he wanted to divorce his wife and the Church wouldn't let him so he killed the monks and chopped off his other wife's head and started his own Church where he could do whatever he wanted because he was in charge.

In one abbey, in a town where grown-ups apparently like squelching about in the mud and listening and dancing to music, King Arthur was buried. He was a hero because he fought many battles with the Knights of the Round Table against his number one enemy Mordred, who killed him in the end, and he defended

180

Britain against the Saxons, who were German invaders. But maybe he didn't even exist, because if he *did* exist, it was supposed to be during the Dark Ages, when no one really wrote things in books, and as George's T-shirt says, *History depends on who wrote it*. So someone, many centuries later, probably played a prank and made up all the tales of the king and his knights, and of Merlin, the wizard, the Quest for the Holy Grail and the dragon in the kingdom of Camelot . . . After *Doctor Who* and *Sherlock Holmes*, *Merlin* was my favourite BBC show.

In the gift shop I bought *10 Best Arthurian Legends Ever!* The Quest for the Holy Grail was one of the chapters.

The Holy Grail was this vessel or special object. It could be a dish, a stone, a plate or a cup . . . anything.

The Holy Grail fixed things! It could stop bad things from happening.

The medal was like the Holy Grail.

I had it already but you had to know how to use it to make it do good things.

I had to use it the right way. I had to put it where it belonged. It had power.

It was a powerful force.

This was a Quest.

What if it was the bronze disease that was making it lose its powers?

What if that was also why Monsieur Renoir gave it to me?

It needed to be fixed, cleaned and polished before it could carry out its work.

181

But first, I guess, I had to figure out what all those words meant.

That was part of the fixing.

We had computer class after break, which was great because Mr Matthis gave us ten minutes of free time where we could do anything we wanted on the computer as long as it was *legal*. 'Remember, young ones,' Mr Matthis always said at the beginning of the class, 'I have all your passwords. Stay clean. Play nice.' I had to get on the case. The medal was still at the bottom of my backpack. I wanted to take a look at it again but I couldn't exactly show it to a class of sixth-graders who would all want to touch it; before I knew it, it would come back to me in smithereens.

I didn't know what to look for.

And then I remembered the '--WA--' we hadn't been able to figure out.

'Hey,' I whispered to Jin, 'what's the crossword clue solver thing Wendy was talking about in class?'

Jin shrugged.

I googled *crossword clue solver*.

I guess it was basically a cheat code for crosswords.

I chose '6' words.

I filled in '--WA--'

There were fifty-two results!

I printed them all out. Eight pages! Luckily Mr Mathis got called out of the classroom by another teacher.

I looked at the screen. There were words there I'd

never heard of: *abwatt, aswail, bewail, diwans, kawaka, luwack*. I mean, it could be anything!

I looked and looked at the screen. I was stuck. My eyes were all glazed over. I blinked. Where was inspiration when you needed it? Then I thought of Mum, who said that the internet could be a FORCE OF EVIL, so I logged out and went into a Word document and I looked at that and then I started writing. A letter.

Dear Monsieur Renoir,
Thank you very much for the medal. I still have it. I don't know if you know it but it is damaged on the one side where the name is supposed to be. Why did you leave the medal on our doormat?
Robert Sartori

I thought about adding the stuff about the Holy Grail but there wasn't much time left, and anyway I wanted Monsieur Renoir to give me his side of the story just in case I'd got it all wrong.

I looked at the screen. Wasn't I supposed to add something before *Robert Sartori*?

Sincerely, I typed.

Jin leaned over.

'What are you doing?' he asked.

'I'm writing a letter to Monsieur Renoir,' I whispered.

Jin read it.

'Are you going to mail it?'

I didn't know.

'Maybe.'

I printed out the letter and folded it. After class, I put it in my backpack.

The triplets, Manuel, Jean and Philip, were still not back from wherever they had gone – could they please stay there for ever – so Jin and I didn't have to dodge them during the lunch break. We went over to the benches around the basketball courts and I showed Jin the results from the crossword clue solver.

We read out the meanings of the words we didn't know.

'Maybe it's *aswail*. Maybe the guy got attacked by a sloth bear in India and—'

'That just sounds weird, Jin.'

'It could have happened.'

'It said *France*, remember.'

'Maybe the aswail attack happened after France.'

'You're not helping, Jin. Maybe the private's name is *Edward*.'

'It's *BEWARE*,' said Jin.

But he was just saying it to creep me out.

'--WA-- came right at the end of all the other words,' I said. 'It was the last thing.'

'BEWARE,' said Jin again.

'It could be BEWARE,' I said. 'People put that in signs at the beginning or end.'

In Zimbabwe, Grandpa had a metal sign on the gate saying BEWARE OF THE DOGS. Other people had signs saying DOGS: BEWARE! Some had signs saying BASOP! which is Zimbabwean for BEWARE!

184

'Or it could be . . .'

I went down the list with my finger.

'REWARD!'

Jin looked at the list again.

'What do you think REWARD means? Reward for what? The medal?'

I shrugged. And then I thought of Mike's words again.

Shame or fear, guilt.

What if he'd stolen it from someone, and was using our place to stash it away? What if we were accomplices to a crime? What if it wasn't even real, like Mum said? Or if he'd bought it on eBay?

But why would he leave it on our doormat?

'Jin,' I said, 'I think it was stolen.' I said it very slowly.

'You mean Monsieur Renoir . . . stole it?'

I shrugged.

'Hey, we can give it back. The reward is ours. We are HEROES!'

'Shhhh,' I said. 'We don't even know who to give it back to. We can't give it to Monsieur Renoir.'

'The poli—'

'They'll arrest us and put us in prison and—'

'*I* didn't take it.'

'Gee, thanks, wise guy. Do you want a biscuit?'

'Ask him if he stole it.'

'That's rude.'

'I guess. Ask him if it's his, in the letter.'

'Okay.'

*

In science class I tried to ask Mr Childs about bronze disease but he said I was off topic and we could discuss this another day. Didn't he know we were running out of time?

When I got home, I typed a new letter.
I added the question and then I read it again.

> *Dear Monsieur Renoir,*
> *Thank you very much for the medal. I still have it. I don't know if you know it but it is damaged on the one side where the name is supposed to be. Is it yours? Why did you leave the medal on our doormat?*
> *Sincerely,*
> *Robert Sartori*

I didn't know if I should apologize for scramming up the stairs when he asked me *What is it, BOY?* But I couldn't exactly say *I'm terrified of your blazing eye,* could I?

I went down the stairs and I stopped by Monsieur Renoir's door. I breathed in, out, and then I did it. I shoved my letter under his door and I ran like mad up those steps.

Chapter Fourteen

Halloween

Mum did not approve of Halloween. She said it
was a horrible celebration. She did not like trick-or-
treating and I was still not allowed to go around with
a bag collecting candy; I couldn't even go around the
apartment building.

*George: She's afraid of perverts: it's the same reason
she won't let you use the men's toilets.*

Me: I thought they were paedo—

*George: Same thing. She thinks they'll entice you
inside and start groping you, bro.*

Me: That's just evil.

George was allowed to go last year, with friends,
around two blocks of the neighbourhood. But Dad
tailed them all the way. George said it was embarrassing,
but he came back with a loaded bag.

The school had a 'trunk or treat'. Some parents
parked their cars at the school parking lot, decorated
them with pumpkins and lanterns and opened their
trunks, which they had filled up with sweets. We
kids went around *trunk*-or-treating' (get it?). Mum

said that this was a SAFE environment. But we weren't allowed to wear scary costumes in case we frightened the younger kids. That was the whole *point* of Halloween. You couldn't even put a white sheet over your head with two holes for your eyes and wander around saying 'oooooo oooooo ooooo'. You couldn't even wear Darth Vader masks or fool around with lightsabers. George said that was lame. No self-respecting middle-schooler would be caught trunk-or-treating in an elf costume.

Jin and I had arranged to meet near the basketball court, then we were going to walk down to the parking lot. I was dressed as a pumpkin, which was actually the costume I wore for the Escalade last year.

George (who was dressed as the devil): VERY original, bro.

There was something funny about George's costume. He looked kinda bulky. What was under that black sheet?

Mum: Now that's what's called the pot calling the kettle black.

George: Huh?

He dashed out of the door before Mum could finish explaining that it was an expression used to say that a person is guilty of the very thing they are accusing another person of. PUMPKIN – DEVIL – HALLOWEEN.

Jin was some kind of insect.

'Roach,' I said.

'Nope.'

I stepped back to take a better look.

'Grasshopper?'

'Nope. Not an insect, a crustacean.'

'I give up,' I said. 'What is it?'

'Prawn. TIGER prawn.'

'Hmmm . . .'

'My mum made it from our old curtains and Su's old ballroom dancing dress, that's all this pink.'

'Hmmm . . .'

It was cold out but we couldn't exactly wear coats over our costumes. I was too round for mine and Jin had too many sticking-out parts. We filled our bags pretty quickly and then we went into the school building to warm up a bit. Both our noses were running. I wiped mine with a leaf part on my arm, and Jin wiped his with one of his mandibles, I think that's what it was.

'So, did you post it?' he asked me.

'No, I put it under his door.'

'Wow. Do you think he's read it?'

I shrugged. How would I know?

'Do you think he'll want it back?'

I shrugged again.

When we got home, George was in the middle of an argument with Dad. I don't know how he'd changed his costume, but he was now dressed in full-combo Call of Duty gear. He even had a dog tag. It was a dog tag like soldiers wear in war. I'd read all about them in Horrible Histories.

'Take it off,' said Dad.

'Can I keep it?' He was taking pictures with his phone.

'Take it off, George.'

'Can I kee—'

'Now,' shouted Dad.

'Okay, okay,' said George, taking it off. 'Chill.'

Dad took the dog tag.

He was pretty mad.

He had also confiscated George's bag. Yes, my bro had taken a thirty-five-litre trash bag (not previously used) to collect his candy in (swag, I guess). And he was putting up a fight for it.

'They're MY teeth.'

'Settle down, young man, you heard what the orthodontist said, no sticky stuff with those braces on. You want a mouthful of cavities?'

'It's NOT fair.'

My bro sounded like a five-year-old. A devil/Call of Duty five-year-old.

'Tough luck,' said Dad.

'What about pumpkin face?' He was pointing at me.

'He's not heaving around a garbage bag, is he? And he has zero cavities. He eats fruit and vegetables.'

Dad, you're making me look bad.

'Mr Perfect,' growled my brother.

Yeah, sure, that's grown-up. That's real swag.

Dad held out a normal-sized bag for my brother, like the one I was carrying.

'You can go through the garbage bag and pick enough to fit in there; the rest goes in the trash.'

'I don't want it.' And just like a five-year-old, he stormed off into the playroom and put his headphones on.

Dad was standing there, the garbage bag on one side, the normal-sized bag in his hand. He picked up the garbage bag, and the dog tag dropped on the floor. I picked it up. I wrapped the chain around my fingers and put the tag in the middle of my palm, and then I turned the tag over. It had Dad's name on it and some numbers and *Rome*. Just like in Switzerland, Dad had to go to the army when he was eighteen. Now you don't, only if you *want* to be a soldier. It's a good thing that I'm Italian and that I'm no good at football.

Dad looked at the dog tag and then at me. His lips were tucked into each other. It looked like he was trying to keep from crying. I had never seen Dad cry.

'Dad, are you o—'

'Yes, Robert, I'm happy that you don't have to do military service.'

I didn't remind him that George might become Swiss and then he would have to go into the army.

'I had a friend,' said Dad, 'we were doing military service together. We were very different. He came from the countryside. I was a city boy. He was picked on because of the way he talked. I tried to help him out, protect him, but you can't be with someone one hundred per cent of the time. One day . . .'

Dad shook his head.

'Come on,' he said. He reached out his hand and I put mine in his.

191

'I can go through the bag, Dad. I know which ones he likes.'

'Thanks, Robert. But I think we'll just throw the whole lot out.'

I guess Dad was trying to teach George a lesson.

Taking the garbage out, I thought of Dad's dog tag and what had happened to Dad's friend and how Dad had tried to protect him but couldn't be with him one hundred per cent of the time. And then Monsieur Renoir, flying his plane in the forest in Kenya, bombing the Mau Mau. I thought about shame and fear and guilt. About the medal with holes in it. FOR VALOUR. And the words on the piece of newspaper that had not disappeared. 1916, PRIVATE, INFANTRY, FRANCE. And Aunty Delphia; God had heard me pray for Aunty Delphia – and I was a boy, Robert, in a plane, and I knew that everything belonged together and I had to find out how.

Chapter Fifteen

Stand-Off

There was an envelope lying on Monsieur Renoir's doormat.

It said *THE BOY*.

I knew *I* was THE BOY.

I picked it up.

I looked at Monsieur Renoir's door and then I scooted up the stairs. I put the envelope in my backpack. I was going to open it tomorrow. I wanted Jin to be with me.

At morning break we went and sat on the stairs that went down from the playground to the basement where the gym was. We were forbidden to sit there but it was the only place where we could get some privacy. We took the risk. I took out the envelope from my coat pocket.

'THE BOY,' read Jin. 'That's kinda scary.'

I nodded. It was. I felt the chills going up and down my spine. It wasn't written grown-up style, in cursive writing, but in straight, blocky letters: THE BOY.

'Here goes,' I said, opening the envelope. I don't

know why but I closed my eyes. And then I opened them. There was one piece of paper, black, folded in half.

'It's black,' said Jin.

'Hmmm.'

This wasn't good.

This wasn't good at all.

'Open it,' Jin said.

'*You* open it,' I told him, giving him the paper.

He pushed it back to me.

'It's yours. Open it. Come on, Robert, break's almost over.'

I opened it.

WE HAVE TO TALK, we both read, together.

Jin and I looked at each other.

I swallowed.

'He sounds mad,' Jin said.

I swallowed again.

The bell rang.

We scrambled out of the stairs and ran as if something was chasing us and snapping at our heels. We were doomed, DOOMED.

WE HAVE TO TALK.

In white, crayony-like. Everything in block. An order. A command.

WE HAVE TO TALK.

We quickly ate our lunch and scooted down to the playground. Jin and I had to work out a plan. But the triplets – yes, they were back – were waiting at the end of the ramp. George called the kids 'The Three Missing Dwarves'. They were tiny but dangerous, and when they needed muscle they had Tanya on stand-by mode.

'Hey, Robert-oh and Ji-nee, hand it over.' That was Manuel, the youngest, apparently, and the meanest.

'Hand *what* over?' said Jin.

I was leaning backwards. I thought that maybe we should back up the ramp, go back to the cafeteria. Or we could stall them here (*not* provoke them) until reinforcements arrived.

'Everything in your pockets.' That was Jean, the eldest and the dumbest.

'Or what?' said Jin. I looked over at him. What had got into him? Usually we just ignored them or ran. Jin was doing something different. He was standing his ground. Even the triplets were confused. Manuel turned to Jean. Jean turned to Philip.

'Just hand it over,' said Philip.

'Or what?' That was me. Jin looked at me and smiled.

I couldn't help thinking that something in Monsieur Renoir's note had got into us both. We were in this together.

And maybe it was Aunty Delphia too.

Mum told me how Aunty Delphia used to take her bicycle and cycle all the way to Hillside Dams just to walk in the bush. And once Aunty Delphia got into a fight with a gang of boys who were stealing birds' eggs and smashing them on to tree trunks. Aunty Delphia came home with a black eye but she'd managed to save an egg and she nursed that egg and the bird hatched and she taught it to fly.

My eyes were blinking really fast.

Sometimes you had to do things out of your comfort zone, that's what Aunty Delphia said. Well, I was doing one of them now.

I guess the triplets thought I was afraid and I was going to cry like a baby.

They stepped closer. We didn't back away. We didn't run. We stared them in the face. We had bigger things to worry about. Monsieur Renoir wanted to talk. Three dwarves, what were they? Nothing. NOTHING.

'You're going to get it now,' said Jean, and they started running towards us, but then all the kids came rushing out of the cafeteria and swarmed us. We made our getaway. We couldn't go down the stairs again because there was an actual playground supervisor blocking them. When you needed one, they were nowhere; when you didn't need one, they were in the wrong place! We looked around the playground. The triplets were at the far end, where they were pushing and shoving in the Beyblade showdown arena. Any moron could play that game; you just needed to throw the Beyblade as hard as you could to knock out your opponents. What was the fun in that! Bakugan was way cooler; you had to THINK. You had trap cards and gate cards that gave you power-ups and ability cards that gave you special powers. But no, Bakugan was banned in the playground. Pokémon was banned. Why? Because they used cards. Cards that you had to have to work out what you needed to beat your opponent. Mum said that the school probably thought they were encouraging some kind of gambling, betting. Adults should just stay out of kids' games and let us have FUN.

'There,' said Jin. He was pointing to the ping-pong table. No one was playing. We sat underneath it.

I took out the envelope again.

And then the black paper.

We looked at the paper.

We read the words.

'What do you think he wants to talk about?' Jin asked.

'Everything, I guess. The medal, and why he gave it to me.'

'Maybe he'll tell us if he stole it.'

I was glad that Jin said 'us'.

'Maybe.'

'What should we write?'

I shrugged. I didn't know if I wanted to write back. We thought and thought but we couldn't think of anything.

'Let's go and *do* something. Maybe the answer will come when we're not thinking about it,' I said.

That was Mum's trick. When she got stuck in a story she went for a walk or made dinner; she just let her mind take a break and the solution always popped up, out of the blue. She said that sometimes the brain craves a distraction, as long as it isn't the internet.

We steered clear of the Beyblade crowd. We went up to the basketball court. There were some fifth-graders and we joined them. I did 'the Robert', which was getting the ball into the net by hitting it on the board. I didn't miss once. Smooth. Just as I was about to throw my sixth throw, it happened. Just like Mum said, the idea popped into my head. The magic carpet! I told Jin all about it. Jin didn't seem too convinced.

'It works,' I said. 'Promise. And if we both sit on it, we'll know what we have to do. We have to try.'

We had to sit on the carpet and let our minds travel. We'd fly as high as the carpet wanted us to and the answer to Monsieur Renoir's letter would come.

I knew it.

Chapter Sixteen

The Magic Carpet

Jin and I organized a play date: it wasn't even Wednesday which was a half day (Swiss kids were luckier; they didn't even *go* to school on Wednesdays).

George: Enjoy it while it lasts – come middle school, it's a full week, no more baby stuff.

We were supposed to spend at least an hour doing homework, but after our snack Mum was so busy with her vampires that she left us to get on with it, without supervision.

I showed Jin all the stuff I'd googled.

'I think I've worked it out,' I said.

I was looking at the list of medals that had been stolen or lost.

Like Sherlock Holmes, I was trying to make deductions and conclusions.

I checked the ones that had 'infantry'.

I checked the ones that had 'private'.

It didn't leave me with very many.

One of those had been stolen in 1920 and I didn't think Monsieur Renoir would have been old enough.

Another was stolen in 1935. Monsieur Renoir was *still* not old enough.

That left only three.

'I think it's one of these,' I told Jin.

One was stolen in London in 1962.

One was stolen in Scotland in 1960.

One was stolen in a museum in Vancouver in the 1950 or 1960s. A fake one was put there instead.

I looked to check the ones that were for actions in 1916.

None of them. Zero.

'I just don't get it,' I said.

'Maybe they forgot to put it in.'

'We need the carpet,' I said.

I went on the balcony and took the carpet to the playroom. George wasn't around and there was no way we were going to freeze to death outside. The temperature was one degree Celsius and there was wind. We'd literally be flying out of the balcony.

'*That's* a magic carpet?' said Jin.

'Uh huh,' I said. 'It doesn't work if you don't believe.'

I sat on it and wriggled down right to the end. The two of us just about fitted.

'What do we do now?' asked Jin.

'Close your eyes.'

We closed our eyes.

After one minute Jin said, 'And now?'

'It doesn't work if you're not patient.'

'Is this like yoga?'

We were sitting cross-legged, just like in yoga.

'Ooooom,' said Jin.

'Shhhh.'

'It's not working,' said Jin, and he wriggled off the carpet.

I stayed there with my eyes closed.

'Robert, do you—'

'Shhhh,' I said.

The carpet lifted off and took me with it and we sailed over all of Geneva and I was far, far away in the clouds. And there was Monsieur Renoir in his plane waving at me.

'*Bonjour, Robert.*' His voice boomed out from the plane.

'*Bonjour, Monsieur Renoir.*'

'*C'est très joli ici,*' he boomed.

'*Oui, oui.*'

And it *was* beautiful, flying between the fluffy clouds.

'*Au revoir, Robert, j'ai du travail à faire.*'

He waved and his plane looped around me and zoomed down where he had some work to do.

'Robert, Robert!'

I opened my eyes. It was Jin shaking me.

'What?'

'Your mum's calling you.'

I scrambled off the carpet.

'Yes, Mum!'

Mum was standing in the middle of the lounge. The car keys were dangling from her hand. She had her boots on. Something was wrong. We didn't walk with shoes in the house.

'Come on, guys, hurry up, we have to go to the airport, come on, move.'

'The airport, why?'

'Come on, Robert, move, your aunt's arrived.'

But Aunty Madeline had only just left. Was Gregory that much in *luuurve* with my brother?

'But Aunty Mad—'

'Aunty Delphia,' said Mum. 'She's here.'

Mum was already out the door. She was holding the lift open by keeping her hand on the button, which she never did. She was always shouting at George when he did that; what if someone else wanted to use the lift, what if there was an emergency?

'Is Cynthia with her?'

'Robert! Move. I don't know.'

Mum drove like Dad to the airport. Fast.

At the airport, she parked the car and then walked so quickly we had to run to keep up with her.

Aunty Delphia wasn't in the arrivals area. Mum went to the information desk and asked if everyone from the flight had arrived and then gave Aunty Delphia's name. The lady told her to wait there and made a phone call.

A policeman came and told Mum to follow him, and then he looked at us and said, wait here.

Mum told us not to move from the information desk; she wouldn't be long.

But we stayed there for ages. Finally, Dad came; Mum had called him.

He drove us over to Jin's house and he left me there too. He said he had to go back to the airport.

It turned out to be a sleepover. On a school night! That had never happened before.

Jin and I sat on his bed. We were each writing a letter to Monsieur Renoir. We couldn't use the computer because Su was doing her homework.

Dear Monsieur Renoir, I wrote.

Mum says that you fought against the Mau Mau. I've read about them in Wikipedia. I know the Royal Air Force bombed the Mau Mau in the forest. Do you feel bad about it? Is that why you gave me the medal? I found a piece of paper in the box with the medal. I could only read some words: PRIVATE, INFANTRY, FRANCE, 1916, REWARD (I think). My mum's a writer and she puts words together to make a story. So this is the story I think these words make. There was a private, an ordinary soldier, in the infantry, who was fighting in France in World War I, 1916. He did an ACT OF VALOUR and he was awarded the Victoria Cross. His medal was lost or someone stole it. There is a reward for whoever returns it. Am I right?

And Aunty Delphia is in Geneva. Thank-you.
Sincerely,
Robert Sartori

I read it out to Jin and then he read me his.

Dear Monsieur Renoir,

I think you stole the medal from the hero because you were jealous and wanted one for yourself. Maybe you think you were braver than the hero fighting the Moo Moo. Am I right?

Jin

'Hmmm,' I said. 'It's Mau Mau.'

Jin just shrugged.

'We should send both,' he said.

'Okay.'

We found an envelope and folded both our letters. We put them inside. I put the envelope in my backpack.

'Can I see the medal?' asked Jin.

I took it out.

I turned it over.

'We have to do something,' I said. 'We have to fix it.'

I had all the printouts from Wikipedia about bronze disease back home.

'We can't do it on our own. It's too complicated.' I tried to remember some of what I'd read. 'You have to put the medal in different mixtures called carbonates.'

'That's in sodas,' said Jin. 'We can dump the medal in some Coke and see what happens.'

'No ways.'

I looked outside the window. It was raining. Really hard. And the wind was blowing the trees backwards.

I kept thinking about the tsunami, about all that rain pouring into the lake, and the wind whipping it up, and all the tiny earthquakes happening on the shore and a big, terrible wave—

'Robert,' said Jin. 'Do you think it's even real? Maybe it's just a fake.'

I had thought about that too. Mum had said it must be an imitation, but when I looked at it I was sure it was real. But what if it wasn't really old, what if Monsieur Renoir was just playing a game? What if it was a forgery? I had read about forgeries in Horrible Histories and in Young Sherlock Holmes. What if Monsieur Renoir was playing a prank?

'We should ask him,' said Jin.

I took out the letters. I gave Jin back his.

'You ask him,' I said.

Jin took his letter and wrote down at the bottom:

Is the medal a forgery? Did you make it look old on purpose to trick us?

Jin gave me a T-shirt to wear because I didn't have my sleepover changing-over clothes. It was SO tight I could hardly breathe. I took it off. I put on my old T-shirt. It didn't smell *too* bad.

When I woke up, it was still raining. It hadn't stopped all night. This wasn't good. This wasn't good at all.

Jin's dad was driving us to school.

'Mr Park, can we listen to the news?'

'Sure, Robert.'

He turned the dials on the radio but he didn't know

where the English channel was. Their radio was set on a Korean one.

'I'm sorry,' he said.

'That's okay.'

It was raining so hard, Jin's dad had to put his windscreen wipers on *fast* mode and they were swooshing as fast as they could but the rain kept on flooding the windscreen. I wanted to go home to see Aunty Delphia. But we were already at school. We buttoned up our coats and dashed into the school and we both still got wet. I watched the rain falling. Would it ever stop?

Dad came to pick me up. The rain had stopped but the road was like a river. Our car was swaying in it.

'Is Aunty Delphia home?' I asked.

He didn't answer for a while. He was concentrating hard to keep the car from swaying off the road.

'No,' he said, when we were waiting up on the ramp for the garage doors to open.

'She's still at the airport?'

'No,' he said.

'Is Cynthia still with Grandma and Grandpa? Is she safe? Will they come and take—'

'Robert, I don't kno— Yes, she's still with Grandma and Grandpa. She's safe.'

He drove the car down the ramp. The garage was flooded. He drove out again, the water splashing like mad.

'Dad, do you think the tsuna—'

'Robert . . .'

Dad drove to the parking spaces in front of the building.

There was one umbrella in the car. Dad gave it to me.

'Don't run,' he said, 'especially on the marble.'

The marble floor in front of the building got really slippery when wet; Madame Badon fell and broke her shoulder once.

Even with the umbrella I still got wet; not as much as Dad, though; he was drenched.

'Where is she, Dad?' I asked him while we were waiting for the lift.

Dad sighed. Water was dripping from his nose.

'They're keeping her in a refugee centre until all the paperwork's done. It won't be long.'

'Is it the one near Balexert?'

'Yes,' said Dad.

'It's dirty, Dad.'

Dad said that was the thing with Geneva. It was so small that rich and poor lived virtually together. And then I heard him tell Mum that the Swiss didn't want refugees to think Switzerland was a soft touch. The Red Cross was fighting to keep Switzerland's doors open. I was sure that's what Henry Dunant would have wanted. I would ask him next time.

We got in the lift.

'Why is she there, Dad?'

'Because under Swiss law she is a refugee and she has to be process—'

The lift door opened and Dad didn't say any more.

I couldn't put the letters under Monsieur Renoir's door because Dad was with me.

Football practice was cancelled so George stayed at home 'multitasking': checking Facebook and YouTube and studying for his Chinese exam, which was going to be marked in China. Next year he was going to China with his class. The good thing about the internet, Dad said, was how easy it was to connect with different people; for instance, George was already chatting with some Chinese high school 'friends' who played football, and they swapped videos of their awesomeness. George said these guys were swag because they were Asian. I was starting to think he was racist. The only people he never said were swag were white (unless they called a country after themselves, like that Rhodes guy, or maybe if they were M and M, a rapper guy).

The magic carpet was still laid out in the playroom but George was so busy that even his sense of smell was clogged up.

I took the carpet to the lounge. Dad was on the phone. He was speaking to Mum. I went past him into Mum's study. We were not allowed to touch anything in there. Mum's computer was still open but the screen was shut down. There were papers on her desk. I leaned over. I didn't touch anything.

Blood, I read.

I pushed Mum's chair against the wall. I put the carpet on the floor. I sat on it. I closed my eyes. I was sailing up, up, and then a gust of wind blew me so hard

I almost fell from the carpet. I had to hold on to the edges so tightly. The wind kept blowing and I looked down and the water in the lake was rocking back and forth, pushing and heaving against the lake walls, and the ropes holding the boats to their anchors snapped off and the boats were free and capsizing in the waves that were growing and growing and water was crashing over the walls on to the promenade, over the streets, the cars, and more of it was coming, the waves higher and higher, and the carpet swung over it all and then there was a plane and Monsieur Renoir was in it and he said, follow me, and the carpet sailed away from Geneva and followed Monsieur Renoir in his plane. We sailed away over the snow-capped mountains and the wind stopped and it was calm and then I heard Monsieur Renoir's voice, we've arrived, and the carpet landed on something soft. It was sand! We were on the beach! Welcome to Jamaica, Monsieur Renoir said. Look at all this sand, look at all these palm trees. I looked at the sand, at the palm trees. And look at this water, Monsieur Renoir said. Isn't it just lovely? It was. Then Monsieur Renoir said, I fancy a swim, don't you? I did. I leaped off the carpet and I ran into the water and Monsieur Renoir was shouting behind me, 'Oh no, stay on the carpet, there are landmines, and sharks, but it was too late, I—'

'Robert!'

'Landmines, sharks . . .'

'Robert, what are you talking about . . . what the heck, you're crying.'

'I . . . I . . .'

George swept the carpet from under me and my butt hit the ground. He waved his arm at me.

'Robert, calling Robert.'

I was back but my body was shaking, my teeth chattering.

'What the heck? Are you cold?'

'Monsieur Renoir told me to follow him and I did and he took me to Jamaica and there were landmines and sharks and he told me too late and I got off the carpet and—'

'Okay, okay, chillax, it was a daydream . . . no, daymare, as in nightmare but during daytime. Bro, we have to take this carpet out. It stinks.'

'I think he did something bad, George.'

'Who?'

'Monsieur Renoir.'

'Yeah, he called us *mer*—'

'No, something really bad, and now he feels guilty, and the medal—'

'Medal, what medal?'

I told George about it, and then I showed it to him. I even told him I'd lied about it to Mum. Then I showed him the letters.

'Seriously, bro, this is so screwed,' he said.

'You swore.'

'*And?* Mum and Dad aren't here.'

'Where's Dad?'

'Gone to the office, so I'm in charge.'

This was the first time ever I'd been left alone in the house with George.

'What are we going to do?'

'Kick ass.'

Kick ass? Were his new Chinese friends adding to his vocabulary?

'How?' I asked, even though I didn't understand what 'kick ass' meant.

'We're going to shake him down.'

'Huh?'

'We're going to go down there and ask him what's up. We are going to have a talk, like he asked for.'

'I don't think—'

'We are. And bring that medal.'

Yes, sir! Who *was* this guy?

We took the lift down to *entresol* (George never used the stairs). I stepped out of the lift and George followed.

Now what?

George put his finger on the buzzer and rang the bell. It was loud. I waited. George waited. I was ready to run. I didn't feel too good. George rang the bell again. It was louder.

There was a crocodile in there!

'Let's go,' I said.

George rang the bell again.

I had a bad feeling.

The crocodile was moving towards the door and he was going to put his mouth on the door handle and—

'George!'

'Okay, okay, put your letters under the door.'

I didn't want to.

'I think I'll give him his medal back.'

'It's not his,' said George.

I didn't have the medal any more. George had it in his hand. I remembered Dad's dog tag and George putting it around his neck, doing his swag poses, taking pictures. I had a really bad feeling.

'Just give it back to him, George.'

'No.'

'It's not yours.'

'It's not his.'

'Give it back.'

'No.'

'You can't wear it. It belongs to a hero.'

'So?'

'You can't put it on Facebook. You can't show it to your friends.'

George looked at the medal in his hand. He was rubbing it with his thumb.

'You're damaging it,' I said. 'It should be in the box.'

George stepped back in the lift and went up without me.

'Clueless Nimrod,' I shouted. (Thanks, Dilbert.)

I stood looking at Monsieur Renoir's door. Where was he? What if he was inside and he had heard everything? EVERY SINGLE WORD. What if he was looking through his peephole right at this very minute? What if he was looking at me standing there in front of his door? What if— I dropped the letters on his doormat and ran upstairs.

*

Mum and Dad came home together. Mum was very tired. She went in the bathroom and stayed there for even longer than usual. Mum said the bath was her de-stressing time; it was also the place where she got ideas. Sometimes she had a bath in the dark with just a candle that smelled of flowers.

Dad made us an omelette. He was great at making omelettes and I liked helping him by breaking the eggs into the bowl. I put on my Garfield apron. Dad took the eggs from the fridge.

'We'll keep it simple today,' he said. 'A plain omelette with fish fingers.'

'Yes, CHEF!'

Dad smiled. I loved *MasterChef*. Dad did too. We were a great team. George couldn't cook anything. He didn't even know how to boil pasta. The only thing he could make was *pane, olio e sale* – bread, oil and salt – which was a snack Dad used to have when he was a boy in Rome; his grandmother used to give it to him after school for *merenda*. Mum said it was unhealthy; bread already had way too much salt and then to add even more salt was just madness. Mum had read studies that said children should only have a pinch of salt a day. George *poured* salt over his food; he didn't even taste it first.

I cracked the eggs, one by one. *Success*, not a single eggshell in there.

'Dad,' I said, while I was beating them up with a fork.

'*Si?*'

'Is it okay to lie sometimes?'

'Hmmm,' he said. 'Give me a hypothetical.'

'A *what*?'

'What do they teach you in that school of yours? Give me an example where you might lie and you might think it would be okay.'

I beat the eggs a bit more. I was thinking. I couldn't really say the word 'medal' or 'Mum' or 'Monsieur Renoir'.

'Well?'

I gave him the bowl of eggs.

'Good job, sous-chef.'

'Say if you told someone that you didn't have something but you had it and they thought you had given it back because that's what you told them but you still had it.'

'That's pretty confusing, Robert. Basically someone has something and they told someone they didn't have it. They lied.'

'Yeeees?'

'I guess the question is, *why* did they lie?'

I thought about that.

'There was this other person who would have started touching it if they knew about it but then that person went away . . .'

'So why did they *continue* to lie?'

'Maybe they were scared. Maybe they wanted to keep the thing for a bit longer and then maybe they would give it back.'

'Why?'

'Because . . . because they were in a mystery and they wanted to solve the mystery, and the medal, the thing . . .'

I don't think Dad heard the medal bit; he was busy flipping the omelette.

'Maybe they wanted to protect the thing, Dad.'

'Because?'

'Because it was precious and the person felt that they were given it to look after.'

'Hmmm,' said Dad. 'I guess lying in that instance might be forgivable, but at some point he'll have to come clean to someone; it's a burden to carry around a lie.'

I took *The Complete Worst-Case Scenario Survival Handbook* from my shelf. I read 'How to Fend Off a Shark' again. Next time I was at the beach I'd make sure to have a sharp object with me at all times so I could poke it in the eyes, over and over. 'How to Escape From a Giant Octopus' I couldn't take seriously. It sounded like something in a cartoon. The other one that made me laugh was 'How to Detangle a Bird Caught in Your Hair'. Close your eyes and wave madly? 'How to Control a Runaway Camel'. 'How to Foil a UFO Abduction'. 'How to Treat a Tongue Stuck on a Pole'. 'How to Survive Awkward Elevator Silence'. 'How to Track Your Teenager's Movements'. I was looking for 'How to Get a Medal Back and What to Do Afterwards'. I was stumped. And then I had it. BLACKMAIL. But with what? How about if I made public the video that Dad took when George was five years old and did 'dance' in Ferney; the one where he was on the stage wearing tights with a frill round his waist and he was dancing holding hands with a girl. I thought about that. I shook my head. Nah. He was only five. Mum *made* him do it. Everyone has embarrassing videos when they're that age.

And then I *definitely* had it!

I waited till we were both in our beds.

'George,' I said.

'What?'

'If you don't give me back the medal, I'm going to tell Mum and Dad that you're married.'

'What?'

'On Facebook.'

'You snitch.'

'*And* that she's sixteen. *And* that she's French. *And* that she doesn't go to the international school. *And* that she goes to Ecole de Budé.' Some of the girls in that school smoked. Marijuana.

No more Mr Nice Guy from me. He was going to pay.

'Okay, okay, you can have it.'

'Hand it over. Now.'

'It's in my underwear drawer.'

'Gross.'

I got out of bed and opened his drawer. I dug around there for ages until I finally found it right at the back. I took it out and switched on the light.

'Turn it off, I'm trying to sleep.'

'I have to see it.'

'It's already on Facebook. Twenty likes. Pathetic.'

He was such a loser. I put the medal back in its box. My backpack was in the hallway, so I just put the box under my bed.

'You shouldn't have—' I said, but he was already asleep.

I took my reporter's notebook. I strapped my Lego band with its figurine torch around my head. I pressed down the figurine's body. I switched off the bedroom light. I bent over the notebook. I looked down at the survival book on the floor full of all the ways to survive all kinds of danger, all the ways people had to keep themselves safe from things, animals and other people. I loved Geneva because there were NO murderers like in New York. I looked down at my notebook and I remembered the Venn diagrams I was learning on the Mathletics website. I drew two ovals crossing over. In one of them I wrote down *Monsieur Renoir*. Underneath that I wrote down *Mau Mau*. And underneath that, *1950 something*. Then I went to the free space in the other oval and I wrote down *Soldier, infantry, private*. And below that I wrote *World War I*. Below that, *1916*. I looked at my Venn diagram. I chewed the end of my pencil. And then I wrote in the crossing-over space the thing they had in common: *The Medal, Victoria Cross*.

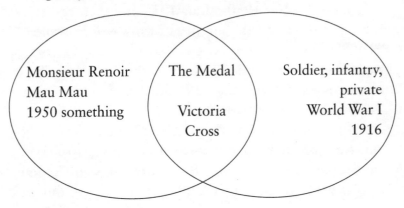

The story was there. The drawing was telling me something.

Monsieur Renoir met the private somewhere and took the private's medal.

I thought and I thought.

Where did Monsieur Renoir and the private meet?

Did they meet in Kenya?

Did the private fight in World War I and then go to Kenya with his medal and fight the Mau Mau? Was that even possible?

I needed to do some maths. How old did you need to be to be a soldier anyway? I thought and thought. In Switzerland you had to finish school. Most people finished school when they were eighteen. So, say the private was twenty, because he was already a soldier when he fought in World War I, how old would he be in 1950 something when he met Monsieur Renoir? I scratched my head. We had only just started doing word problems in class. I wrote down the sentence: *If the private is twenty in 1916, how old is he in 1950?* That was kind of easy: 1950 minus 1916 and then add it to 20. I put down all the numbers of my word problem. HELP! I needed Mum! I needed Dad! I needed George, no, not George, I needed a calculator! I tried three times and crossed out the answers and then I got my final answer. The private would be fifty-four. And Monsieur Renoir? How old was he in 1950? I didn't know; he must be just starting out to fight in Kenya, so maybe he was eighteen or twenty. But wait, Monsieur Renoir was in his eighties, so in 1950 he would be . . . I did the word problem again. He'd be about thirty! That was old to be starting out in a war, wasn't it?

I closed my eyes and tried to imagine thirty-year-old Monsieur Renoir and a fifty-four-year-old private (were you always a private if you left the army?).

Did the private die fighting the Mau Mau? I didn't think so. Fifty-four was too old to be a soldier, wasn't it?

Did Monsieur Renoir take the private's medal?

Did the private give the medal to Monsieur Renoir? Maybe they were friends?

And then I thought of something else.

Did the medal even belong to the private?

Then I remembered that Monsieur Renoir was actually British.

Did Monsieur Renoir and the private meet in England?

I went back over the pages of the notebook. I read my notes and the printouts I had stuck in.

There were medals that had been stolen in England, medals that had mysteriously disappeared.

Was this one of them?

But none of them were for actions in 1916.

Did Monsieur Renoir leave England to go to Kenya with the medal already in his pocket?

Was the . . . was the medal a good-luck charm, like . . . like footballers with their crucifixes around their necks (which Mum said was disrespectful if you weren't a practising Christian)?

The Venn diagram was sprouting questions and

questions in my head. My head was full of so much thinking. I rubbed my forehead. I took off my torch. I put the notebook on the floor. I put my head on the pillow and thought that there were millions and millions of people in the world and millions and millions and millions of people never met each other and only a few of them did, like me and Monsieur Renoir and Monsieur Renoir and the private, and that when that happened your world changed and you became someone else's story. I was in Monsieur Renoir's story now. I was in the private's story. I was in the medal's story.

Chapter Seventeen

Girls

I was going to a birthday bowling party with Jin. I didn't really like birthday parties. I liked bowling. It was Wendy's party. Wendy was great. We were on the same table in class and she didn't read pink books. She read Percy Jackson. She knew about the Greek gods and the Norse ones. Sometimes, at break, when Jin was on the football pitch, we would sit together and talk. The only annoying thing was that when we did this everyone, even Jin, said I was her boyfriend, and she was my girlfriend. Mum said that she found it very difficult to accept how the school allowed so much kissing in the hallways. She had seen it herself. Teenagers stuck to each other in every possible way. Disturbing.

Once, in Payot, Mum showed me a book called *How to Talk to Girls*. It was written by a nine-year-old. There was a *heart* on the cover. A nine-year-old! Didn't the kid have anything better to do? Couldn't he write a book about how to tame a dragon or something? Sad.

I looked out of the car window. Phew. The lake was calm. The water was blue and not grey, like when it rained too much. The boats were still on the water. The swans were there. Everything was in the right place. I tried to imagine the mini earthquakes. Were they happening right at this very second? Could the fish feel them? Could the swans?

We drove across the Mont-Blanc Bridge. The flags along the bridge were fluttering about but not so much as when it was really windy and it looked like they would snap off their poles. I looked over at Monsieur Rousseau sitting high on his chair with a book on his knee and a pen in his hand. There he was on his island, looking over Lake Geneva, which he loved so much, but *no*, they had turned him round again so now he had his back to the lake just like when they first put him there; some Genevois in the olden days didn't want him to be there at all because they didn't like what he had to say about how rich people should help poor people, so they made a compromise: he could be there but he couldn't look at the lake, and then they turned him round, and now they had turned him back again. I didn't think it was fair to do that on his three hundredth birthday. I liked Monsieur Rousseau. I had asked him many questions. He was a philosopher.

'What did you get Wendy?' Jin asked.

'A book.'

'Boring.'

I shrugged. It wasn't. I had the same book. It was the book of *How to Do Everything*. There were lots of cool things to make, do and explore. It showed you how to do stuff like sawing somebody in half, walking

222

on a tightrope, using chopsticks, making and flipping a pancake. Dad and I made the best pancakes ever from it.

'What did *you* get her?'

'A Barbie.'

In my head, I slapped my forehead. I *knew* Wendy was going to hate that. She'd told me that Barbies were stupid. But I didn't say anything to Jin.

There were twelve of us. Wendy chose me for her team. We won. I got three strikes. Wendy said I was the best. She opened her presents. She got lots of pink and purple stuff. She opened my present. The cover was a shiny, silvery blue, the letters in bright red.

'Perfect!' she said. 'It's so perfect. Thanks, Robert.'

I was embarrassed but also very happy.

'That's okay,' I said. And then she started reading it right there. I wanted to tell her to try out the pancakes but I could already hear someone whispering *boyfriend*. It was Jin. Sometimes even your best friend betrayed you.

Dad picked us up and I was mad with Jin. We sat in the back, not talking.

'Did you guys have fun?' asked Dad.

We didn't answer.

'Hmmm,' said Dad. 'Did the girls give you a hard time?'

'Wendy LOVES Robert,' Jin said.

'She does not.'

'Yes she does.'

'Tanya LUUUURVES you.'

'Gross.'

'Kiss kiss kiss, oh Jin, oh Jin . . .'

'Guys, calm down.'

Jin punched me on the shoulder. I punched him back.

'Guys!'

We dropped Jin off. I didn't say goodbye.

'The more you react, the more they tease,' Dad said when we were on the road again.

'It sucks. He's my best friend.'

'Even best friends have fights.'

I knew that, but DID IT HAVE TO BE ABOUT A GIRL?

'Wendy liked the book. She said it was perfect.'

'Good.'

'She didn't say anything about Jin's Barbie.'

'Maybe that hurt Jin's feelings.'

I thought about that. Dad *could* be right. Maybe Jin *was* hurt. Maybe he was upset with Wendy. We couldn't let a girl come between us, even if that girl was Wendy.

I phoned Jin when I got home. We were best friends again; I don't think we had stopped being best friends even when we were fighting.

'Did you check if he left something?'

'No.'

'Go and check, and phone me back.'

'Okay.'

Everyone was busy. Mum had gone out to see Aunty Delphia. Dad was on the phone with his boss, who didn't believe in weekends and family time. George was busy with his usual stuff. I could sneak out.

I sneaked out. Slowly, gently, I opened and closed the door.

I crept down the stairs.

I stopped.

Monsieur Renoir's door was wide open.

I stood on the stairs. I clung to the railing. I peered over. There were voices. Men. I leaned right over. Boxes on the landing. One. Two. Three. A voice was growing louder, nearer . . . *Oui, oui, toutes, toutes* . . . I scrambled back up again. Could they hear me breathing? I heard *thud, thud, thud*, and something being dragged. The boxes. Footsteps. I rushed up to our apartment. I heard the lift opening, the boxes being pushed into the lift, and then I looked at the lift. I heard it opening on the ground floor. What was going on? I crept back into the apartment. Dad and George were still occupied. I phoned Jin.

'Something very strange is going on,' I said.

'What, *what?*'

I told him all about it.

'Wow. Did you see him?'

'No. But I think I heard him. He said, "*Oui, oui, toutes, toutes.*"'

'What did he put in the boxes?'

'I don't know.'

'Go and see.'

'I can't.'

'Why not?'

I didn't want to tell Jin that I was scared.

'You're not scared, are you?'

'No.'

'So go.'

'Okay, I'll—' But I was saved by Mum, who came bursting into the room, and Aunty Delphia was with her!

But she wasn't the same Aunty Delphia as the one in Zimbabwe.

She was smaller.

She was thinner.

She was sadder.

She was old.

She didn't have beads in her hair. She didn't have any hair. It was all shaved off.

'Hello, Aunty Delphia.'

She was standing in the hallway. She was holding a plastic bag in both hands; she was holding it really tightly like she was afraid if she didn't someone would come up and snatch it and run away.

'Delphi, it's Robert. He said hello.'

Aunty's eyes moved around and then she found me but she didn't smile or say 'Robert! It's you!'

She looked at me and tears started falling down her cheeks. I was making Aunty Delphia sad.

'She's tired,' said Mum. 'Come, Delphi, relax in the lounge while we get your room ready.'

Mum tried to take Aunty Delphia's hand but Aunty Delphia wouldn't let go of the bag, so Mum put her hand under Aunty Delphia's elbow and moved her through the hallway into the lounge.

'George,' Mum called out as they were passing the playroom, 'come and say hello to your aunt.'

George didn't hear her. His headphones were on.

'George!' Mum shouted. Aunty Delphia made a funny scream. It wasn't a scream exactly but a sound as if she was in pain.

'I'm sorry, Delphi.'

George was standing in the doorway.

'Hello, Aunty D,' he said and raised his hand to give her a high five, which was what he always did to her in Zimbabwe. But Aunty Delphia didn't look at him. She didn't raise her hand. She was mumbling something and banging the plastic bag against her chest.

Dad was standing in the lounge and he made room for Mum and Aunty Delphia to get in.

He went to George and put his hand on his shoulder. George was almost as tall as he was.

'Your aunt is very traumatized. We have to look after her. It will take time but she will come back to herself.'

George didn't say anything. He looked very grown up and serious.

We had to move everything out of the playroom because Aunty Delphia was going to stay for a while. George didn't complain that we had to move the computer to our bedroom and that he would have to hang out with his friends in the lounge or in our room.

By the time it was bedtime, I felt very tired.

I said good night to Aunty Delphia. She was sitting in the lounge, the plastic bag still in her hands, looking straight ahead. I don't think she heard me.

*

On Mondays and Thursdays, the football pitch was reserved for Year Fives and Sixes during lunchtime.

Jin scooted off to the football pitch. Wendy was sitting on the bit of grass behind the basketball court. She had *How to Do Everything* on her lap and she was concentrating on a page. I looked around the playground. The triplets and Tanya and Tom were fighting it out with the Beyblades. Everyone else was by the football pitch. I went over to Wendy.

'Hi,' I said.

She looked up.

'Hi, Robert. This is such a great book. Thanks.'

I looked around the playground again – *all clear* – and then I sat down next to her. That book was pretty heavy to carry in a backpack. She must really like it.

'I can tightrope-walk,' she said. 'It works. I've been practising.'

We looked through the pages together until we got to the very end. Then we just sat there and I was getting cold; I was getting up when she said, 'Do you believe in the gods?'

'You mean the Greek gods?'

'All of them,' she said. 'The Norse ones too.'

'I don't know,' I said.

'I do.'

'I think they're just stories.'

'But they're so real.'

'They're cruel.'

'And just.'

I guess she was right. The gods always had a good reason for cutting someone's head off, or plucking out their heart, or killing their children.

'Who's your favourite?'

'Hmmm,' I said. 'I guess Hades. He has a tough jo—'

But I didn't get to finish because all of a sudden there were kissing sounds everywhere. We were surrounded. The triplets, Tanya, Tom, and the rest of the Beyblade gang.

'Robert's got a girlfriend.'

'Wendy's got a boyfriend.'

They were singing it, in our faces.

'Stop it,' Wendy shouted. 'Just stop.'

But they sang even louder.

'Stop,' shouted Wendy.

But they were having way too much fun. They were going to go on for ever.

I'd had enough. I stood up. Wendy stood up too.

Manuel took a step. He was right in front of me.

'Ooooooo, Robert's going to kiss Wendy. Smoooch. Smoooch.'

'Stop it,' I said.

Manuel's mouth opened, and then he closed it, and then he opened it again. He looked like a fish. He couldn't believe what he was hearing.

'You asked for it,' he said. 'You're going to get a knuckle sandwich.'

He struck his fist against his hand. And then he ground it. His lips were clenched together. What was his problem?

I don't know why, but I didn't move. I didn't duck. I didn't run away. I stood there and I looked him straight in the eye.

'You better run,' he said. 'Or you're going to get it.'

I was waiting for it. I didn't know what I was going to do when he knuckle-sandwiched me.

He raised his fist; here it came. I didn't flinch – well, maybe just a little – and just when I was expecting it to make contact I heard:

'Yo, what's going on? Are you dissing my bro?'

It was George. With his crew.

I loved my brother SO MUCH!

The sixth-graders beat it.

George and his crew were looking at Wendy and me. George shook his head.

'Kids,' he said, and walked off.

And suddenly, I was popular.

I was the brother of *that* guy.

Everywhere I walked I heard '". . . dissing my bro?" Did you hear him? He's so cool.' And they were trying to *sound* like George. Sixth-graders wanted to *be* George. They thought I was the luckiest guy alive because George was my brother. The triplets were on Facebook even though it was illegal and they were begging George to be their 'friend'. I was surrounded by George wannabes. Everyone wanted a piece of me, everyone wanted a play date so that they could be in the same house as George, be *near* him. It was exhausting. I just wanted things back the way they were. Jin said I was crazy. We were set for life!

*

When I got home, I went down the stairs again to check the mailbox. There was no mail. I was locking up the mailbox when the buzzer of the foyer door went off and the door slid open. I looked. It was him. He couldn't see me because of the mailboxes. He was standing in the doorway holding a handkerchief to his eyes. He walked into the foyer and that's when I should have scrammed, but I didn't. He put the handkerchief in his pocket. He shook his head. His shoulders were all hunched. He looked up again. And that's when I ran.

I stopped by our front door, breathing really hard. There was something about how he'd looked standing in the foyer that made me feel kinda sad. That wasn't right. He was Monsieur Renoir.

Chapter Eighteen

The Play Date

Wendy invited me for a play date. Even though she was a girl, I said yes, and no one made any comments when I got in her car on Wednesday. I was Mr POPULAR. Wendy lived in France. In France there were murderers, not as many as in New York, though. She lived in a house not an apartment. We went downstairs to the basement, which was where people who lived in houses put their children's playrooms. Sometimes they were dark and pretty cold but Wendy's was cool. There wasn't a single pink anything. The walls were a bright blue. There were bookshelves from floor to ceiling against two of them. Mum would love it. There were two couches and a TV and a computer. There was another desk with a microscope on it. A telescope was looking out of a window. It felt more like a hangout room than a playroom but Wendy didn't have any older brothers or sisters. I suddenly felt very strange; I guess I was feeling shy. It was just the two of us with no one around. She wasn't Jin so I couldn't do something random like shout MERRY CHRISTMAS or something. I just wanted to go home.

'I found this,' she said.

I looked down at her hand. She was holding a tooth.

'Gross,' I said. And then I had one of my random thoughts: *It's Gregory's tooth! Found!*

'It's not human,' she said. 'It's a cat's.'

It was still gross.

'Come and look at it under the microscope. I found it in the park.'

Mum never let us pick up anything off the ground. She would freak out if I picked up an actual tooth, a cat's tooth. I'd have to wash for fifteen minutes with soap *and* antibacterial wash.

'Look.'

I looked, and it looked even more gross.

'Do you see the cavity? Poor cat, it must have really hurt. I'm going to be a veterinarian when I grow up.'

'My aunt's a veterinarian.'

'Really?'

'Yes.'

And then I started telling her all about the animals I'd seen in Zimbabwe, and how my aunt knew everything about them, and I didn't feel so strange any more.

'I don't know if she's still a veterinarian. She had to leave Zimbabwe. She's here now.'

'Why?'

'Bob the Butternut's men hurt her.'

'Who's Bob the Butternut?'

I told her who he was.

'She has to take *antiretro*something. I have to google it.'

'We can do it now.'

We went to the computer and I typed in *antiretro*.

The management of HIV/AIDS, I read, the first result from Google. It was from Wikipedia.

I didn't want to read more. I knew that something was wrong with Aunty Delphia. Wendy leaned over me and read the next bit out.

'The management of HIV/AIDS typically includes the use of antiretroviral drugs, which are medications for the treatment of infection by retroviruses, primarily HIV. Different antiretroviral drugs restrain the growth and reproduction of HIV.'

Wendy stopped. She put her hand on the mouse. I knew she wanted to click on HIV but I snatched the mouse away.

'She's sick,' I said. 'She's taking medicine. She's going to be well.'

I was being rude. I waited for Wendy to go running up the stairs to tell the babysitter (we *aren't* babies!) that our play date was over and she should phone my dad to pick me up.

'Okay,' she said.

Okay what?

She looked around the room.

'Do you like chess?'

'Yes!'

She took down the chess set from one of the shelves and that's how we spent the rest of the play date. She won and that was okay.

*

When we were waiting at the lift, I told Dad I wanted to do some exercise; I'd been cooped up all day so it wasn't a lie. I *did* need some exercise. I went slowly up the stairs. I stopped. There was an envelope on the doormat and I knew straight away what was written on it.

THE BOY.

The door was closed and there wasn't a single sound coming from the room. Was Monsieur Renoir in there? Was he watching me? I bent down and picked up the envelope. It was heavier than before. Maybe he had written a real letter. I didn't run up the stairs this time. I walked slowly. And I kept looking back at Monsieur Renoir's door in case he . . . in case he opened it, I guess.

I just *had* to open the envelope. I couldn't wait for school. Jin would understand. This was an emergency. What if there was something DEATHLY important in there, something I needed to know RIGHT now?

I went to go and say hello to Aunty Delphia, but the door to the playroom was closed.

'She's sleeping,' said Mum.

George was away on a school camp. He wouldn't be back until next week. I went to my room. I sat down on the bed. I closed the door. I waited to see if Mum was going to call me, but she was already in her study. I opened the envelope.

BOY, I read.
Youth is nothing but a mirage, a trick. You experience it barely and then it disappears. You make your mistakes, those, those last for ever,

a lifetime. And so it is. I am here, an old man, dying, perhaps already dead. Who knows. Do you believe in ghosts, Boy? Of course not. But I am a ghost. You have seen me. What a horrid creature that thing is, you have thought. It is true. In youth, I would have thought the same thing. Horrible, horrible creature, yelling at a boy for what, for what? A bit of noise, noise. I held the medal, that damned thing, in my hand and I said, I will be true to this, to this moment, I will live my life forever true to this, but how could I, one who had taken what was not his because of, because of fear, fear, and now here it is, here I am, lost, dying, dead. So Boy, the child comes to me now singing, dancing, whispering in my ear and I know that death is close, if I am not dead already. Did you see the men with the boxes the other day? Did you see me? They cart away my life, my life, piece by piece, and I tell the child, go off now, go off, go with them, leave me alone, leave me in peace, but he stays, he stays, and I hear the thing whistling, whistling down and I say, child, run, run, but he laughs, shouts, refuses to listen, and he stands still, holds out his hand to catch the mighty thing falling from the sky. How do you know what it is that you hit? How? And so it is.

His writing was large and it was in cursive.

There were two other papers. Our letters. Monsieur Renoir had written his answers on top of our questions.

Dear Monsieur Renoir,

I think you stole the medal from the hero because you were jealous (NO, PERHAPS) *and wanted one for yourself* (YES). *Maybe you think you were braver than the hero fighting the Moo Moo* (NO). *Am I right?* (IN A WAY)

Jin

Is the medal a forgery? (AS FAR AS I KNOW, NO) *Did you make it look old on purpose to trick us?* (REALLY, HOW ODD)

I picked up mine.

Dear Monsieur Renoir,

Mum says that you fought against the Mau Mau (THAT IS TRUE). *I've read about them in Wikipedia* (WHAT IS THIS?). *I know the Royal Air Force bombed the Mau Mau in the forest* (TRUE). *Do you feel bad about it?* (NO) *Is that why you gave me the medal?* (NO) *I found a piece of paper in the box with the medal. I could only read some words: PRIVATE, INFANTRY, FRANCE, 1916, REWARD (I think)* (OH YES, THAT). *My mum's a writer and she puts words together to make a story. So this is the story I think these words make. There was a private, an ordinary soldier, in the infantry, who was fighting in France in World War I, 1916. He did an ACT OF VALOUR and he was awarded the Victoria Cross. His medal was lost or someone stole it.*

237

There is a reward for whoever returns it. Am I
right? (YOU ARE CLEVER, BOY)
  And Aunty Delphia is in Geneva. Thank-you.
  Sincerely,
  Robert Sartori
DO THE RIGHT THING, BOY.

There were chills creeping all over my body. I took the papers and ran into the hallway. The door to the playroom was a bit open. I pushed it. Aunty Delphia was sitting on the bed, her feet on the carpet, her hands on her knees.

'Aunty Delphia,' I said. 'Can I come in?'

She looked up.

'Robert,' she said. Her voice was soft like a whisper.

I stepped into the room.

I was standing there with the papers in my hand.

'Aunty Delphia,' I said, 'I think Monsieur Renoir did something really bad. Look.'

I put the papers on her lap. Her hands didn't move.

'Read them, Aunty. Read them.'

She looked down at the papers and then she looked at me. And then she picked up Monsieur Renoir's letter. She was reading it.

'It is a story,' she said when she was finished.

I nodded.

'It is not for a child, not for a young boy,' she said.

It *was* for a young boy. Monsieur Renoir wrote it for me.

'Monsieur Renoir—' I said, but Aunty Delphia

238

was looking through the plastic bag that was on her pillow. She was taking out clothes. Cynthia's clothes. I remembered them from our time in Bulawayo. There was Cynthia's pink jersey. There was Cynthia's yellow T-shirt with a shiny pink bunny on it. There was Cynthia's green skirt. Aunty Delphia was putting them against her face. She was rubbing her face in them. She was breathing the smell of the clothes. She was breathing in Cynthia. And then she took her face away.

'Robert,' Mum said. 'I hope you didn't wake up your aunt.' Mum was standing behind me. She had plastic bottles in her hand filled with pills.

'No,' I said.

'That's good. Why don't you go and watch some TV.'

Mum never let us watch TV during the week. What was going on?

She went to the kitchen. I heard the tap running.

I took the papers from the bed.

'Thank you, Aunty,' I said.

I waited a bit but she didn't say anything. She was lying on her side facing the window, her hands under her head.

I went into the lounge. I sat down on the couch. Dad had gone back to the office. It was so quiet.

I turned on the TV. I watched a bit of *Ben 10* but I just couldn't concentrate. Monsieur Renoir's letter kept butting in.

What did Monsieur Renoir mean that he was a ghost?

Who was the child whispering in Monsieur Renoir's ear?

Did Monsieur Renoir have a grandson?

Monsieur Renoir lived alone.

Was Monsieur Renoir keeping the child prisoner?

Why was the child standing waiting to catch the thing in the air?

Was the thing a bomb?

Didn't he know about bombs?

Did he think they were something to play with, like a ball?

Where was the child?

Was the child outside?

He was playing and shouting, and Monsieur Renoir could see him?

Was the child in the forest?

Was Monsieur Renoir waving to the child?

Was Monsieur Renoir shouting to the child, go, go away, a bomb is coming?

Did the child hear?

Was the child a ghost that came to Monsieur Renoir when he was sleeping?

Was the child alive?

Did Monsieur Renoir drop a bomb on the child's father in the forest and now the child was coming to haunt Monsieur Renoir?

Monsieur Renoir was full of guilt and fear.

He took someone's medal because he was afraid.

He took the medal.

Monsieur Renoir flew a plane in the forest.

He dropped bombs.

Lots and lots of bombs.

Monsieur Renoir killed the Mau Mau.

Was Monsieur Renoir a hero?

The little boy was coming to Monsieur Renoir.

He was a ghost.

Like Monsieur Renoir.

My head hurt.

I went and stood by the window. It was really dark outside. It was only four o'clock. I watched the bus draw up at the bus stop; it was all lit up inside. There was an old lady getting out with a little dog on a leash.

Mum said that when you became really old, you remembered things that had happened many, many years ago as if they had just happened.

Was that happening to Monsieur Renoir?

Mum read an article in the *Tribune de Genève* that said there were many more dogs in Geneva than children. Mum said that was because there were many old people in Geneva who were lonely. Dogs were like their children.

Was Monsieur Renoir lonely?

Was he so lonely he dreamed about a young boy who was laughing and shouting and whispering in his ear?

Aunty Delphia said that Monsieur Renoir's letter was not for a young boy.

Monsieur Renoir wrote the letter to me.

Maybe I wasn't a young boy any more. Maybe I had grown up.

*

I heard sirens. They were getting louder and louder and then I saw the ambulance turn in to our building. I watched it go down the ramp and park right in front. And then I saw them pull out the stretcher. The concierge was waiting for them. I watched them hurry into the building. I ran to the front door. I opened it. I didn't hear them clatter up the stairs. That was strange. I waited and waited. Not a single sound. And then I thought, the park! I ran down the stairs. I passed Monsieur Renoir's door. It was closed. I went all the way down. The door to the park was wide open. The wind was blowing in.

And then I saw them wheel the stretcher in.

It was Monsieur Renoir.

His eyes were closed.

Chapter Nineteen

The Fall

Monsieur Renoir was not dead. He was badly injured. He had broken his legs and his hip. Mum said that she didn't think he would be coming back to his apartment. She thought that he was probably going to go to an old people's home like the one just opposite our building.

The concierge said that Monsieur Renoir had fallen from his balcony.

How did Monsieur Renoir fall from his balcony?

I stood on our balcony. There was a frosted glass wall around it. All the apartments were built with them. It was fifty-five centimetres high. Mum measured it when we were small. She wanted to change it and put a proper wall but the building administrator said that was not possible. All the apartments had to look the same outside. She said that she was always afraid that a terrible accident would happen. There were also gaps between the bits of glass. They were fifteen centimetres wide. Mum said that she could imagine us somehow squeezing through them. When we were small, she had Dad tape bamboo mats all over the glass so that we wouldn't be tempted; we wouldn't see that there might be a way to go through.

Monsieur Renoir was old.

Did he climb over the glass and tip over? I'm one hundred and forty centimetres tall. I could climb over the glass and tip over.

Was it an accident?

Mum said it was an accident.

George: She's trying to protect you, bro. He was trying to kill himself. Suicide epic fail. Seriously, from entresol?!

Nonna said that if you killed yourself you went straight to hell. Suicide was a mortal sin. Only God decides when it's time for you to go.

Nonna's God sounded a bit like a Greek god.

Mum said that she thought God was more compassionate.

George: It's dumb to kill yourself. Seriously, what is the point? You don't even know you've succeeded.

We were in Marino's. Every Sunday when George didn't have a match we came here for pizzas. George didn't like it any more because on his birthday all the waiters came to the table and sang 'Happy Birthday' out loud. He covered his face with his hands through the whole song. He was very embarrassed and upset with Mum and Dad for telling everyone that it was his birthday.

Mum and Aunty Delphia weren't with us. They were at home.

It was Armistice Day. It wasn't a Swiss holiday because Switzerland didn't really fight in any war. It was a French holiday. It was also a holiday in England except they called it Remembrance Day. It was a holiday in America too. They called it Veterans Day. There were going to be parades in all the countries. Soldiers who fought in World War I (were there any still alive?) and World War II and in other wars would be there. In England the soldiers pinned poppies on their coats. The poppies are bright red and they remind people of all the soldiers who have died in wars. Mum read me a poem about the field full of poppies where thousands of soldiers died in World War I.

Monsieur Renoir was a veteran.

He fought in a war.

Was flying planes and dropping bombs fighting?

'Dad, you know in Kenya they had the Mau Mau?'

'Yes.'

'And the British pilots bombed the Mau Mau in the forest.'

'They did?'

'Yes. And Monsieur Renoir was a pilot and he bombed the Mau Mau.'

'He was, really?'

'Yes, so did he actually *fight* in the war?'

'In the war against the Mau Mau? How do you know all this, Robert?'

'Mum told me, Monsieur Badon told her.'

'Uh huh. What do you mean?'

'He was dropping bombs. Is that fighting?'

Dad thought. He tore off a piece of bread.

'*Dad?*'

'I'm thinking, Robert. It's a hard question. It's an ethical question. Did the Mau Mau fight back? Did they have rockets that could bring down the planes? Did they have guns that could shoot at the planes?'

'I don't know.'

'If one person who is so much stronger is beating up someone much weaker, can you call that a fight?'

Dad was talking to himself.

'Fascinating, Robert. Fascinating.'

And if that person 'won' the fight, could you call them a hero?

Our pizzas arrived. Mine was a margherita. Dad was always trying to get me to be more adventurous, but Mum wouldn't let me have pizza with prosciutto crudo or cotto or salami; she had read studies about the high levels of carconi, the chemicals that give you cancer, in them. Dad said that he'd grown up on prosciutto, but Mum said that that was different because in the olden days they didn't put all those chemicals in the prosciutto but lots of salt. George had a *pizza Calabrese*, which had lots of salami in it. It wasn't fair. Mum gave up on George because of all the arguing (basically, he won), and so when he turned fourteen he was allowed to order whatever he wanted even if he was filling his body up with cancer. I mean, I wasn't even allowed salmon any more because Mum had just read a study saying it was full of mercury and that damaged people's brains. So I was stuck with plain tomatoes.

Dad made George take off his headphones and his cap before he could eat.

'Yo, Dad,' said George. 'Neymar's going to play for Manchester City. Seriously, Dad, *Manchester City*. Lame.'

'It could be worse,' said Dad. 'It could be Chelsea.'

George hated Chelsea.

'Racists,' he said.

We left Marino's and we ran to the car because it was so cold. There was already snow on the mountains around Geneva. Last year the mountains had so little snow in January that we had to go and ski on artificial snow during our ski week at school. But then the ice storm happened.

'Dad, can I visit Monsieur Renoir?'

The question just came out of me.

'I'm not sure if he's still in the hospital, Robert.'

'Monsieur Badon will know.'

Mum and Aunty Delphia had gone for a walk. That was what Dad said. Mum left a note on the kitchen counter. I saw the note first and I read the words *Centre médical d—*

Dad had to go out to a meeting with his boss. On a *Sunday*. He left me alone with George. My life was in his hands. Was this becoming a habit? Did Dad and Mum think I was mature enough to be left alone with my older bro? I *was* growing.

George closed the bedroom door, which meant that he was skyping his Facebook 'wife'. *Gross.*

I went into the lounge. I could play Skylanders but it wasn't that much fun when you played alone.

The phone rang. It was Jin.

'Is he dead?'

'No.'

I thought about that. I hadn't seen him, with my own eyes. What if the grown-ups were lying, to protect me?

'I don't think so. Mum says he's alive.'

'Did you see where he fell?'

I hadn't. I was avoiding the park ever since his accident. It gave me the heebie-jeebies just to think of him lying on the grass.

'Go and see.'

'No.'

'Are you scared?'

'No.'

'So go and see.'

I hated it when Jin was bossy.

'He might have dropped something.'

'What?'

'I don't know. Go and see.'

'I'm doing my homework.'

'We didn't get any homework. You're scared.'

'I'm not.'

'So—'

'Okay, I'm going.'

'Phone me back.'

The bedroom door was still closed, so I just left without telling George. It was his fault. He was supposed to be supervising me. I walked down the steps slowly. Ever since the accident I didn't like going up or down those steps, passing Monsieur Renoir's door. It was closed. And then, I don't know why, I flung out my hand and pushed down the door handle. The door was locked. I sprang down the rest of the stairs. Was I mad?

I took a huge breath and stepped outside. There was no one in the park. It was all drizzly and cold. Mum and Aunty Delphia must be frozen. I stepped close to the grass. I looked to where Monsieur Renoir had fallen. Was there blood on that patch of grass? I climbed up the ledge and I was on the edge of the grass. I looked up at the balconies.

I took another breath.

One, two, three big steps and I would be there.

One. Two. Three.

I was standing where Monsieur Renoir had fallen.

I jumped away.

Away from Monsieur Renoir's body.

I looked up to the balcony. The window was open and the curtain was blowing in it! Why was the window open? Had Monsieur Renoir forgotten to close it? I looked down at the grass again. There was some dog poo there. A dog had pooed where Monsieur Renoir had fallen. Had the dog smelt Monsieur Renoir there? I heard a sound coming from the balcony. I looked up. A woman was standing on Monsieur Renoir's balcony. She was smoking a cigarette and rubbing her shoulder with her hand. And then a boy joined her. She said something to him and he went back inside.

'Robert!'

For one moment I thought it was the woman calling me and so I looked at her.

'Robert!'

I looked further up. It was George.

'Robert, what the heck?'

I ran back inside.

Monsieur Renoir's door was open. I heard voices. And then, just as I was about to turn away, the boy stepped out from behind the door. He was very, very pale and thin. I could see the veins through the skin on his forehead. 'My name's Jack,' the boy said. He had a British accent.

Jack.

Monsieur Renoir had said 'Jack' at the post office.

Was this the boy?

And then the woman's voice shouted, 'Jack, damn it, close the bloody door!'

I watched the Armistice Day, Remembrance Day, Veterans Day parades on TV. Some of the soldiers were very, very old; they were in wheelchairs. They were sitting thinking of the wars they had fought, remembering everything. Some of them had fought the war on foot, some of them on horses, some of them in ships, some of them in planes. They had used their hands and guns and missiles and bombs. In our Peace and Conflict unit we talked about just wars. A just war was a war you fought to protect your country from invasion. You fought a just war for freedom. A just war was the right thing to do. Hitler had to be stopped; he was a very evil man; he would have kept killing more and more people. Terrorists hijacked planes, smashed them into buildings, bombed people. They turned people into bombs. They had to be stopped. The United Nations decided when a war was just. We went with the class to see the United Nations building in Geneva. There were the flags of all the countries in the world. We went into the big room where all the important people of countries talked about human rights. But the real United Nations is in New York. That's where they decide about the wars.

A fact: Switzerland only joined the United Nations in 2002. Dad says it took them that long to decide if they wanted to be part of the world community. Mum says what's even worse is that women only got the right to vote in the smallest canton in Switzerland in 1991. *Sexists*.

In August, when we were in Zimbabwe, I watched the Heroes' Day celebrations on TV. There were thousands of tanks rolling by and soldiers marching and then Bob the Butternut started talking. Grandpa came in the lounge and told me to change the channel; he already had a headache without having to endure *that man*.

Grandpa was a war veteran.

The camera zoomed in on a soldier in a wheelchair, all the way up close to his face. He had fought in World War II. There was something shiny on the man's cheeks. It was tears.

I thought about the Mau Mau. Were they evil too?

Did they kill and hurt other people? Did they have to be stopped? Was that a just war? Were the Mau Mau veterans?

'Robert,' said George when we were in bed.

'What?'

'Someone messaged me about the medal. Don't tell Mum or Dad, okay?'

I sat up in my bed. I couldn't believe what I was hearing.

'Robert! Don't tell Mum and Dad.'

'Okay.'

'They want to buy it.'

This wasn't good.

'Who?'

'I . . . I don't know. I just got this random notification from someone; they want to see the medal and buy it.'

'What do you mean random, you're not supposed to—'

'Shhhh,' said George. 'I can't keep track of all my friends on Facebook. They have friends who have friends. It gets all messed up.'

'You should tell Mum and Dad, not . . . not about the medal, but that some random person—'

'No ways! Are you crazy?! They'll ban me from Facebook for ever.'

'Did you write back?'

'Yes.'

'What did you say?'

'I said the medal wasn't mine.'

'And?'

'They wrote back. They don't care. They want it.'

'Tell Mum and Dad.'

'I deleted the messages and marked him as spam.'

'I told you not to put it on Facebook.'

George didn't say anything for a bit.

The piano prodigy started ramming his fingers on the keys. The Fifth Symphony. Again.

When he paused for his break, George said, 'We should put it on eBay.'

I had a bad, bad feeling.

I dived under the bed. I coughed. I sneezed. There was so much dust it was clogging up my nose, my throat. I felt around for the box. Nothing. Nothing. N— Yes, there it was. The box was still there! I opened it. I felt the medal.

It was a good thing that Mum wasn't keeping track of chores; George hadn't vacuumed under our bed for ages.

'George, you can't—' but he was already sleeping.

I slept with the medal tight in my hand, keeping it safe.

Chapter Twenty

The Boy, Jack

I had a cold and a cough so I stayed home from school. Mum had a meeting with a writer friend of hers who was in Geneva from London.

'Be good with your aunt,' she said. 'I won't be too long.'

'Could you ask her if she's going to write a children's book?'

'I will.'

I always asked Mum to ask her writer friends that. I was supposed to stay in bed the whole day, but it was boring just staying in bed, doing nothing. I couldn't read because my head hurt a bit. I got out of bed. I would have some cereal and then think of something to do. Aunty Delphia was in the kitchen.

'Good morning, Robert.'

She sounded almost like the old Aunty Delphia.

'Good morning, Aunty.'

'Should we have breakfast together? I was just about to make myself a cup of tea.'

'Yes, Aunty.'

I took out the cereal, the milk, my bowl and spoon. I sat down opposite her.

'Aunty Delphia, did Grandpa fight?'

She looked up from her tea.

'Fight?'

'In the war, for Zimbabwe?'

Aunty Delphia put her cup of tea down. She looked over my head and I turned round to see what she was looking at. But there was just the glass door and, out of that, there was the view of the park.

'Yes, he did,' she said.

'He fought for Bob the Butternut?'

Aunty Delphia's lips moved a little.

'I mean . . .'

'He fought for the people, for freedom.'

'It was a just war.'

'Robert, are you learning this at school, or is it all the books you read? Yes, it was a just war because it stopped racist policies.'

'Grandpa is a hero.'

'He doesn't have any medal, but yes, I think he is a hero. But don't say that to him. He will get very upset if you say that.'

'Why?'

'Because . . .' Aunty Delphia looked down at her tea again. 'Because he is very disappointed in how things have turned out.'

Aunty Delphia was sad again.

'Did he kill people?'

Aunty Delphia looked at me very hard.

'I don't know, Robert. He doesn't talk about those days.'

Everyone had been in a war. Monsieur Renoir. Nonno. Grandpa. Even Dad had been in the army. Even Dad knew how to hold a gun. Even Dad could go and fight. Even Dad could kill people. If Dad had gone and fought in a war and if he had killed people, would he be the same Dad? Would he still like to play basketball with me? Would he still watch *MasterChef* with me? Would he still let me break the eggs when we made omelettes? Would he still shout '*Sogni*—' before I went to sleep?

Aunty Delphia was writing some letters at the dining room table so I couldn't switch on the TV because that would disturb her. I went into Mum's study. She still had the same papers on her desk but she had put a red cross over *Blood* and some of the papers were crumpled up. Mum was having trouble with her vampires. My carpet was still on the floor but I didn't sit on it. I sat on Mum's armchair and I looked outside. You could see the primary school across the road. It was eleven o'clock and the kids were coming out for their lunch break. Swiss kids were so lucky. They had a two-hour lunch break; they left the school and went home. Some of them went to town or to Balexert and then to McDonald's or they played PlayStation in Fnac.

The lollipop lady was very busy. There was a boy with a woman crossing when the lollipop lady wasn't ready. The lollipop lady ran to the middle of the pedestrian crossing and said something to the woman. I leaned closer. The boy was already on the pavement.

It was *that boy.*

I sprang up from the chair. I knocked my knee against a table leg but I didn't think about it. I ran out of Mum's study. I tugged my coat from the coat stand and it almost fell on me like it always does when we overload it. It banged my head but I didn't think about that. I pushed my feet into my trainers. I didn't do the Velcro straps. I flung open the front door and dashed down the stairs. I ran across the foyer and out into the parking space. I jumped up the step, fell and banged my knee. I didn't think about that. I stood on the pavement. I looked left, I looked right. Drat, I couldn't see them. I looked left again, then right, and then . . . there they were at the bus stop! The bus was turning the corner. I ran across the road. A car hooted. I didn't think about that. The bus had stopped. I didn't have a ticket. I didn't think about that. I watched them jump on the bus, in the middle section. I jumped on too, at the back. They were sitting near the doors. I sat on one of the seats on a raised platform so that I could see them. The woman kept looking at a paper in her hand and then up at the screen that showed which stop was next. When it said *Coutance*, the woman said something to the boy and he stood up. I stood up too. They got off. I got off. I was shivering. I was still in my pyjamas. They waited by the bus stop. I waited too. The number 5 came and they got on it. I did too. The bus went on and on. I had never been on the number 5 before. I was a bit afraid. I looked out of the window. Where were they going?

Everyone was getting off the bus. It was the end of the line. I stood up. I got off. The woman was looking at her piece of paper again. She grabbed hold of the boy. They crossed the road. I ran after them. They stood in front of a building. There was a plaque on it. *Hôpital Cantonal de Genève*. I was suddenly very cold. Monsieur Renoir was in there. They were going to see him. I walked slowly behind them. They went into the hospital; they looked at the plaques on the walls and then the woman went to the reception and showed the lady there the piece of paper. I heard, '*Monsieur Jacques Clift? Oui, un instant.*' The woman waited while the lady looked down at her computer, and then the lady said, '*Au deuxième étage, deux zero quatre.*' Room 204. The woman pointed to the piece of paper and said, 'I don't speak French. Write it down.' The lady did. And then she pointed to where they should go. The woman walked quickly and the boy had to run to catch up. I went behind them. No one stopped me. They took the lift. I waited. I took the next one. I stepped out of the lift. The boy and the woman were gone already. I walked slowly until I was standing just next to the door. The door was open and I looked quickly inside. The boy and the woman were standing next to a bed and Monsieur Renoir was lying there, tubes coming in and out of his body.

'We can't stay long, Jack,' the woman said, and then

the boy turned his head, and his eyes opened wide when he saw me.

I turned and ran.

There was a policeman at the door. He stepped aside to let me in. Mum was crying. Dad put his hands on my shoulders and gripped them so hard it hurt. George came rushing in the room.

'Robert, what the heck!' he shouted.

Aunty Delphia was standing behind George. When she saw me, she sat down on one of the dining room chairs.

The policeman unclipped his radio from his shoulder and started talking.

'*On l'a trouvé,*' he said. '*Il est là avec sa famille.*'

He clipped his radio back and then looked down at me.

'*Jeune homme,*' he said. '*Ça va?*'

I said yes, and then he asked me where I had been and I had to tell the whole story. Dad was standing there shaking his head and Mum had her hands over her face.

'What the heck!' said George again.

Dad shouted, 'Out, out,' to George and George went out.

The policeman told me how I had made everyone worry, how the whole police force in Geneva had been mobilized to find me, how I could easily have been hurt.

I said I was sorry. I was crying.

I waited for the policeman to ask me to show him my bus ticket. He would arrest me and throw me in jail. I would be gone for a long time. I started to cry even more. My teeth were chattering.

The policeman shook his head and then he left.

Mum made me go and have a warm bath. Later, I was coughing even more. When she took my temperature I had a fever. Which was a good thing. I didn't get busted too badly. I wasn't allowed to buy any new books for the next six months.

George: Oooooo, I can't buy a book, ooooo.

Aunty Delphia came to my room. She sat on the edge of my bed. I'd been in there for three whole days, hacking away.

'Well, Robert,' she said. 'What you did was, of course, very naughty. We were all so worried. You should have seen your brother. But I must say I'm amazed at your sense of adventure, at your resilience.'

Aunty Delphia was smiling. Not a smile that showed all her white, straight teeth, but it was still a smile and it made her look young again.

'Your mum tells me that was quite a journey you took, and in your pyjamas too.'

I nodded.

'You were searching for truth. You wanted to get to the root of something. That is admirable. You are a warrior,' she said.

Aunty Delphia was like that. She said things you didn't expect. She said things that Bob the Butternut and

260

his people didn't want to hear. She said you couldn't go into a National Park and just say it was yours and start killing the animals there. She said animals had rights too.

I had found Monsieur Renoir. He definitely wasn't dead.

'Shall we play a game of tsoro?' she said.

'Yes, yes, Aunty.'

I loved tsoro. It was invented in Zimbabwe. When we played in Zimbabwe, Grandpa just scooped holes in the dirt and we used stones. But he made me a wooden set and gave me lucky bean seeds in a leather pouch to take back to Geneva. Some games take ages to finish, like Monopoly but much more fun. Just when you think you are close to winning, you make a wrong move and the game starts all over again.

We played on my bed. We put seeds in our rows, three in each hole. That's called sowing. I had the two top rows, Aunty Delphia the bottom ones. Then Aunty Delphia scooped up three seeds; she dropped one in a hole, then the next one, and she was just about to drop the last one when she moved her hand away and said, 'Robert, you showed me a letter.'

'Yes, Aunty.'

'Was it from this old man who is in the hospital?'

'Yes, Aunty.'

She sowed the seed in a hole and she captured my seeds. She played some more moves, capturing more seeds until she sowed a seed in a hole where she couldn't capture any of my seeds. And then it was my turn. I sowed. I captured her seeds, I sowed again, I captured some more, and then it was back to her.

'I don't remember what was in that letter very well,' she said, while she was sowing.

She captured some of my seeds.

'Aunty, he said he fought against the Mau Mau and he's a ghost and there's a boy who keeps whispering in his—'

I dropped the seed I'd just picked up on the floor.

'What is it, Robert?'

'Do you . . . do you think I'm the boy who won't leave him alone?'

Maybe I had made Monsieur Renoir so sad he . . . maybe I'd been bothering him so much and he—

'No, Robert.'

She put both her hands on my face.

'Listen, Robert. You have a very beautiful, generous heart and that's why this old man, this lonely old man was talking to you. You helped him.'

Aunty Delphia sniffed and then she wiped her eyes with her fingers.

While she was plotting her next move, I looked up at the Aladdin lamp.

It wasn't just a teapot.

A beautiful, generous heart wasn't a pure one, but maybe . . .

I made a wish.

But I guess it was more than one wish. I tried to pack it all in there.

Aunty Delphia won but not very quickly.

'Rest now,' she said.

I fell asleep.

When I woke up, it was dark in the room. There was a *squeak squeak* sound near my bed. I switched on the light and blinked. On the floor next to my bed there was a cage, and in the cage there was a hamster. The hamster was going round and round on a wheel.

The hamster was mine! It was Aunty Delphia's present.

'Your mum thinks he might just keep you out of any further mischief.' Aunty Delphia winked.

I had been begging Mum for *ages* for a pet. I don't know how Aunty Delphia convinced her. She was the best aunt ever!

'He's in good hands,' said Aunty Delphia. The hamster was going round his plastic tunnels, exploring.

I knew that Aunty Delphia didn't like to see animals in cages. She was making an exception for me.

'Thank you, Aunty Delphia,' I said.

I named him Zeus.

Aunty Delphia told me all about hamsters, and she even showed me his tiny penis.

Monsieur Badon told Mum that the woman was Monsieur Renoir's granddaughter and the boy was his great-grandson. Monsieur Renoir wasn't alone in the world. He had a family.

On Saturday I felt much better. Mum let me go out to flood my lungs with fresh air.

George: Tag him with an ankle monitor.

HA HA HA. Hilarious, bro, hilarious.

'Can I go and buy a *marmite* in Migros?' I asked Mum.

'Yes. But take your phone.'

Yes, my adventure had got me a cell phone!

George couldn't believe it. I was supposed to be under punishment. And I was getting hamsters, and cell phones, and *marmites*. His point was proved. I *was* a spoilt brat. The family's *chouchou*.

But it wasn't a smartphone. It only did what phones used to do in the olden days.

Mum made sure that I was all wrapped up. I had to put on a fleece *and* a coat, gloves, a hat, a scarf. It looked like I was going off to the mountains. It was sunny outside and the thermometer on the wall on the balcony said nine degrees Celsius. Zimbabwe is upside down to Switzerland. In June, July, August, it's winter. Christmas happens when it's really hot. When we were in Zimbabwe and the temperature was fifteen degrees Celsius, Grandma and Grandpa said that it was freezing and Grandma wouldn't go outside the house without a blanket over her shoulders.

I walked down the stairs. It seemed like ages since I had done that. Monsieur Renoir's door was closed. I hurried down.

The park was full of people. There were dogs running about without their leashes. I heard someone calling, 'Robert.' I turned round and looked up. Mum was standing on the balcony waving. I waved back.

I turned round again and walked across the park. Teenagers were hanging around the benches. I went up to the playground. When I was little I loved the big slide. Mum wouldn't let me play in the sandpit because people let their dogs run loose in there. Mum had read a study about dog poo and how sticking your hand in it and putting your finger in your eye could make you blind. Gross.

The boy was sitting on a swing.

He wasn't swinging. He was just sitting there, very still. He looked like he was thinking very hard. I walked up to the swing.

'Hello, Jack,' I said.

He blinked and blinked like he had sand in his eyes and then he rubbed his eyes as if there really was sand there.

'Hello,' he said, in his British accent.

'What are you doing?' I asked him.

'Thinking,' he said.

'I thought so. About what?'

He shrugged. I thought he was thinking about Monsieur Renoir, his great-grandfather. I didn't have any great-grandfathers. They were both dead. He was lucky.

'How old are you?' I asked.

'Eight.'

I don't know why, but I didn't think he was *that* boy, the boy in Monsieur Renoir's letter.

It was a HUNCH.

'I'm going to get a *marmite*.'

'Marmite,' he said. 'You have it here?'

265

He said it the British way. I was polite; I didn't correct him.

'Yes, come, I'll show you.'

He slid off the swing. I looked around but the woman wasn't there.

We walked without talking till we reached Migros. We went inside and I showed him the *marmite*.

'That's not marmite,' he said.

'Yes it is.'

He shook his head.

'Marmite comes in a jar like jam.'

I shook *my* head.

'*Marmeet*. It's for the Escalade.'

'Wow,' he said.

Exactly. That's how I was when I saw one for the first time. A cauldron made of chocolate! Just chocolate, and inside the cauldron – he couldn't see that because there was a chocolate lid covering the cauldron – there were vegetables made of marzipan. On the sides of the cauldron there was a marzipan Geneva coat of arms: a key and an eagle. It was in a box with a plastic window and along the box's sides were scenes from the Escalade: 11–12 December 1602, the Duke of Savoy's soldiers scaling the city walls, and Mère Royaume pouring boiling soup over them.

I picked up the box and went to the counter and paid for it. I was going to put it on my shelf in my bedroom and count down to Escalade day – it was still three weeks away – when, like all kids in Geneva, I'd take the cauldron out and smash it and gobble everything up.

We walked back to the playground. I let Jack carry the cauldron half of the way.

'Don't drop it,' I said.

We sat down on one of the steps. My phone started ringing. I answered it.

'Yes, Mum. Can I stay in the playground for a bit? Yes, Mum. Bye, Mum!'

I put the phone back in my pocket.

'I can stay,' I said.

We watched a couple of babies in the sandpit. If only they knew what they were putting in their mouths.

'Were you sick?' he asked.

'Yes, I was.'

He nodded.

'Did you stay in the hospital for a long time?'

Huh?

Ohhhh . . . *that's* why he thought I was in the hospital. Before I could stop myself, I blurted, 'I was following you.' Well done, Sherlock Holmes.

His eyes almost popped out of his head.

'You *were*?'

I nodded. 'I got into a lot of trouble after.'

'We went to see Great-Grandad.'

'I know.'

'He tried to kill himself.'

'Oh,' I said.

I was getting cold. I stood up and did some jumping jacks. He watched me. He wasn't wearing a coat, or a hat, or a scarf or gloves. He wasn't even wearing a fleece. And I bet he didn't have a vest on.

I took off my coat, my hat, my scarf, my gloves.

'Great-Grandad's rich and he's going to make us rich.'

I didn't think Monsieur Renoir could be *that* rich. He lived in a small apartment.

Maybe Jack saw that I didn't really believe his great-grandpa was rich, because he said, 'He sent me a present.'

You didn't have to be rich to send a present to your great-grandson.

'An elephant tusk.'

Okay, he was just making stuff up now.

And then I remembered the brown box in the post office. It was pretty big. But an elephant tusk? Maybe a baby elephant, and that was even worse.

'That's illegal,' I said to him.

He looked at me.

'An elephant's tusk. You aren't allowed to have it. It's ivory.'

'It has pictures on it.'

In Zimbabwe, Aunty Delphia showed me a room full of elephant tusks. Some of them had carvings. Was he really telling the truth?

'A man, a very, very tall man, came to see Great-Grandad after you left.'

I didn't think you had to be very, very tall to make an impression with Jack.

'We had lunch with him in the cafeteria. He bought me an ice cream.'

I didn't know what to say about that. I guess it was

nice of the very, very tall man to buy him an ice cream. Swiss ice creams were pretty good.

'He showed Mum a picture.'

I was getting cold again.

'Jack, I'm goi—'

'It was a medal.'

I stopped dead in my tracks.

'A medal?'

'Great-Grandad might have it.'

I was really, really cold now.

'He said it wasn't Great-Grandad's. There's a reward. Lots and lots of money.'

I had to say something. I blurted out, 'I've got a hamster. His name's Zeus.'

I sounded like a moron. Guilty person, over here.

Jack didn't say anything.

'Do you want to see him?'

He nodded.

'Let's go,' I said.

I put my coat, my hat, my scarf and my gloves back on. Once we came out of the playground, Mum would be able to see me from the balcony.

We took the stairs and I stepped aside for Jack to go to Monsieur Renoir's apartment and tell his mum that he was going up to ours to see my hamster. But he didn't go near his door.

'Your mum,' I said. 'Don't you have to—'

'She's not in.'

He pushed down the door handle. It was locked. He shrugged and looked up at me. Wow. His mum left him alone in the park. *And* he was only eight. *And* he didn't have a coat or a scarf or a hat or gloves. *And* . . . I looked down at his shoes; he was wearing trainers and not mountain boots with thick socks. *Boy*.

I tried to hold my breath.

Didn't the smoky, musty smell bother him?

And then I remembered the crocodile. He was probably in there gnashing his teeth, waiting to—

'Great-Grandad's place is full of—'

And then he slammed his hand over his mouth. I guess he wasn't supposed to talk about what was in there.

We went up to the fourth floor, which was really the fifth. I explained it to him while we were walking. I told him all about *entresol*, how his great-grandpa lived in the in-between world.

Mum had the phone in her hand when we came in. She was just about to phone me again.

'Hi, Mum,' I said. 'This is Jack. Monsieur Renoir's great-grandson. He's come to see Zeus.'

Mum looked at him.

'Hello, Jack,' she said. 'Does your mum know you're here?'

'His mum's out,' I said. 'Come on, Jack, he's over here.'

As long as Aunty Delphia was with us, Zeus was living in Mum's study. Mum said it wasn't hygienic to have a hamster in our bedroom.

Zeus was sleeping. He slept throughout the whole day. George said he was so lame. What was the point of him? And then, at night, when everyone else was asleep, he went wild on the wheel. Wendy said that you can train hamsters to stay awake during the day and to sleep at night, but Aunty Delphia said that was cruel, it was forcing the hamster out of its natural, biological rhythms; who knew what physical and psychological damage would be done – *can you imagine if we humans were made to sleep during the whole day and forced to be awake at night?* Mum rolled her eyes and said that rodents couldn't be compared to humans, and Aunty Delphia said that was where she was wrong; why did she think they did all those tests on cosmetics on hamsters . . .

We couldn't even *see* Zeus because he was sleeping under the straw behind the wheel.

'You can come for a sleepover,' I said. 'He'll be awake.'

Mum made us a snack of toasted cheese sandwiches with a glass of milk each.

Jack ate his sandwich so fast that he started coughing and choking. I patted him on his back a couple of times.

'Great-Grandad sent me a card with the elephant tusk.'

'What did it say?'

'Sorry.'

Sorry?

What was Monsieur Renoir sorry for? Was it for the elephant tusk? Was he sorry that an elephant had been killed for it? Was he sorry that he was giving it to Jack? Maybe he wanted to give Jack something else.

271

'Mum said he should be sorry all right.'

His mum didn't sound like a very nice person.

'He did a very bad thing in Africa. He should be in prison. He ran away.'

I felt chills all over.

'That's what Mum said.'

It was hot in the apartment. In Switzerland they put the heaters on very high because of all the old people. He pushed up the sleeve of his T-shirt. I stared at his arm. It was black and blue and more blue. He saw me staring and he pushed down his sleeve.

'Did you fall?' I asked him.

He said, 'Kind of.'

'Where's your dad?' I asked him. I was just trying to change the subject.

His face became a funny shape like it was crumpling.

'I don't know,' he said.

I tried to think of something that would make him happy. I was stumped.

Then he said he had to go.

'What if your mum's not back?'

'I'll wait outside.'

I wanted him to stay a bit longer. I thought of things we could do, something I could show him that wouldn't be asleep and hidden like Zeus.

'I've got a medal,' I blurted out.

What was wrong with me? Was I like one of those criminals who want to be discovered?

I took him to my room and showed him the medal. I didn't tell him that his great-grandpa had given it to me. He didn't ask if he could touch it, but he looked at it very hard.

'Mum wants it,' he said.

'I didn't steal it. Monsieur Renoir gave it to me.'

'Who's Monsieur Renoir?'

And then I had to tell him the whole story about when he yelled at George and me. His eyes opened really wide and the veins on his forehead looked as if they would pop out from his skin and blood would pour out. I told him about the name plaque next to the buzzer that his great-grandpa had never removed – hadn't he seen it? He shook his head. And then I told him about the medal on the doormat and the letters. I was exhausted when I finished. He looked like he didn't understand most of it.

'Are you going to give it to the tall man?'

I didn't know who the tall man was.

And suddenly I felt really scared.

What if he found out that I had the medal and he came after me? What if – what if he was like a bounty hunter? What if he captur—

'I have to go,' Jack said.

He looked down at the medal again.

I put the box behind some books on my shelf. He was watching.

'I trust you, Jack,' I said. 'Monsieur . . . I mean your great-grandpa said I was to do the right thing. I don't know what that is yet. When I know, I'll tell you. Shake on it.'

I held out my hand. He held out his. We shook.

273

His hand was so tiny it was swallowed up by mine.

I walked him out the door and took the steps down with him to *entresol*. I saw him knock on the door and then open it. His mum was home.

Chapter Twenty-One

Baby

Mum and Aunty Delphia were crying in the lounge. They were hugging each other. George and I were standing there looking at them. Finally they untangled and Mum looked over at us. She wiped away her tears with the back of her hand.

'Hi, guys,' she said. She was smiling.

'What's wrong? Why are you crying?' I asked.

'Nothing's wrong,' said Mum. 'We've just come back from the clinic and your aunt's been given the all clear.'

'She doesn't have HIV?' I said.

'How did you kn—'

'That's right,' said Aunty Delphia. 'I'm HIV free, but I have to do one more test later just to be extra sure. But for now, it's good news.'

'Are you crying because you're happy?'

'Yes,' said Aunty Delphia.

'What's wrong, George?' Mum asked.

I turned to look at George. He was standing very still.

'George?'

'Nothing. I'm . . . I have some homework,' and he rushed off. George *never* volunteered to do his homework. Something *was* wrong. Then Aunty Delphia stood up from the couch and said, 'Wait, George. Can your homework wait a bit? Can you come and walk with me to Migros? I need some strong hands to help me with the bags.'

There wasn't an answer from George.

'George,' my mother shouted. 'Your aunt's talking to you.'

Aunty Delphia grabbed Mum's wrist. 'Leave him,' she said. 'He's a young man. He'll come when he's ready.'

I didn't understand why George was so upset. Aunty Delphia was fine. She wasn't sick. She didn't have the virus in her body. She wasn't going to die.

I went into the kitchen. George was sitting at the table; his head was resting on his hands.

'George, Aunty Delphia's fine,' I said.

I thought maybe he didn't understand.

'She's not fine,' he said.

'Yes she is. Didn't you hear Mum? She doesn't have—'

'It's not that, Robert. She was—'

And then he got up.

'She was what?'

'Nothing, nothing.'

'Tell me,' I said.

'You're just a baby. You don't get it. You think Aunty Delphia's going to be all smiley faces now because she isn't sick; well she's sick because of what they did to her, you moron.'

Why was he upset with me? And Aunty Delphia wasn't sick, that's what I was trying to tell him.

'I'm not a baby.'

'You are.'

I punched him on the shoulder, nearly on the shoulder. He grabbed my hand and twisted it. I screamed. Mum and Aunty Delphia came rushing in.

'What's going— George!'

'Jane,' said Aunty Delphia. 'I'll just go outside with George. Come, George, let's go.'

I looked up at George. He had tears running down his cheeks. What was going on?

When they were gone, I asked Mum what AIDS was and she explained it.

'Is that why the nurse told us not to touch anyone else's cuts or blood?'

'Yes.'

'Is it in the air? Can you breathe it?'

'No, Robert.'

'What about if you touch something or someone with AIDS?'

'No. As long as you don't touch blood or a fresh cut.'

'Are you sure?'

'Absolutely.'

'George says Aunty Delphia *did* get sick.'

'I think he means another kind of sickness, Robert. What happens to your mind and heart when you are hurt. Do you see what I mean?'

'I guess.'

'If someone hit you, you would get over the physical pain, wouldn't you, but you'd still hurt inside, and that can take much longer to heal.'

I think I understood. I mean, I'd never been hit before; okay, George had just twisted my arm really hard and that didn't hurt any more but I still felt hurt about it. And I guess he still felt hurt by my punch, even though it wasn't that hard and I missed most of his shoulder.

They were gone for a long time, and when they came back they didn't have any bags from Migros. George went to lie down on his bed with his headphones on. I went and gave Aunty Delphia a hug. And when I looked up at her she was smiling, but not her real, true smile.

Later George said he was sorry for calling me a baby.

I said that I was sorry I'd punched him.

I wasn't a baby, but George *was* my older brother; he knew much more stuff than I did.

He was right about Aunty Delphia.

Chapter Twenty-Two

L'Escalade

At the Promenade de la Treille:

Soldiers fighting with swords – a duel!

Cannons firing away, *Boom! Boom! Boom!*

Hands clamped over ears.

Babies screaming.

Boom! Boom! Boom!

Soup ladled out from the huge cauldron bubbling away on the fire.

At La Place du Bourg-de-Four:

Blacksmiths in breeches and leather aprons busy making horseshoes.

I closed my eyes every time the heavy hammer hit the iron.

'What's that?' I asked Dad.

When I was smaller, I just watched the blacksmiths, but now I wanted to know what everything was, how it all worked.

'A bellows.'

'What does it do?'

'Watch.'

A man with ginormous biceps was pushing down on the huge bellows, pushing air out into—

'What's that?'

Dad looked down at the booklet. He read the French word *forge* but he couldn't translate it to English.

'George,' said Dad. 'Translate this on your phone.'

George rolled his eyes.

'I'm doing something, Dad.'

'Do this, make yourself useful.'

George tapped in the word.

'Forge,' he said.

'Yes,' said Dad. 'What's the translation?'

'Forge, it's the same word.'

'Okay,' said Dad, 'I guess it means a place like an oven. So the bellows pushes air into the forge to keep it burning.'

Another blacksmith put the metal into the—

'What's that?'

'A smelter,' said Dad. 'You'll see why it's called that in a second.'

Another blacksmith took out the molten—

'I get it, Dad, it's *melted*.'

'That's right.'

'Wow,' said George in his sarcastic voice.

The molten iron, red hot from the smelter, and now – my favourite part – the blacksmith picked up a huge hammer and raised his strong hand, over and over.

'My ears are ringing, Dad!'

'Wow,' said George. 'Can we go now?'

'Dad, if he misses—'

'Bye bye, hand,' said George.

Another blacksmith joined him; the two of them hammered away on the same piece, *ring ring ring*, over and over.

'Look, Dad, they've done it. It's a horseshoe!'

'Wow,' said George, 'Can we *please* go now?'

Bands – drums, flutes, trumpets – marching from the Hotel de Ville –

Seven-year-old me: Dad, can we stay here?

Dad: It isn't a hotel, Robert. It's where the government of Geneva meets.

Seven-year-old me: Do they sleep there?

Dad: Hmmm. I don't think so.

– through the cobbled streets of the Vieille Ville.

Olden-day Genevois in knee breeches and stockings giving out *vin chaud* and soup from the wooden taverns behind the Cathédrale Saint-Pierre.

Infantry and cavalrymen in steel helmets doing exercises.

Ladies in long dresses and capes and fancy hats; servants with aprons and bonnets and baskets under their arms.

A wild pig – a boar, Dad said – on an olden-day spit, turning in the fire.

There was something happening everywhere!

I was a traitor, a Savoyard – a *soldat coiffé du morion*, said the *Bulletin de la Compagnie de 1602*, *Ceux de 1602*, which was written for the Escalade in 1977; Mum found it at the book market in the Place de Madeleine.

George took one look at me when I put the costume on and rapped, 'Yo, check it out, bros, Peter Pan's in da house,' and he flicked the *morion* off my head. My *morion* wasn't made of metal. It was made of grey felt. But I was holding the Genevois flag. Red and gold.

I watched the Duke of Savoy's troops try to climb up the walls of the cathedral with their ladders. George was sitting on one of the benches. He was on his phone. He didn't care about soldiers and swords and halberds and muskets and hats with tall real feathers, banners and iron helmets and galloping horses; he didn't care about the heroes of 1602 – Mère Royaume with her soup, Dame Piaget who threw the key to the back gates out of the window so that the Genevois could attack the Savoyards from behind, and Isaac Mercier who raised the alarm – and that they were all here in the old town today. He didn't care about all that *fancy dress*, he said. Lame *and* gay. Mum didn't like George using 'gay' like that. She said it was offensive to people who were gay. It was homophobic.

George: *I'm only joking.*

Mum: *If you're the only one laughing, it's not a joke.*

George: *My friends laugh.*

Mum: *Enough. I don't want to hear you use that word like that.*

George: *Oui, Maman.*

I didn't really understand why 'gay' was offensive. Gay meant you were happy but it also meant that a boy loved a boy the same way Dad loved Mum. Loving someone made you happy. It made you gay. Mum said that certain words mutated and became something else; they had meant one thing before and then they meant something else. She didn't like George's rap music because of the words.

At least he wasn't one of those teenagers who celebrated L'Escalade by running around and throwing eggs and flour on each other and anyone else who was in their way.

Mum and Dad were sitting on a step sipping their wine. I booed the Savoyards and cheered the Genevois. The Savoyards were expelled. Geneva was safe. We all clapped and cheered. And then we sang *'Ainsi périssent les ennemis de la République!' Thus perish the enemies of the Republic*, I sang, waving my flag. I knew all the words off by heart.

'Veux-tu une *médaille?*'

It was a girl. She was wearing a bright red dress and a white bonnet. She had a small basket under her arm. It was full of medals.

'*Combien?*' I asked her.

'*Seulement un franc.*'

I had five francs to spend. I picked up a medal. It had a picture of a soldier standing next to a horse, and a red and yellow ribbon, the colours of Geneva. I gave the girl one franc and pinned the medal to my soldier coat. Even though I was dressed as a Savoyard I was really a hero. I had expelled the Savoyards. I marched over to George. 'Look,' I said. 'Isn't it cool?' George looked and nodded and went back to his phone, and then he looked up again.

'Hey,' he said. 'Do you still have that medal?'

The boy in *A Medal for Leroy* buried his father's medal in a field in Belgium where his great-grandfather had died. It was the right thing to do.

'I still have it.'

'You better do something. The guy keeps harassing me.' George sounded really worried.

'What . . . what does he say?'

George didn't tell me to go away.

'I'll show you. I just got another notification.'

I sat down next to him.

'Here,' he said. He handed me the phone.

I think what you have may be the real deal. It must be returned. Reply and no questions will be asked as to how it was acquired. You are in the possible possession of a stolen item. In all confidentiality. L.

'He keeps hacking into my password. I've changed it hundreds of times. I keep blocking him.'

George sounded panicky, which made me nervous.

This was serious.

'Give it to me,' he said. 'I'll delete it.'

I gave him the phone.

'What's his name?' I asked.

'He just signs "L".'

'Can't you found out who he is? I mean, Facebook has rules, doesn't it? You can't be anonymous.'

'I don't care who he is. I just want him to leave me alone. It's creepy.'

It *was* creepy. What if the guy knew where George lived? What if he wanted that medal so badly? What if he was a really bad guy? What if he told the police? What if the police thought we'd stolen it? What if I was a thief now?

'L for loser,' I said.

I guess I just wanted to make George feel better.

It worked.

'That's it! I'm being punked.'

'Punked?'

'Someone's pranking me. They're trying to freak me out.'

I didn't know about that.

'George—'

But he was busy on his phone again. I hoped he wasn't replying to that message. He didn't know for sure it was a prank, but I supposed he must be right. Who else would be stalking him? It had to be a joke.

It was night-time and the main procession had arrived at the cathedral. There were torches, olden-day ones, which means branches set alight, and the band was playing. There were banners and flags. We followed them. There was Mère Royaume with a huge *marmite*. There were so many people. Mum held me tight. I sang and sang and sang.

When we got home, I took the *marmite* from the box. I smashed it on the dining room table. I saved some chocolate and marzipan carrots and turnips for Jack.

Chapter Twenty-Three

The Land of In-Between

Jack opened the door.

'Come in,' he whispered.

I stepped inside.

I coughed. That smell was everywhere.

It was dark.

He closed the door.

He didn't ask me to take off my shoes like Mum asked visitors at home.

I followed him, one, two, three steps, and then I was no longer in Geneva. I was in Africa!

Elephants and lions and zebras and antelopes and leopards leaped off the walls.

Teeth and tusks.

Animal skins swept over every wall; they were even on the ceiling.

And on the floor Jack showed me what everything was.

'Look, this is an elephant's leg. It's too heavy. I can't lift it.'

I had to bend over to see it.

It *was* an elephant leg! And they had made it into a stool.

Poor elephant!

'This is an elephant tusk,' he said. He was holding an ashtray.

I stepped over something sharp. I almost fell.

'Be careful,' he said. 'There's a crocodile.'

I jumped.

There *was* a crocodile!

His head was poking out from under the low table, his mouth wide open, his teeth sharp and waiting; the rest of his body fat and swollen under the table like he had just had a meal.

There were eggs, lots and lots of eggs on the table.

Jack knew what some of them were.

'Ostrich egg, crocodile egg, snake egg.' The snake egg was covered with a snake skin.

He didn't touch them. He pointed to them.

I thought of all those eggs hatching, little baby ostriches and crocodiles and snakes in the room, alive!

There were chairs covered in zebra skins.

There were drums covered in skins.

There were spears and shields on the walls.

Masks!

'It's like *Jumanji*,' I said.

'*Jumanji*, what's that?'

'It's a movie where these kids play a game and then all these animals from Africa come alive and start attacking them in their house. It's scary but fun.'

'Imagine if these animals came alive,' he said.

I could but I didn't want to think too much about that.

'Where's your mum?'

Jack shrugged.

'Dunno. She's gone to meet someone. She said she'd be back tomorrow.'

'Tomorrow?'

'Yes.'

'Who's coming to look after you?'

He shrugged.

'No one. I can look after myself. I know how to make toast and everything.'

He was eight years old! George didn't know how the toaster worked.

'Aren't you scared?'

'It's a'right. I've done it before.'

This place was spooky. I'd be terrified to close my eyes.

'Sit over there,' he said.

I sat on the zebra.

Sorry, zebra.

Aunty Delphia would be so mad if she was here.

He went to another room and came back pushing a box.

'I found this in the closet. In Great-Grandad's room. Come and help me. Mum wants to throw it out.'

I went over to help him. I put my hand over my nose.

'It stinks,' I said. 'What's in there, rats?'

'You'll see.'

We had to clear a space for the box. We rolled away

the animal skins. We pushed away the chairs and moved the drums.

He opened the box.

It smelt horrible.

'It's a skunk,' he said. 'Well, not *all* the skunk, just the smelly bit.'

I clamped my hand over my mouth and nose. I didn't know if I should be breathing or swallowing this smell.

He pulled something out from the box.

A tail!

And then he pulled something else out.

Another tail!

'That's a rabbit. This is a monkey.'

He shuffled more in the box. Shouldn't he be wearing gloves or something? I thought of all the antibacterial wash Mum would make me use if I touched anything in there.

He brought out packets and packets of things. They were in ziplock bags.

Leaves.

Grass.

Herbs?

Teeth.

Bits of animals, plants?

And then he stuck his hand right underneath and brought out a big brown envelope.

'They're pictures.'

He poured them out on to the floor.

They were black and white. Old. Like pictures that you found at the market.

There were pictures of men next to dead animals, guns in their hands.

A lion. An elephant. A crocodile.

There were pictures of huts and children playing outside them.

There were pictures of a forest. So many trees.

There were mountains. And rivers. And a big lake.

There were pictures of jeeps and men standing beside them with guns.

'Look at this one,' he said, picking one up. I didn't want to touch it. He put it on the table. I peered over.

There was a line of men tied to a rope by their hands. They were black.

He put another picture on the table.

It was a hut burning.

There were pictures of lots of things but not a single picture of a plane. Not one.

I waited and waited for one to turn up.

In the forest.

By the huts.

In the bush.

Next to the jeeps and the men with guns.

But they weren't there.

Air force pilots loved their planes. They loved posing with their planes. Why wasn't there a picture of Monsieur Renoir posing with his plane? Didn't he love his plane? Wasn't he proud to be a Royal Air Force pilot?

'Do you think he's good at football?'

'Who?'

'*Him.*'

He showed me the picture. The sides were blackened like they had been in a fire. In the picture was a boy. He was wearing just a pair of shorts. No T-shirt. He wasn't wearing any shoes or trainers.

There was a ball at his feet. Not a real ball. A ball like the ones I saw in Zimbabwe, made of rags and plastic bags.

'His name's Luke,' he said.

'How do you know?'

He turned the picture over.

LUKE, in block letters.

I looked at the words very hard.

Monsieur Renoir had written them.

He knew a boy called Luke.

Was this the boy who came and whispered to him, the boy who would not run away?

Was this the boy who stood with his hands stretched out?

I don't know why but I said, 'Can I have it?'

Jack looked at the picture.

I thought that he'd say it didn't belong to him, that it belonged to his great-grandpa, that I already had the medal, but he said, 'Okay.' I touched the picture; I took it from him.

'There's something else,' he said. His hand was already in the box. I could only see half of his arm now. What if there was some magic in there, something in there that bit and when he took out his hand there wouldn't be a hand but a—

'Look!' he said.

He put it down on the table.

My heart jumped and thumped.

I'd seen it before.

'Open it,' he said.

It was the leather book with the patch of animal skin.

'You open it,' I said.

He shook his head.

'You're older,' he said.

That was the trick I used on George but I just couldn't reach out my hand and untie the string. Maybe it was thinking about *Jumanji* and what happened when the kids opened the box, all the bad things that came rushing out, but I just had this feeling that something terrible was in there and I didn't want to touch it.

I was saved by my phone. It was vibrating in my pocket. I took it out. It was Mum. It was a message. It was time to come home.

'We'll look inside another day,' I said.

He nodded.

And then I thought of something.

'Do you want to have a sleepover? Mum won't mind. I have sleepovers with Jin, that's my best friend, all the time.'

He was thinking about my invitation. I thought he would say yes. How could he stay alone in this spooky place? All night! It was mad.

He shook his head.

'Can't,' he said. 'Mum said to stay here.'

'You could come back really early tomorrow. I've got an alarm clock.'

He thought about that.

He shook his head again.

'Can't.'

And that was it.

'Don't tell your mum,' he said.

He stretched out his arm.

We shook on it even though I felt bad about promising not to tell Mum. Mum would never leave me alone in an apartment, not even for one minute. Mum would do something if she knew. She might even call the police.

'Okay,' I said. 'If you change your mind, just come, any time, day or night.'

I felt better after saying that.

And then he showed me something else. He got it from the cabinet in the toilet behind the front door.

My heart stopped, and then it went crazy. It hurt.

Monsieur Renoir's eye was looking at me.

It was blazing, in a dish.

It was made of glass.

At home I read Monsieur Renoir's letter again and I looked at the boy.

He looked like he was my age, but skinnier.

He was looking at the camera with a serious face.

Are you him? I asked him.

Are you him, Luke?

Are you the boy who stood there with your hands

293

stretched out, waiting to catch something falling from the sky?

I had to write a letter to a child soldier for French class. The child soldier was in the Congo, where they speak French. Madame Thorens said that it was voluntary, only if we really wanted to and if our parents said we could. I asked Dad, who thought about it, and then he asked Mum, who thought about it, and then they said yes but I couldn't sign the letter with my real name, I had to use a pen name. Madame Thorens would post the letters and they would reach a boy somewhere in the Congo. The Congo was a huge country in Africa. There were many forests there. Mum had a book about a child soldier. The child soldier wrote the book. Mum said that organizations like the Red Cross helped him to start all over again and to become someone else. I'm proud of Dad.

> *Salut, child soldier,*
>   *Je suis un garçon de dix ans. Je vis en Suisse mais je ne suis pas Suisse. Je suis Zimbabwean et Italien. J'aime le basket, lire et jouer avec mon meilleur ami, Jin. J'espère que vous êtes heureux. Que voulez-vous faire quand vous serez grand?*
>   *Un garcon*

I wanted to ask the child soldier other questions.
Did you miss your mum and dad when you were a soldier?

Did you shoot a gun?
Did you kill anyone?
Were you afraid?
Did you ever see a plane drop a bomb?
Do you have bad dreams?

Chapter Twenty-Four

Le Marché aux Puces

Flea market day, and I had a plan!

In December, the market happened earlier because of Christmas. Mum loved the market for everything. She said that you never knew where inspiration would come from or what 'thing' would offer a solution to a problem in a story. Her books were full of her finds from the market. Last market day she found a World War II ration book (No. 3) that belonged to a woman named Mary who lived in New York and who was seventy-seven years old. There were still some stamps left in the book, and Mum had her faraway look while she was holding it.

Dad loved the market for the old cameras that he would find and the discussions he would have about them with the stall owners.

I loved the market for the same reason as Mum. You just never knew what you would find, what you would *have* to have; for example, I found the baseball mitt and ball (five francs), one Lego Star Wars X-Wing Fighter (fifteen francs, with the manual), one Lego Creator Dinosaur (ten francs, with the manual), one Lego Aqua Raider (five francs, without the manual), a whole box of Bionicles (five francs, without the manuals), a whole set of Pokémon cards (four francs), a Super Mario DS game (ten francs).

George always hoped that the market would happen on a Sunday when he had a match. He was lucky this time; his match was in Oberwallis. Oberwallis was almost three hours from Geneva so we weren't going to watch him (Yeah!).

Dad was taking the lake shore route. The box was in my coat pocket. I looked out of the window. We were already driving past Versoix. In summer, we went to the beach near there and George and me – *George and I* – and other kids would swim to the platform and push each other in the water. Then we passed Coppet. I loved the castle up on the hill. That's where Madame de Staël – for a long time I called her Madame de Style – a very important woman writer, lived, a long time ago. She used to have parties – Mum called them *salons* and *soirées* – for other writers.

Aunty Delphia was with us. She didn't want to come at first but Mum said that if she didn't then she'd stay behind too. She was sitting with her hands crossed on her lap. She looked tired and old again. Her head was leaning against the window. She wasn't looking outside. Her eyes were closed.

She missed Cynthia.

She had nightmares. Sometimes I heard her crying.

She was depressed.

She was taking pills to try and make her feel better. They were yellow and orange, like candy. Sometimes she forgot them on the kitchen counter. I asked Mum what they were.

Even though she was healthy, she was still sad.

It was sunny. There were lots of market stands lining the promenade. It was the last market before Christmas. I had my favourites. We started at the end near the pêcheurs with their nets and cages, like we always did. I had to be patient.

I saw Jean and Simon, two kids who always had cool stuff. Mum said that one of these days we'd go through my old toys and rent a space at the market. The problem was, I didn't like parting with my stuff. I loved having it there in case I ever needed it again.

'*Salut*,' I said to Jean.

'Hello, Robert. We have something *très* cool.'

I liked the way Jean said 'cool'. *Coooooolll*.

'*Quoi?*'

Jean ducked under the table and dug around in a brown bag. He came back up again. He had a white dinosaur in his hand.

'Hmmm . . .' I said.

'It moves.'

'Hmmm.'

He went back under the table, dug around the bag again and came back up with a remote.

He started pressing the buttons.

I looked at the dinosaur on the table. It was very still.

Jean shook the remote, pressed more buttons, but the dinosaur didn't move one centimetre.

Jean turned to his brother.

'*Simon, qu'est-ce qui se passe ici?*'

Simon was a bit like George. He had hair that was way too long and a baseball cap sitting high on his head and Beats hanging around his neck. He was playing something on his phone.

'*Quoi?*'

'*Il ne marche pas.*' Jean showed Simon the remote.

Simon shrugged.

'*C'est la pile,*' said Jean.

I wasn't interested in the dinosaur even if it *could* move, and then what? What was the point of a moving dinosaur? Besides, I had Zeus. I looked through their comic books. There was a *Titeuf and Astérix*, which I bought for two francs.

'*Au revoir.*'

'*Au revoir, Robert.*'

We stopped and bought some sausages with bread from the usual guy, who had the dirtiest fingernails ever – Mum always made sure to snip off the crusts and the end bits of the sausages he'd touched. I chose the normal sausages because the white ones just looked creepy; it was veal and I knew what veal was now, a baby cow. We sat on the benches by the water. I liked watching the ducks and swans wander among the boats. There were some kids on the pier throwing chunks of bread at them. The pieces were too big and it made me think of the movie Mum likes so much, *About a Boy* – the boy is really a man who refuses to grow up and the boy is actually the mature one. Anyway, the boy throws a whole loaf of stale bread in a pond and the loaf hits the duck and kills it; it doesn't sound very funny but it is, in the movie. Mum says the book is even better because you can build your own picture, which is the magic of words.

The stall I needed to go to was across the road, in the square, just behind the fountain. Dad was busy with his cameras. Mum and Aunty Delphia and I crossed the road, and then Mum took Aunty Delphia to the café to have something hot to drink because she was shivering.

'Stay in the square,' said Mum. 'Do you have your cell phone?'

'Yes.'

'Is the battery still full?'

I put my hand in my pocket and took out the phone; the box almost fell out.

'Yes, the battery's full.'

Monsieur Brion – he had this plaque with his name on it – was sitting down behind a little table loaded with two bottles of wine, bread and a pot of fondue. I didn't like fondue. I didn't like the smell of the cheese. I didn't like how the bread and cheese got stuck in the back of your throat and you had to make yourself swallow. Mum said that fondue was unhygienic: people who weren't even family (Dad ate a lot of fondue with his colleagues at Café du Soleil) sharing the same pot of fondue, some people putting the spears of bread and fondue so far down their throats they were almost touching and scraping their tonsils and then dipping the spear into the fondue, again and again, and all this in winter when there was flu and all kinds of viruses and bacteria . . . Dad said how about in Zimbabwe, people ate from the same *sadza* plate, even licking the stew and *sadza* off their fingers before they dipped into the plate again; Mum said that was in the rural areas and people were more educated now.

I love chocolate fondue. Mum bought a chocolate fountain at the *kermesse* and for my birthdays it's become a tradition. Jin and I dip lots of different types of fruit in it. My favourite are kiwi and strawberry. George makes Mum very angry because he dips marshmallow after marshmallow and when Mum says that's enough he finds some butter biscuits and dips those in. There is no way George is going to eat fruit, even if it is covered in chocolate. He has an unhealthy diet for a champion sportsman, if you ask me.

Monsieur Brion was small but he was eating a lot of fondue and chugging down glass after glass of wine and wiping his mouth with his arm. I watched for a bit and then I went up.

'*Bonjour, Monsieur Brion.*'

'*Bonjour, jeune homme.*'

My hand was in my pocket, clutching the box, but I couldn't make it bring out the box into the open for Monsieur Brion to see.

I started looking at his trays of medals.

There were medals for all kinds of bravery. There were medals for all kinds of heroes.

Switzerland didn't really have any war medals. Switzerland didn't believe in war. But Monsieur Brion was French and the French believed in wars and medals. The French had medals for *every single war* they had ever fought in, all the way back to *hundreds* of years ago. They had lots and lots of medals. And he had medals from other countries too. He kept his really special ones in two locked cabinets. I guess Monsieur Brion came to Switzerland to sell his medals because people were richer and Switzerland was an international place, full of bankers and big bosses of companies.

'*Alors, jeune homme, comment puis-je vous aider?*'

I was looking down at the crate of books and olden-day newspapers Monsieur Brion had by his medals. I guess I was just stalling or trying to work up my courage. There was a bright red book with gold Chinese writing. Monsieur Brion bent over – he almost knocked the table over – and reached out and took out the book.

'*Ah, L'Art de la Guerre. Un classique.*'

The Art *of War?* How could war be art? Art was . . . art was . . . paintings and drawings and writing books. Mum was an artist.

Monsieur Brion sat down again. He opened the book and turned its pages. He showed me the pictures. Pictures of ancient Chinese men on horseback, fighting.

War was everywhere.

The book was all in Chinese. Maybe George could read it. Maybe he could find out how war was an art. Did it mean the *pictures* of war? Pictures of battlefields and soldiers. Pictures like Caravaggio's, which we saw in Florence. They were scary but Dad said it was *how* they were painted that made them great art. Mum read to me 'The Charge of the Light Brigade' from an old leather book she bought at the market; she said it was a poem about the Crimean War where many, many soldiers died.

Theirs not to make reply, Theirs not to reason why, Theirs but to do and die, Into the valley of Death rode the six hundred.

It was a beautiful poem about an ugly thing.

George wasn't allowed to have war games like Assassin's Creed or Call of Duty on his PlayStation. Mum said war was ugly and brutal and playing it with real-life graphics where you went around shooting and killing everyone desensitized you to the consequences of violence in real life. She said that there were studies to show that.

George: Seriously Mum, like I'm going to get a gun and go around killing random people?

Mum: That's not the point, although some people have gone around and killed people because they've been desensitized. The point is that I don't want you to grow up thinking it's okay to hurt people.

George: I'm not a baby.

Mum: You're my baby.

George rolled his eyes.

I went for it. '*Monsieur Brion, avez-vous une Victoria Cross.*'

'*Une Victoria Cross?*' He put the book down.

'*Oui.*'

'*Une Victoria Cross d'Angleterre?*'

'*Oui, Monsieur Brion.*'

'*Non, non.*' Monsieur Brion shook his head. '*Seulement une Croix de Guerre. La Victoria Cross, elle est rare. Très rare. Les Anglais ne sont pas comme les Français. Ils ne sont pas très généreux avec leurs médailles.*'

My hand was almost squashing the box. I had to bring it out. I *had* to.

'Monsieur Brion—'

But then Monsieur Brion stood up, almost knocking over the table again.

'Ah, monsieur, I have been waiting for you. I have it here.'

Monsieur Brion's English sounded just like French.

And then he looked at me and said, '*Au revoir, jeune homme, au revoir.*'

The man was wearing a hat and a big baggy coat and everything about him was very grey.

He said, 'Good afternoon, Mr Brion.'

He was British.

Monsieur Brion looked down at me again.

'*Au revoir*—' and then he stopped and looked up at Monsieur X.

'Ah, this young man has been asking me about the Victoria Cross. I tell him how rare they are, extremely rare.'

The man looked down at me.

I looked up at him; boy, did it hurt my neck to look all the way up there.

'Indeed,' he said. 'I would gladly part with

thousands of pounds for one of those. Every now and then one crops up at an auction. Do you have one, young man? There's been some chatter on social networking sites.'

I let go of the box. Chills were going crazy all over my body.

'Nnnn—'

The man laughed.

'Of course not. If you had one of those, I'd have to kill you for it.' And then he laughed again.

Haw haw haw.

I went over to the next stand, which was full of old dolls, so I moved on to the next, which was full of old maps. I stood there. I could still see Monsieur Brion and his visitor. Mr Brion was giving him a long thin box. The man opened it and then he stepped back and took out a pair of glasses from his pocket; he put them on and then he looked at whatever was in the box. And then Monsieur Brion and the man talked. Monsieur X handed Mr Brion an envelope. Mr Brion looked inside the envelope. He felt whatever was in there with his fingers and then he nodded and shook hands with Monsieur X and then Monsieur X left and went into the café where Mum and Aunty Delphia were.

My phone vibrated. It was Mum. I ran to the café. Mum and Aunty Delphia were sitting right by the door. I sat down next to them and looked for the man. I couldn't see him. I looked again. I leaned way over. There he was, sitting at a table behind the cigarette machine. He was still wearing that coat and hat. His head was bent down. He was looking at something on the table. I got up.

'Where are you going?' asked Mum.

'The toilet.'

Mum looked at me.

'Can't you wait?'

'No, Mum, I can't.'

'I'll go with—'

'Mum!'

'Okay, but use the ladies'.'

I walked slowly past the man. He was too busy looking at the medal to notice me. I wanted to stop to see what the medal was like but I was scared he would look up and see me staring. I walked all the way to the back, to the toilets. I *did* need the toilet. I looked at the women's. I looked at the men's. I went to the men's.

When I walked back, I bumped into his table, not on purpose; the man looked up and he saw me.

'You're the boy,' he said. 'The one with Mr Brion.'

'Yes.'

'So, you're interested in medals?'

'Hmmm . . .'

'Just the Victoria Cross then, is that right? Is it for a school project?'

'Nnnn—'

'Robert.' Mum tapped me on the shoulder.

'Good afternoon,' Monsieur X said, lifting his hat. 'I was talking to this young fellow, Robert, about his interest in the Victoria Cross. We met at Mr Brion's stand.'

306

Mum looked at the man and then at the table. He had left the box with the medal open.

'Is that from Monsieur Brion?' Mum asked.

'Yes.'

'It's beautiful.'

'It's Russian. Cost quite a penny but worth it. They'll be happy. I—'

Mum's phone rang.

'Excuse me,' she said. She answered it. 'Okay, we're coming.'

She put the phone back in her bag. 'I'm sorry, we have to get going. Come on, Robert, Dad's waiting.'

'It was nice meeting you,' she said to Monsieur X.

Mum said that besides interesting objects, you never knew just *who* you would find at the market and what stories they carried with them.

As she was walking away, she turned to Monsieur X. 'You know, our neighbour has—'

'Mum!' I shouted. 'Let's go.' I grabbed her hand and pulled her out of the café. From outside, I saw him stand up and look at us. If he reached out his hand he could touch the ceiling. Was he going to follow us? But then he sat down again and wrote something on a piece of paper.

George had won his match 3–2. He had scored two goals, one of them a penalty. And he had made one assist. It was his last match for Lancy FC.

'I bossed them.'

He didn't have any pictures or videos to upload on

Facebook because Dad wasn't there to take them, so he just looked over all his Greatest Hits.

'George, do you know there's a book in Chinese called *The Art of War*?'

He was concentrating so hard on his past glories he didn't hear me. He was writing down his TOP TEN goals and linking them to video footage.

'George!'

'Huh?'

'A book in Chinese called *The ART of WAR*?'

'Yeah, Mr Lu told us.'

'Why is it called "art"?'

'I don't know.'

'What's it about?'

'How to boss a war. It was cool. Better than Confucius.'

'But why is it art?'

'Robert, who cares?'

I did, but I knew George would say, 'Do you want a biscuit?'

I went to Dad. He was taking apart a camera he'd bought at the market.

'Dad?'

'Yes?'

'Is war an art?'

Dad put the camera down. 'Is war an art?'

'There's a Chinese book that says it is. It was on Monsieur Brion's stand.'

'I think it's just a way of saying how to do war well.'

'What do you mean? You mean, like, kill more people?'

'*Forse no*, *forse si*, actually kill *fewer* people but still get what you want from the war, so if you're fighting to get more land, *maybe* it shows you how you can do this without losing too many of your soldiers or completely destroying the enemy.'

I thought about Dad's answer but I still didn't get why it was art.

'War can't be art, Dad. It's not beautiful.'

'That's right, it isn't, but maybe for some people the idea of a military campaign, the planning of it, its execution, that's what they think is beautiful, what they believe is an art.'

'So *anything* can be art.'

'You'll have to ask your mum that.'

And then I remembered something.

'Did you tell Mum about the lake, that it's having earthquakes and there could be a tsunami?'

'I did. But she's given up on the vampires.'

'Why?'

'She couldn't give them enough to think.'

I thought about her paper where she had crossed out *Blood*.

'She'll come up with something,' Dad said. 'She always does.'

What would Monsieur X do with the medal? Would he sell it at an auction? Would he put it on eBay? Would he keep it?

What was he writing down in the café?

And then I knew who he looked like.

THE GRIM REAPER in *Billy & Mandy*, except that he didn't speak with a Jamaican accent and I didn't think he was going to become my best friend forever any time soon.

He looked like he might have a scythe buried in his big baggy coat and that he'd use it to swipe off my head and take off with the medal. I had to be SO CAREFUL.

And then I almost fell over. Was I dumb?

The tall man.

Jack.

The very, very tall man.

Monsieur X was a very, very tall man.

Chapter Twenty-Five

The End of the World

It was the seventeenth of December. I looked at the Advent calendar Mum had got for me. It was Lego Star Wars. I hadn't opened any of the boxes. I hadn't even made my Christmas list. Mum noticed.

'Robert,' she said. 'Do I have to *force* you to make a list this year? You're running late.'

She was right. Last Christmas I started my list in September.

'Can't I do it on the twenty-second?'

She looked at me as if I wasn't well.

'The twenty-second! Of course not. I . . . Father Christmas can't get everything done in two days.'

At least he would have *two* days. In Italy he had to do it in *one* day because over there we opened our presents at midnight on the twenty-fourth; we kids could open ours straight after dinner, which was usually finished at about eleven o'clock.

'What's going on, Robert?'

'Nothing,' I said.

Mum put her hand on my forehead.

'You seem to be all right. I don't—'

'Ah, I think I know what it is.' Aunty Delphia had stopped her letter writing.

'What is it?' asked Mum.

'Nostradamus. The Mayan calendar.'

I nodded. 'Yes, Mum, he says the end of—'

'Yes, Robert, I know, but you're not falling for such a prank, you're too smart for that.'

'How do you *know* it's a prank?'

'Because he said it without any scientific proof or theory or logical reasoning.'

'And Robert,' said Aunty Delphia, 'the animals would tell us if something was coming up.'

'They would? How?'

'Well, for instance, before the tsunami, all the animals started trying to reach higher ground. They could feel the earth's vibrations long before humans could. By now we'd be seeing, for something as enormous as the end of the world, the animals doing very strange things.'

'And they aren't?'

'No. And you know I'm an expert. If the animals aren't convinced, the world's safe.'

I trusted the animals.

I opened the boxes of the Advent calendar in mega-fast time. I made up the figurines. The clone troopers, R2D2, Master Yoda. They looked cool. And then I started on my list. I looked up the list of the Young Sherlock Holmes books that I didn't have and wrote them down. I wrote down a booster pack for Skylanders. And then I couldn't think of anything else. What was happening to me? Was this it, my Christmas list? Sad. Was this growing up?

The phone rang. I was closest so I picked it up.

'*Bonjour.*'

'Good afternoon, grandson, is that you?'

It was Grandpa.

'Yes, Grandpa, it's me, Robert.'

'So, grandson, have you been putting that catapult to good use?'

'Not yet, Grandpa.'

'Not yet! Did I hear correctly? Are there not pigeons there still?'

'Yes there are, but we are not allowed to catapult them.'

'Not allowed! Who says this? Don't tell me it is your aunty with her animal rights who's preventing you. Bring her—'

'No, Grandpa, it's Geneva.'

'*Geneva? The police?* And so what do you do with these pigeons?'

'We feed them.'

'You *feed* them?'

'Not me, Grandpa. Other people, mostly an old woman who brings them packets of bread.'

'The birds over there are fed on bread. And what are people eating? The birds? So you have to strike them down with the catapult.'

'No, Grandpa. We're not allowed to eat the pigeons.'

'And why not?'

'Because . . . because . . . I don't know, Grandpa.'

'So what do these pigeons do, just get fat on people's bread?'

'Yes, Grandpa, and sometimes they come and make a mess on the balcony.'

'A mess, what kind of mess?'

'They poo on it.'

'What's *poo*?'

'You *know*.'

'Oh, you mean *ka ka*.'

Grandpa and Grandma came to Geneva once during Christmas, so Grandpa didn't see the pigeons and all the mess they made.

'Even the birds in Europe are spoilt. But I thought people there went hunting? Didn't you show me a forest, last time, where people hunt?'

'Yes, Grandpa.'

'So you must go with your catapult and hunt.'

'Yes, Grandpa. *Grandpa . . .*'

'Yes, grandson.'

'Are you a hero?'

'Am I a hero?'

'Yes. Aunty Delphia says you fought for the freedom of Zimbabwe.'

'I did, grandson. But that was a long time ago.'

'Aunty Delphia says you don't want to be a hero.'

Grandpa was silent for a long time, but I could hear him breathing.

'It is like this, grandson, in life you must do what you believe is right. A long time ago, for me, it was to go up to the mountains and fight with a gun. Now I am older

314

and I think, was that the right way to fight? Would it have been better to fight with knowledge? To educate myself to a high standard and to show the white man that, look, you think I am not a human being but I am a doctor and when you need a doctor do you think you will go running away because it is a black one, only if you are a complete idiot and then there is no hope for you. Do you understand, grandson?'

I didn't know if I really understood.

'So it's better *not* to fight?'

'No, no, I did not say that at all; you have to choose, and only the moment when you have to choose will you know which is the best way to fight; sometimes it is clear, sometimes it is not so.'

'Okay, Grandpa, bye, Grandpa.'

'Goodbye, grandson . . . wait, here's your grandmother.'

'Hello, Robert. How are you?'

'I'm fine, Grandma.'

'That's good to hear.'

'*Grandma . . .*'

'Yes?'

'What did you do while Grandpa was fighting?'

Grandma didn't say anything for a while. She coughed.

'You mean, in the bush war?'

I didn't know it was called that.

'The war to free Zimbabwe.'

'Yes. Well I was a nurse, my dear. I was working in a rural clinic. Just hold on, Robert, Grandpa wants to talk to you again.'

'Grandson, listen carefully now, your grandmother, she is the real hero. The *real* one. She raised her four sisters and two brothers *single-handedly* and she looked after the community *tirelessly.*'

Then Grandma came back on the phone.

'Goodbye, Robert, your parents will tell you our surprise later. Bye bye.'

Then they talked with Mum and Aunty Delphia.

It was the best surprise, ever!

Cynthia was coming to Geneva. She was coming with Grandma and Grandpa. Dad had arranged all the papers. They were going to be here for Christmas. Uncle Stewart, Aunty Madeline and Gregory would be here too. The house was going to be very full with the whole family.

I took out the medal. I put it in my palm. I blew on it. I lifted my palm right up to my mouth. I kissed the medal gently. I don't know why I did that.

The End of the World couldn't come.

Chapter Twenty-Six

The Festival of Lights

Tomorrow was the Festival of Lights at school. We were celebrating Christmas, Eid, Hanukkah, Diwali, Chinese New Year, Santa Lucia and St Nicholas. Our class was having an apple bobbing stand. I asked Jack if he wanted to come.

'What do you do?' he asked.

'Lots of stuff. There's games and face painting and Father Christmas, not the real one, just a fake one, and lots and lots of food. It's fun.'

'I don't know if Mum will let me.'

'You can come with us.'

'I'll ask her,' he said, but he didn't sound like he thought she would say yes.

We were in Mum's study. His mum was sleeping and he'd sneaked out.

Zeus's cage was between us. At least this time he wasn't hiding.

'Let's wake him up,' I said.

I opened the cage. I stroked Zeus gently like how Aunty Delphia showed me. I kept stroking until finally

317

he opened his eyes. He didn't look too upset. I put my hand under his stomach and lifted him out of the cage.

'Do you want to hold him?'

Jack shook his head.

I didn't know what to do with Zeus so I just put him down, which was a BIG mistake. He scurried away, and because I hadn't closed the door, he went straight outside the study.

'Mum!' I shouted 'Zeus's escaped! Close the doors!'

But it was too late. There were too many open doors. Too many hiding places. He could be anywhere now.

Everyone was called into action, even George.

Mum was cross. The rodent was going to go everywhere.

'He better not be in the kitchen,' she said.

We searched and searched. We couldn't find him anywhere.

We took all the cushions away from the couches. We looked in boxes, under the heaters, behind the curtains. Nothing. Zeus was gone.

'Probably cat food,' said George.

'George!' shouted Mum.

There was a cat next door. What if . . . what if Zeus had dashed out of the door and the cat had found him; what if Zeus was freezing outside and he caught a cold or pneumonia or froze to death—

'I found him!' called Aunty Delphia.

Aunty Delphia was in my bedroom.

'Oh no!' shouted Mum.

There were books scattered all over the floor. Zeus was in Aunty Delphia's palm.

'He was behind your comics,' she said. She gave him to me. He was fast asleep.

'Thank-you, Aunty.'

'Robert . . .' Mum's voice sounded strange, and then I saw what she was looking at.

The medal box was on the floor.

She picked it up.

'Is this what I think it is?'

'Mum, I—'

'Busted,' said George.

Mum opened the box. She looked at the medal and then she looked at me.

'I am very disappointed in you, Robert,' she said.

Mum had never ever been disappointed in me before.

'Did I hear wrongly or did you not say that you had given this medal back to Monsieur Renoir?'

'It's not his,' I said.

'Robert!'

She looked over at Jack.

'Jack, you'll have to go home now,' she said.

'Mum—'

She didn't even look at me.

'Goodbye, Jack.'

When Jack had left, Mum told George to leave the room too. And Aunty Delphia. And then it was just Mum and me.

She sat down on my bed.

'Why did you lie, Robert?'

I couldn't open my mouth.

'Robert, I want some answers.'

'I . . . I didn't want Gregory to start touching it.'

'Gregory . . . what . . .?'

Mum looked like she was going through things in her head, remembering.

'Oh,' she said. 'And when Gregory was gone, why did you continue to lie?'

It was like Mum was an echo of Dad.

'I . . .' I didn't know where to begin, how to explain it to Mum. 'I have to keep it safe,' I said.

'It's Monsieur Renoir's medal.'

'It isn't.'

'Robert—'

'He told me.'

'He *told* you?'

'Yes, he wrote a letter. I showed it to Aunty Delphia.'

Mum's eyes opened wide.

'Can I see this letter.'

Mum wasn't asking me. She was telling me.

I took the letters from my backpack.

She read them all. She shuffled the papers and she read them again.

She put the medal on my shelf.

'We'll talk about this when your dad gets home.'

'I'm sorry, Mum.'

Mum looked at me and then she gave me a hug.

'You're growing,' she said. She ruffled my hair and then she left the room with the letters.

I looked down at Zeus. I wasn't mad that he had

knocked down the books. I was happy that the cat hadn't got him.

And I don't know why, but it was okay that Mum knew.

I lay down on my bed and I put Zeus on my chest.

I fell asleep.

I heard Dad's voice. First I thought it was in my dream, but then I felt his hand on my forehead. Was he checking my temperature? I opened my eyes.

'I hear you're in trouble,' he said. He lifted Zeus from my chest. 'And I hear this guy is partly responsible.'

I sat up.

'Can I take a look at this medal?'

I took the box from the shelf and opened it.

'And you think it is real?'

I nodded.

'Your mother says you want to keep it safe.'

I nodded. 'But it's damaged, Dad.'

I took the medal from the box and turned it over.

The holes didn't look like they were any bigger.

'I think we should give it back to Monsieur Renoir, Robert.'

'But it's not his.'

'That may be so, but it's his responsibility to fix what he did wrong.'

'But he wants *me* to fix it, Dad.'

'He shouldn't have given it to you and he shouldn't have asked you to make it right. We have to give it back to him.'

'Can we wait, Dad, until he comes back?'

Dad looked down at the medal.

'Dad, we can't give it to that lady. She'll sell it. We can't.'

Dad sighed.

'Okay, Robert. When Monsieur Renoir comes back from the hospital, we give it to him. Agreed?'

'Yes, Dad.'

I didn't get punished for lying, because Mum said I'd learnt an important moral lesson. George said that was just typical, I was such a *chouchou. Even if you burn the house down they'll be saying, oh, our* chou, *it's not his fault, it's okay . . . GEORGE, why did you leave those matches lying around . . .* So I could go to the Festival of Lights. Jack could come too. His mum wasn't home most of the time. She'd found some English people near the train station and she drank beer around there.

The school was all lit up. I showed Jack my star on the Christmas tree. My wish at the back of it was for PEACE, which George said was what dumb blondes in beauty contests wished for all the time and *they* never got it. He was lucky Mum didn't hear him because I was sure she would have told him off for making use of stereotypes again. Anyway, if dumb blondes wished for peace, they weren't so dumb. I had put a lot of glitter on my star to cover up the splodges of jam and milk; I made the star while snacking. I took Jack upstairs to the cafeteria where all the stalls were set. I had twenty francs to spend.

Jin was waving at me from a stall at the back.

'Come,' I said to Jack. 'My best friend's over there.'

I started walking, but when I turned round, Jack was still standing in the same spot.

'Come on, Jack.'

But he wouldn't move.

I had invited him here so he was my guest and I had to look after him. That was one of Mum's golden rules.

I went back to where he was standing.

'What's wrong?'

'I want to go back home,' he said.

'Why, it's fun here.'

'Robert, you should see those toys over there. They're made of wire.' Jin had come over.

'Come on, Jack.'

'Come on, Robert.'

I didn't know what else to do; I just took Jack's hand and pulled him along. He didn't snatch his hand away. He let me pull him along. I knew that the triplets, if they saw me, would call me *gay*, but I didn't care. Jack was afraid and lonely and I was just being his friend, kinda like an older brother, and that felt good.

We looked at the wire toys. They *were* cool. There were animals: giraffes and elephants and frogs with beads fixed on them, but the best things were the cars and the airplanes. And there were some made from soda cans *and* wire.

Over by the vending machines, George was signing

autographs for some star-struck fifth- and sixth-graders. And I was sure he was making them pay.

Mum bought us some samosas from the Indian stall and we ate them watching the girls getting their hands painted with henna. Wendy was there. I hoped Jin wasn't going to start with the girlfriend business.

'Hi, Robert.'

'Hi, Wendy.'

I looked around to see if the triplets were around. Nope.

She had a red dot on her forehead and she kept touching it.

'It's a bindi,' she said. 'It's my third eye.'

'Huh?' said Jin.

'That's what Fatima's mother said. Look at Fatima. She's wearing a sari.'

'Huh?' said Jin.

'It's what Indians normally wear when they're in India.'

'Huh?' said Jin.

'I can moonwalk,' she said. 'Watch.'

And she did.

'That's so cool,' I said.

'I learnt it from *How to Do Everything*.'

'Wow,' said Jin, but he said it the way George would have said it. Was he becoming a teenager before his time?

And then Jack just slid across the floor. He was so smooth it was like the floor had grease and he was sliding through it. And he was just eight years old.

'How . . . how did you do that?' I asked. 'Did you learn it from a book?'

He shook his head.

'You could enter a competition or something. You should show George, he'll be so jealous.'

George thought *he* had all the moves. And *I* had the moves like Mick Jagger.

'He— Hey, look at that giant!'

I looked to where Jin was pointing.

It was him.

The Grim Reaper, standing by the bake sale, and he was looking right in my direction.

'Oh,' said Jack, 'Mum.'

Standing beside the Grim Reaper was Jack's mother.

She was wearing a really short, shiny skirt and she had stockings with lots of holes in them.

Jack walked slowly towards her.

'Hello, love,' she said. 'I thought I'd pop in, check out the sights.' She made a funny noise – a laugh, a cough, a shriek. People were staring at her. 'And look who I found snooping about outside the flat.'

She turned to the Grim Reaper.

'What did you say your name was again, love?'

She was tugging on the Grim Reaper's sleeve.

'Richard,' he said. 'Richard Low.'

And something banged in my head.

'That's right, Richard. This is my son, Jack. Remember him? Named him after the miserable old git.'

L.

She was pinching Jack's arm. She almost toppled over. I knew what she was. She was drunk.

'Richard here's done investigations and he thinks your great-grandad might have something that doesn't belong to him.'

She looked up at the Grim Reaper.

'Doesn't he?'

The Grim Reaper nodded.

L for Low.

'Perhaps we should talk about this outside,' he said.

Jack's mother was staggering around, still clutching Jack's arm.

'He says he'll make it worth our while if we give him what he wants.'

Jack's head was shaking.

'So have you seen what this gentleman's looking for, Jack? You seen the medal?'

Don't tell them, Jack. Don't tell them.

She was twisting Jack's ear.

'Excuse me, is there a problem here?'

The principal! Mrs Drake! Dracula! Jack's mother and the Grim Reaper had met their match!

'No, no problem at all,' said the Grim Reaper. 'We were just stepping outside.'

Dracula looked at Jack's mother, who had let go of Jack and was holding on to the Grim Reaper to keep from falling.

'Good,' Dracula said and watched them go downstairs.

I followed them.

And then when they were outside and Jack's mum started going after Jack again, I did the right thing.

'I have it,' I said.

She let go of Jack.

'Monsieur Renoir gave it to me.'

'Monsieur what?'

'Jack's great-grandad. He gave it to me. And I'm not giving it to you. It doesn't belong to him, it doesn't belong to any of you.'

'Listen, you, I'll—'

She lunged towards me. She bumped into Jack, almost knocking him over.

'I'll—'

And then Mum and Dad were standing next to me.

'What's going on here?' said Dad.

'That boy has our property,' said Jack's mum.

'What do you mean it doesn't belong to Monsieur Renoir, as you call him?' the Grim Reaper asked me.

'He stole it,' I said.

'Well,' said the Grim Reaper, 'that's precisely why I want it.'

I didn't understand what he meant. Did he want to steal it too?

'Young man, I'm a private investigator.'

'Like Sherlock Holmes?'

He smiled, kind of.

'Not quite as esteemed, I'm afraid, although I am somewhat renowned in my field. Sometimes I am hired by people to find lost or stolen things. In this particular matter I have been hired by a family who are in the process of tracing their family history and heirlooms. They wish to find the medal of their relative. It was stolen from the Museum of Military History in South Africa.'

He took out a notebook from his coat pocket. It was just like mine! He opened it and flipped through the pages. He took out a picture. He stepped closer to me and stretched out his arm. He showed me the picture.

'That's the young man the medal belongs to.'

It was a picture of a soldier in his uniform. He looked very smart. It reminded me of something, and then I remembered. Nonno.

He told us the soldier's name.

I recognized it! But something was wrong and I didn't know what.

He opened his notebook again, turned some pages.

'It was awarded to him when he was a private in the infantry. He was cited for his actions in 1916 when, severely injured himself, he moved on to open ground and saved three fellow soldiers. A reward – now at five thousand pounds – has been offered for information leading to the medal's safe return.'

PRIVATE INFANTRY 1916 REWARD – the words were ringing in my head.

'The medal's ours,' said Jack's mother.

'If it is the medal I've been looking for, I'm afraid your grandfather is guilty of a crime and liable to prosecution.'

'What, you're going to arrest him in hospital, are you?'

She grabbed Jack's arm. 'Come on, Jack, let's get out of here.'

As she turned to go, she glared at the Grim Reaper.

'You'll be hearing from my lawyer.'

When they had left, I looked at the Grim Reaper. Something *was* wrong. And then I knew what it was.

'But I investigated all the privates and none of them were awarded the Victoria Cross for an action in 1916,' I said.

Richard Low looked at me and nodded, then he flipped through some pages of his notebook.

'You're right,' he said. 'The medal was awarded when he was still a private, but he later became a captain. So maybe you eliminated the captain candidate.'

I nodded. That could make sense.

'So you think it's his?'

'I do,' the Grim Reaper said.

He dug in his pocket again, took out a card and gave it to Dad.

'You can check my credentials here, and you can talk to a family member. The reward is still in place.'

Dad took the card and looked at it for a bit, then he put it in his pocket.

'How did you find Monsieur Renoir?' I asked.

'That,' he said, 'was good old-fashioned legwork. I went to South Africa, to the museum. I looked at their records. Your Monsieur Renoir, also known as Jack

Montgomery Clift, arrived at the museum on April the twentieth at ten past eleven – he signed his name in the visitors' book; he was the only visitor at that time. The medal was discovered missing the next morning. During that time the museum had seven visitors. Six were part of a supervised tour and were monitored by the guide at all times, so it's highly unlikely the thief would be among them. Jack Montgomery Clift, on the other hand, roamed about on his own. He should have been the prime suspect, but this was South Africa just before the end of Apartheid; it was unthinkable that an English gentleman could be accused of such a theft, so suspicion naturally fell on the black staff. The medal was never recovered. I tracked Jack Montgomery Clift finally to Geneva, whose environs, as you witnessed yourself in Nyon, another case took me to. In addition, there has been a picture of a medal posted on Facebook that led me to believe it might really be here.'

George!

So he wasn't the Grim Reaper. He was a good guy.

'Do you think she's going to be any trouble?' Dad asked him.

I knew Dad meant Jack's mum.

'I don't think so. She'll get whatever she can get.'

I had been thinking about everything he had said. And then I knew what else didn't fit, what still didn't make sense.

'But why would Monsieur Renoir put his name down in the visitors' book if he wanted to steal something?

That's so . . .' I looked for a word and I found George's, 'lame'.

'That *is* a mystery,' said Richard Low, ace investigator. 'Perhaps he'll answer that question himself.'

Chapter Twenty-Seven

Peace and Conflict

But we couldn't ask Monsieur Renoir, because he had died in the hospital.

We found this out the next day. It was Monsieur Badon who told Mum. He caught an infection. He died late at night. He was alone.

Jack was sitting on the heaters in the foyer. I used to like sitting there until George told me it would make my penis shrivel up and snap off. Even though I knew it wasn't really true, I had a phobia about it now. It's like the phobia he gave me about bananas. I used to love bananas. I used to eat them all the time. And then George, who hates fruit, told me that bananas dance when they're in your stomach and they do the splits. And that was it. I couldn't eat a banana ever again, not even Mum's super-special banana cake. I didn't tell Jack about the heaters and the penis. He was sitting there, his head on his knees, his hands covering his head. I could hear him sniffing; he was trying to smother the noise of his crying. I stood next to him.

'Hi, Jack,' I said.

He didn't move.

'I'm sorry, Jack.'

I sat down next to him. Too bad for my penis. This was important.

Jack turned his head towards me. His face was wet with tears.

'I'm really sorry,' I said.

Jack sniffed and nodded.

'Mum's happy.'

'Why?'

'She says we're rich now. She's going to sell everything in the flat.'

'Everything?'

'Or throw it away.'

'And the medal?'

Jack shrugged. 'I took this.'

He unwrapped his arms from his knees; the book with the animal patch was lying on his thighs.

'Take it,' he said, 'in case Mum comes.'

I didn't want to take it. I already had the medal. I already had the picture. I felt like I had enough of Monsieur Renoir's things.

'No, that's all right. Keep it.'

'It's Great-Grandad's,' Jack said.

'I know.'

'It's important.'

I knew it was.

'A grown-up should have it.'

He shook his head.

'Great-Grandad wants you to have it.'

'That's—'

I almost said 'crazy', but I stopped myself in time.

'He told me.'

'Where?'

'In the hospital.'

That gave me the chills. His great-grandpa was dead. And then I remembered the letter where he said he was a ghost. I was really spooked.

'We went to see him before. Mum went to get something to eat. He grabbed my hand and said . . .'

It was like listening to a ghost story. I wanted to get up and run across the foyer, up the steps into our apartment, and lock the door behind me.

'. . . give Robert the book.'

I jumped.

'He said that? He said my name?'

'Yes.'

'Did he say which book?'

Jack shrugged.

I thought about that.

'How did he know we'd find the book?'

Jack shrugged again.

'Take it,' he said.

We both heard the lift door opening at the same time. Jack threw the book on my lap; it slipped on to the floor and I lunged for it and put it in the waistband of my jeans. I stretched my T-shirt over it. I shivered. The furry patch on the book was pricking my skin.

It was George. He was on his way to football practice

and he just gave the two of us a nod and carried on walking.

'I'll see you later,' I said to Jack. I walked a couple of steps and then I stopped. I turned round.

'Why don't we read it together?'

It would be safer. It was his great-grandpa's after all. He shook his head.

'I can invite Jin for a sleepover. We can all read it.'

Jack shook his head again. He was scared of the book. Did he think something would leap out of it? Thinking that made me almost drop it.

'He's getting burned,' he said.

'Who?'

'Great-Grandad.'

I almost said how can he be burned if he's already dead, and then I remembered it was the burning when you were already dead. He was getting cremated. I didn't know what to say to that. To be honest, I didn't want to think of Monsieur Renoir lying in flames getting burnt. I kept thinking, even if he was dead, he would feel the flames. They would hurt. And then I could hear him laughing and screaming and smiling that crocodile-like smile.

'Mum says she's not taking the ashes back to England. She said for all she cares, she's going to throw him down the chute, that would serve him right for being a real pain in the arse.'

I just wanted him to stop. Now I had to think of Monsieur Renoir stuck in the chute. I would never be able to throw rubbish down there again.

He gave me a little wave, which was strange. He had never waved goodbye to me before. I wanted to say something nice about Monsieur Renoir because I could tell that he really cared about his great-grandpa, but all I could think of was, 'He had a blazing eye,' and Jack nodded.

I didn't know what to do with the book.

I put it in my backpack. But I didn't like thinking that it was there, so I took it out. I looked around my room and wedged it in with my other books. And that didn't look right either. I left it there and walked about the apartment. Aunty Delphia was cooking in the kitchen. She was having a good day. Dad was still at work. Mum was in the lounge, reading. I went into her study. I rolled up the magic carpet and tiptoed back to my room. I unrolled the carpet and looked down at it and then I took the book from the shelf and put it in the middle of the carpet and rolled it up again. I pushed the carpet under the bed.

I dragged the carpet from under the bed. I unrolled it. The book was not there. I closed my eyes and opened them again just in case they were playing tricks on me. I looked and looked at the carpet. I patted it down as if the book was hiding somewhere. I swiped my hand under the bed – it hit something hard, an edge of something, a book! I dragged it out – *Garfield*. I wriggled under the bed, moved my arms and legs around. There was nothing. I came back out again. I coughed. I sneezed. How could it just disappear? How could it just not be there? I knew it was crazy but I had the creepy feeling that Monsieur Renoir had changed his mind. He wanted the book back and he had come to get it. Monsieur Renoir, the ghost, like he said he was. I looked everywhere in the room in case . . . in case . . . I had rolled it in the carpet and put the carpet under the bed; that was the only place it could be, but I still looked because the book wasn't where it was supposed to be. It was gone. Maybe I was dreaming. Maybe this wasn't real after all. I pinched myself. It hurt. Did you feel pain in dreams? I didn't know. I went out and stood in the hallway. I looked at all of Mum's Chagalls and I just wanted to get into one of them and float in the sky too. I looked closer, I don't know, in case somehow the book had been spirited away there. Nothing. The house was really quiet. When I listened more I could hear George muttering something. He was in the lounge. He was rapping. I think it was his own lyrics.

Yeah . . . yeah . . . yeah . . . yeah . . . yeah . . .

That's how it sounded to me; the stuff in between I couldn't work out.

'George . . .'

'Yeah . . . yeah . . .'

'George, have you seen—'

'Yeah . . . yeah . . . yo . . .' His eyes were closed; he was waving his hand in the air.

'George!'

'What? I'm in the flow here. Can't you see I need my dough—'

He slapped his book shut, and that was when I saw it.

337

It was Monsieur Renoir's book!

George was writing lyrics, *rap lyrics, yeah yeahs and yo yos*, in Monsieur Renoir's book!

'George!'

I snatched the book from him.

'What the heck! Give it back!'

'No, you took it from me.'

'It's not yours.'

'It is.'

'Prove it.'

I couldn't think of anything to say.

'Thought so,' said George. He snatched it back.

'It's Monsieur Renoir's. Give it back, George. Please.'

'Monsieur Renoir's dead.'

'Can I look at it, George? Please.'

'Hey, chillax,' he said. He stretched out his hand. 'Don't read my stuff. Copyrighted.'

I took the book. I turned the pages carefully. There were four pages of George's *yeahs* and *yos* and then blank after blank. There was nothing on the pages. No writing. I had a bad feeling.

'George, did you . . . did you tear some pages out?'

'No, moron, now give it back.'

Maybe, maybe Monsieur Renoir had written things down with invisible ink!

I ran to the playroom.

'Robert! I'm going to kill you!'

'Just a minute!'

I rummaged around in my spy drawer. I took out:
my evidence kit

338

my spy camera
my spy binoculars
my spy radio set
my spy handset
and there it was, my infrared torch that could read invisible ink.

I flashed it on the pages. I fixed my eyes on them. There was . . . NOTHING. It wasn't possible. It just wasn't possible. What did it mean? I was so confused.

I ran into my room. I put the book under my pillow, which was an obvious hiding place but I was in a hurry because I could hear Mum and Aunty Delphia. They were back from the doctor's. The one you talk to.

George shouldered me in the passageway.

'You better hand it over after my football practice, or else,' he whispered.

'Hand over what?' asked Mum.

'Nothing,' I said. 'Just bro stuff.'

George gave me the evil eye. And behind his back, he did the gun sign. I flashed him my peace sign.

While Mum and Aunty Delphia were having tea in the kitchen, I went back to my room. I took the book out. I looked through its pages again and it was just like before. There was absolutely nothing. I felt the furry bit. It still grossed me out. I touched the leather parts. I tugged the string. Nothing. I opened the book to page one of George's lyrics:

Yeah . . . the stars are out, yeah, there's no one about, yeah, my eyes open wide, this is something

that I cannot abide, yeah, I look at the sky, I wish
I could just fly . . . away

from here cause I'm scared, yeah, I wasn't prepared
for this, yeah, just sitting here

in this cold place alone, I look around, yeah, it
feels as if people are watching me.

I wish my mom was here at least she could console
me. Yeah, I think I need her, yeah.

I close my eyes and count to three, I'm so happy
that my friends can't see

me like this, yeah, they would laugh at me to the
end of eternity. I look outside, I

see the wolves. They start howling, yeah, I start
scowling after all I already made a

call to 117 and they said they would be here in an
hour, yeah, it already feels like a

year. I start to scream. I close my eyes hoping that
this is just a bad dream, yeah, I

mean I'm only a teen I'm not ready for this, yeah.
I hear the hiss of the wind, yeah.

*That's when they come. I see my mum and my
dad, man I'm so happy that*

*they are here and my mind clears. Yeah, I'm home
and I see my bro, he hugs me. Yeah. It's all good,
yeah. Yeah.*

Now they made sense, not when George *rapped* the
words.

I looked at the book's spine. And then at the space
where the pages of the book were stuck to the leather.
There was a little gap there. I couldn't see through it
properly, all the way inside. I strapped on my Lego
torch and looked. And there it was. A piece of paper
stuck on the inside. It was all rolled up so that it
looked like a straw. I needed something long and thin
to get it out. It was going to be a delicate operation.
I went to Mum's bathroom cabinet and found the
thing she used for pulling out hairs growing out of
her chin. Tweezers. She said women usually used them
for pulling out the hairs from their eyebrows. When
I asked her why, she said that they thought it made
them look more beautiful. That was just weird. I took
the tweezers to my room and I put it down the spine
of the book. I clamped it round the piece of paper and
then I pulled. I was afraid I would rip it up or break
the book so I kept pulling and stopping, pulling and
stopping. Finally it was out. Yes, it was a roll of paper.
I would have to read it like a scroll. I began to unwind
it. I read.

I knew you were clever, BOY
The Last Will and Testament of
Jack Montgomery Clift

All my worldly goods I bequeath to my great-grandson, my namesake, Jack Clift.

My sins I bequeath to God to do with as he sees fit.

To the family of Luke (surname unknown) I bequeath the truth as set forth in the following pages.

I do hereby solemnly swear that the following confession is written while clear of mind and judgement and that it can be used in a court of law as a legally binding document.

I, Jack Montgomery Clift, served in the Kenya police force from 1953 to 1955 during the height of the Mau Mau insurrection. This was not the posting I had envisioned for myself as a boy or indeed as a young man, but after failure to qualify for the Royal Air Force pilot training course and longing for some kind of adventure to get away from the tedium of my life as a clerk in Manchester, I sought to join the colonial service. I was steered towards the police services. I arrived in Kenya fresh from my training and with an eagerness to prove wrong what I considered to be my instructor's condescending views of my abilities. I took to life in Kenya like a fish to water. I found that I made friends easily there and threw myself into the way of life. I took up with people with means and was thus able to join hunting parties when I was off duty. But how I envied those air force pilots who climbed

342

into their Lincolns and soared high above us dropping their pretty bombs into the forest, and who later would meet at the officers' mess and coolly smoke and drink as though they hadn't a care in the world. They did not have to involve themselves with the hard slog of on-the-ground clearance of the Mau Mau menace. They were not innocent bunnies, the Mau Mau. They were breathtakingly cruel, to their own people above all, their blood oaths binding each member to the tribe, their oath of allegiance breakable only by death.

I was not the only policeman who was afraid. My fellow service members were just the same. And so we acted rashly to conceal our fear of a rabid enemy that thought nothing of torching huts with women and children in them, annihilating whole European families in their homesteads with their pangas and machetes. We were really in the Heart of Darkness.

In time we met like with like. Our cruelty would match, surpass theirs.

And now to the crux of it.

It was Tuesday, 18 October 1955.

I was at the station when reports came in of the sighting of suspected Mau Mau sympathizers, some twenty kilometres from Nairobi. Following operational procedures we set out: three white policemen and approximately thirty homeguards.

I was put in charge of interrogations. This was a promotion of sorts. It was time to prove my worth. I would extract the relevant information by what-ever means it took. I had been witness to several

343

interrogations and I had no illusions as to what was expected, or required.

We reached the village just after ten o'clock. Our arrival had been communicated by the bush telegraph system, so that when we got there we were met by a scene of abandonment. No men were present (that, not much of a surprise), as those not working in Nairobi were, as customary, already soused out at the local beer hall. No women, not in the fields, and not a child ran ragged between the huts, not a thing, even the animals seemed to have fled, not a single African dog, emaciated beyond decency. This abandonment was taken as an admission of guilt by the officers. Orders were given. The huts were torched. We set out in our vehicles to the beer halls and the clinics and the schools and the village hall and we gathered about twenty or so of the villagers. We were reasonable in our demands.

Who are the supporters of the Mau Mau?

We went to each one individually.

Tell us, who is it who supports those murderers?

All lips were sealed.

I had in my hand a grenade. Ridiculous, how it came to be in my hand. One of the homeguards had given it to me as if it was just a child's toy. You pull the pin, then you must throw, he said, and then wait and see. He smiled. His teeth so brilliantly white against his black skin. Try, sir, just try it, it's crazy. These people, they are terrified of these things. They will speak. Aim it for their cattle.

I was proud of my grenade. We policemen always egged each other on about what we had done out there in the bush, what ingenious ways of extracting information we had come up with. And so, when all the questioning and the threats yielded nothing, not a shred of information, I stepped forward into the breach, and the grenade was in my hand like some exotic fruit. The villagers moved back from me. They knew what I held; its capacity for damage.

'One last chance,' I said. 'And then we will get the truth by other means.'

And still they refused to talk. The fear was even deeper in their eyes now that they saw what power I wielded in my hand, but the Mau Mau powers were stronger than mine and this fed my anger, my rage.

'You will not talk,' I said. 'Well then, perhaps this will help to jog your memories.'

I walked ten paces from them and I looked out into an open space. As if by God's grace, a goat had wandered there, and now two chickens and a cow. I looked at all this, which was the village's bounty, together with the straggling maize, and I took out the pin in the manner that I had only just been shown, and I heard somewhere, 'Steady on there,' and I arched my hand and threw the thing and then, only then, as my exotic fruit flew over the field, a figure came darting out running, his arms open above his head as if he meant to catch my fruit. It was his act of surrender – here was our Mau Mau sympathizer – but it was the fruit that got him, that silenced him.

First there was the silence after the explosion. A collective shock.

And then the screams. The unending screams.

No one wanted to know.

No one would look me in the eye – an ironical figure of speech, because I had lost an eye in the explosion – some flying fragment, a piece from the stalk of the straggling maize perhaps, pierced through the retina.

To make matters worse, a Labour Member of Parliament had jetted in, knowing nothing of the realities of serving in this darkest corner of empire, to investigate charges that white policemen had tortured and killed innocent Kikuyu with government-sanctioned impunity. She compared us to Nazis.

I was discharged from the service, full pension and the rest of it to keep things quiet.

I was no longer a wanted man in Kenya.

My friends disappeared.

I went back to England, lived there for some time, and then fled once again. I took off to South Africa. That was in the 1960s, and as luck would have it, there was money to be made. I had lived a frugal life in England, squirrelling my savings, and it was with these that I bought shares in a little diamond franchise. I became moderately wealthy.

Life was good in the Cape, but I was unsettled. I tried my hand in a variety of enterprises, working for a time in a vineyard. I settled finally for opening some grocery shops. Steady and reliable income, for everyone has to eat.

I married. Elizabeth. A fine woman who had come to South Africa from the home country to find herself a husband such as me, who she supposed was a gentleman.

Many years passed in relative tranquillity. The birth of two children: a son, Jack, a daughter, Alice. The death of Alice by drowning.

And finally the death of my beloved wife.

I was once again at sea. Nothing seemed to give me pleasure. I had few friends and my son was away at university in England. Truth be told, we were not close. I hardly knew what to do with myself because at a certain point money seems to make itself.

Until the day when, visiting the South African Museum of Military History, I saw it.

That Victoria Cross.

That emblem of bravery and honour.

Valour.

I wanted it, in that instant, for myself.

What drove me, I cannot tell.

It was an impulse that overtook me. There it was, unprotected. Who would think that anyone would want to steal such a thing, would have so little shame as to claim another man's sacrifice for his own? And a man like me who had done what he had.

But I saw it and I wanted it.

I took it.

It was a compulsion. It left me with no choice, no free will. The cross was everything that I was not, and seeing it lying there, I needed it in my hands to know

347

the truth of that. Once it was in my hands, it was no long journey to my pocket. I waited for something to happen, for God, perhaps, to point his finger of judgement at me, but the room was silent. There was no ringing alarm bell. No cameras. No guards to come tearing in and tussle me to the ground. In that museum of war there were images and artefacts of brutality: the First and Second World Wars, the Boer War, when once again we English had sought to do our duty and had somehow become infected by the darkness of this continent, where in the scorching heat so much evil and savagery abides. Who knew now, with the terrorist released, a man they deemed their freedom fighter like the Mau Mau before them, what other wars would be fought in these lands? But there was also much in the museum that was good and noble and true and should have made any man think twice of tainting it with theft, and for a man such as me who had allowed darkness into his soul, it was unthinkable, unforgivable.

It was a restless night I spent with the medal in my possession. I did not know where to put it. I was seized by paranoia. At any moment the police might break down my door, drag me from my bed, shame me in the newspapers, and my son, my son, the horror of it. But they did not come. Not that night, nor any night after. A write-up in the paper, a mere mention of the theft, a few lines. That was all.

I fled South Africa. Times were uncertain for the white man. Black majority rule, well, I had experience of the ruthless capabilities of a black majority. I sold my *assets. My only regret lay in having lacked the foresight to bury my beloved daughter and wife in England.*

I settled first back in Manchester, but, having invested substantial assets in Switzerland, I decamped once again, this time for Geneva, like many Englishmen have done over the centuries.

It is here that I have set eyes on a boy who every school day takes the steps up to his apartment on the fourth floor, singing. I've watched you time and time again through my peephole as you sing your way up the stairs. On that day when I screamed at you for the noise you and your brother were making, it was only because that day, that day was the very anniversary of the boy's death, the boy whose picture I keep in my possession, pressed into my hands by the heartbroken father that I should forever remember.

The medal I found while clearing things. I have come to an age when death is no longer foe but a welcome respite. So long I had forgotten this particular treachery, but when my eyes set upon it I was once again swept to that day when I stood alone before the casement and saw it. How easy it was to lift the glass lid (had someone forgotten to lock it?) and simply take what was not mine. I rediscovered the medal and saw the damage underneath, the name of the private eaten away by damp, for I had not taken care in its storage.

And then – I hesitate to write this for I am not, in truth, a religious man, but I will write it – a miracle happened. You, in your innocence, wrote me a note and my eyes fall on it now:

349

Dear Monsieur Renoir,

My Aunty Delphia has been put in jail in Zimbabwe by the president. I know that you have special powers. You have Knowledge. You will know the right thing to do. Please help her. Please write back and tell me what we have to do to save her.

How the note agitated me, as though you had seen through me. It was the use of that word: Knowledge. I had Knowledge, you wrote. And that Knowledge seemed to me to be the medal. I knew what I had done. I wrote to you in my vexed state. Perhaps I frightened you with the cryptic nature of my words.

I tried to do the right thing, to find a way to return it, but my courage failed me. You were standing by the stairs, the box dropped, the medal lost for a moment. I had heard you say, 'Monsieur Renoir . . .' – no, it was a question, 'Monsieur Renoir?', as if you wanted something from me. I asked you what it was you wanted, but you fled.

On another day, as I held the medal in my hands, I heard you clatter up the steps, I saw you take a step towards the door, and then another. Your face was right against the door. I watched you raise your hand. Would you dare ring the bell? Your hand went to the bell and then you pulled it back and then you knocked gently on my door. You did not wait for me. You scrambled upstairs. I opened my door and stood outside holding the medal, and it was decided for me. I stepped in the lift and left the medal there on the doormat for you to find. And you will do what is fitting and right.

I put all my trust in you, Robert.

I thought of everything I knew:

Monsieur Renoir hadn't been a Royal Air Force pilot.

He wanted to be a pilot but he had failed the tests.

He had become a policeman instead.

He had done something terrible in Kenya.

He had killed a boy.

The boy had come running, his arms stretched out, waiting to catch not a bomb, but something whizzing through the air. A grenade.

Monsieur Renoir had stolen a medal.

Monsieur Renoir had chosen me to do the right thing.

And now I knew what it was.

I showed the will to Dad and Mum. Dad went downstairs to show it to Jack's mum. He wasn't there for very long. He said she said that she didn't need that piece of paper; Monsieur Renoir had already signed everything over in the hospital.

'It all belongs to Jack,' I said.

And I thought of Jack with the animals and the drums and the masks and the spears and the eggs.

The crocodile.

He would look after them.

*

Dad checked out Richard Low's story and he said that all the pieces fitted. He was who he said he was. Then he showed me the newspaper articles where he had returned lost or stolen medals to families.

'He's a good guy,' I said to Dad.

'Looks like it, Robert.'

Dad took me to the airport.

I opened the box one last time. I looked at the medal.

I felt happy and sad.

I was happy because the medal was going back home.

I was sad because it had become like a friend.

I would miss it.

I hoped they could fix the back.

Would they put the captain's . . . the private's name back on?

Mr Richard Low was off to a new case already. He was standing by the newsagent still wearing that coat. Did he ever take it off?

It was time.

I held out the box.

'Here it is,' I said to Mr Low. I gave him the medal.

'Thank you, Robert,' he said. 'I'll make sure the family gets it back. You're a real hero.'

There was a removals van leaving the parking lot when we got back. The removals men were closing the doors. Inside the van were brown boxes. I told Dad that I would take the stairs. Monsieur Renoir's door was open.

Monsieur Badon was standing outside.

'*Bonjour, Robert,*' he said.

'*Bonjour, Monsieur Badon.*'

He was starting to close the door.

'*Puis-je aller dans l'appartement?*' I asked him. '*Seulement pour un instant, s'il vous plaît?*'

Monsieur Badon shrugged and then he pushed the door wide open.

'*Vas-y,*' he said.

I stepped inside.

It was dark in the hallway as before.

I stepped further in.

Everything was gone.

There were no animals on the walls, on the ceiling. No teeth and tusks. There were no stools made from elephant legs. No crocodile hiding underneath a table. No eggs waiting to hatch on the table. No drums. No spears. No masks. It had all disappeared.

Only the smell remained.

'*Ils sont tous partis,*' Monsieur Badon said behind me.

I hadn't said goodbye to Jack.

'*Le garçon a laissé quelque chose pour vous.*'

I turned round.

Monsieur Badon had a piece of paper in his hand. I took it from him. I looked down.

It had where Jack lived in England.

I laughed out loud.

He lived in Plymouth!

Chapter Twenty-Eight

A Boy's Tale

It was the day after Christmas. I woke up very early. It was quiet and still around me. I got out of bed and tiptoed out of the room. There were so many people in the house but it was silent. Aunty Delphia and Cynthia were sleeping in the playroom. Aunty Madeline, Uncle Stewart and Gregory were sleeping in the lounge. Grandpa and Grandma were sleeping in Mum's study. Zeus was sleeping in the kitchen. But it wasn't so quiet now. I heard *tap tap tap* and then it stopped, and then *tap tap tap* again. I walked into the kitchen and Mum was there on her computer. She looked up and saw me.

'Good morning, early bird,' she said.

'*Guten Morgen.*'

Sometimes I say good morning in German, when I'm really happy, because on my last birthday we went to Legoland in Germany and it was the best birthday ever! And now, this Christmas! And Wendy had sent me a package in the post with a card. In the card she'd written: 'Merry Christmas, Robert!' Inside the packet was a T-shirt. It was blue, but not an ordinary blue; it was like rays of blue coming out from a centre. It made me happy looking at it. I knew what it was. I had seen a picture of a T-shirt looking something like that in the book on *How to Do Everything*. And she had made it, just for me.

And Mum had shown us the air tickets for the writers' festival in Negril. Jamaica, here we come!

And the End of the World, well, that didn't happen.

'What are you writing?' I asked Mum.

'A new story. I've just started.'

'Are there any vampires in it?'

'Nope,' she said. 'I'm done with vampires, virals, whatever name they go by.'

'Then what's it about?'

Mum drew me close and whispered in my ear.

'It's about a boy,' she said.

'A *boy*? Is it a children's book? Does he have magic powers?'

She drew me even closer.

'Yes, he does,' she said.

Finally Mum was writing a children's book!

'What . . . *what* powers, Mum?'

Mum whispered in my ear again.

'He thinks.'

'Oh,' I said.

She looked at me and smiled.

'A lot.'

Robert's Reading List

The Percy Jackson series by Rick Riordan
The Young Sherlock Holmes series by Andrew Lane
Horrible Histories by Terry Deary
10 Best Arthurian Legends Ever! by Margaret
    Simpson
Warriors by Erin Hunter
A Medal for Leroy by Michael Morpurgo
*The Complete Worst-Case Scenario Survival
    Handbook* by Joshua Piven and David Borgenicht
Garfield by Jim Davis
Dilbert by Scott Adams
How to Do Everything by Dorling Kindersley
    Publishing
and
The World Wide Web

Acknowledgements

Many thanks to:
Alex Christofi
Sarah Castleton, and everyone at Constable and Robinson
Griffin
Mary and Stephen
Denise, Debra
Mum and Dad
Fabio
and Riordan